DIANA PALMER

WYOMING BRAVE

HQN™

Recycling programs for this product may not exist in your area.

ISBN-13: 978-0-373-78994-8

Wyoming Brave

Copyright © 2016 by Diana Palmer

This edition published by arrangement with Harlequin Books S.A.

For questions and comments about the quality of this book, please contact us at CustomerService@Harlequin.com.

® and TM are trademarks of Harlequin Enterprises Limited or its corporate affiliates. Trademarks indicated with ® are registered in the United States Patent and Trademark Office, the Canadian Intellectual Property Office and in other countries.

www.HQNBooks.com

Printed in U.S.A.

Dear Reader,

As I write this, we are mourning Jim's brother Doug. We lost him after a long illness. He leaves behind his wife of fifty years, Victoria, as well as sons Rodney, Paul and James and his wife, Jennifer; Valerie and her husband, Wayne; grandchildren and great-grandchildren; sister Kathleen; brothers John and Jimmy; and nieces and nephews.

This book is dedicated to him. He was a twenty-year navy man, a veteran of the Vietnam War. He was brave and kind, and he loved his family and all sorts of animals, most especially his cats, and wild birds.

We will miss him a lot. I imagine him sitting now by a pond in a green meadow, with a fishing pole in his hands. Waiting for the rest of us to show up.

So long for now, Doug. It was a privilege to know you.

Diana Palmer

Robert Douglas (Doug) Kyle
1946–2016
Patriot. Vietnam veteran. Father, grandfather,
great-grandfather. He loved birds and NASCAR,
cats and fishing. We loved him.

CHAPTER ONE

REN COLTER WASN'T WELCOMING. In fact, he was immediately hostile when Merrie Grayling walked in the door of his Wyoming ranch with his brother.

Merrie looked at him and felt as if someone had hit her in the stomach with a bat. He was glorious. Tall, broad-shouldered, narrow-hipped, with beautiful lean hands and a mouth that was chiseled and sensual-looking in a face topped by thick black hair and a straight nose. He was as handsome as his brother, but in a darker way. He scowled at her. But, she could hardly take her eyes off him. He was wearing work clothes; jeans and boots that had seen their share of action in the trenches, along with shotgun chaps and a sheepskin jacket. A black Stetson was set at a slant over one eye. Both glistening black eyes were on Merrie, making comments that he didn't even have to put into words.

She moved closer to Randall, which seemed to set Ren off even more. Randall was tall and blond, with laughing blue eyes and the face of a movie star. He was very different from his brother.

"It's only for a few weeks, Ren," Randall said softly. "She's…well, she's been through a lot. Her father just died and she's had some trouble with a…with that person I told you about." He didn't look at Merrie, because what he'd told Ren wasn't quite the truth. "You have state-of-the-art surveillance and plenty of bodyguards around the place. I thought she'd be safe here."

"Safe." He had a deep, velvety voice. He studied Merrie with his sensuous lips pursed, but he seemed to find nothing enticing in the woman with the long, platinum hair in a braid down her back, her pale blue eyes trained on him like spotlights. She was pretty enough, but Ren had had enough of pretty women. Her figure wasn't easily discernible in what she was wearing. She had on jeans and a sweatshirt, both loose on her slender body, and she wore no makeup. Odd, he thought, for one of Randall's women not to show up in a tight and trashy outfit, batting her eyelashes at Ren and flirting with him. Randall's women were experienced and aggressive. Ren hated having them around. Of course, Randall was usually around to entertain them. But here he was, bringing in an odd female and leaving her while he traveled around the world for Ren, lauding their ranch's prize bulls. Randall was a born salesman. Ren was more introverted, withdrawn. He didn't really like people much. He hated their mother and had no contact with her. But he loved his brother.

He avoided women like the plague since his fiancée, Angie, had been caught with not one, but two other men, only two weeks before they were supposed to be married. Ren called off the ceremony and left Angie to deal with the aftermath. She'd been Randall's girl first, until she realized that he wasn't about to marry anyone. She set her cap at Ren instead, and teased him out of his mind for the three months of their engagement. To Randall's credit, he'd tried to warn his brother. Ren had been in love for the first time in his life, and wouldn't listen.

Angie, meanwhile, had been looking forward to living a life of luxury. Ren chaired a mining company that was Fortune 500. That was in addition to the very profitable purebred Black Angus herd that graced the thousand acres of his ranch, and the champion seed bulls that commanded millions in sales of both young bulls and semen straws (which held bull semen) that were sold internationally. The bloodlines of his cattle were impeccable.

The worst part of their broken engagement was that Ren had read all about himself on Angie's Facebook page. He'd had to buy a new laptop afterward, since he'd thrown the damned thing clear through a window out into the yard. One of the kindest things she'd said about him was that he was a clumsy, boring lover, and his hick ranch was a joke.

Attorneys had taken care of Angie's lies online. He hadn't heard from her again. He hoped he never did. He was never letting another woman get close to him. Once burned, twice shy.

Now he was being stuck with another one of Randall's women. It didn't put him in a sparkling mood. She wasn't going to find much fun here. He'd make sure of that. He was tired of Randall's parade of women.

"She won't cause any trouble," Randall was saying.

Merrie nodded. She didn't say anything. The tall rancher didn't like her. He didn't even try to hide that.

"Delsey!" Ren called.

An older woman came out of the kitchen with a harassed look on her face. She was small and plump, with gray hair in a bun and dark, beautiful brown eyes. She looked at Merrie with faint surprise, then she smiled.

"This is Merrie Grayling," Randall announced to her, putting a comforting arm around Merrie, who was almost trembling from Ren's open hostility. "She's from a small town in Texas."

Delsey shook Merrie's hand. "You'll be welcome here, dear," she said with a wary glance at Ren. She smiled at Randall. "You off again?"

"Yes. To England, to talk to a baron," he added with a grin. "He runs purebred Black Angus and we have some champion bulls we'd like to sell him. He's interested, but the personal touch is what makes sales."

"It does," Ren agreed. His mouth pulled to one side. "I don't have it."

"His idea of the personal touch is a cattle prod," Randall told Merrie with sparkling eyes.

"Only with people," Ren replied, sticking his hands in his pockets. He stared at Merrie. "I don't use cruelty as a tool. My cattle are used to gentle handling. I like cattle."

"Me, too," Merrie said softly, flushing when Ren stared at her. "But I like horses best." She searched his hard face. "Do you have one…that I could ride, maybe?"

"We'll talk about it later." He glanced at his watch. "Vet's coming over to inoculate some replacement heifers. I have to go."

Randall started to hug him, but was met with ice-cold eyes, and put out a hand to shake instead. He gave a wry smile to his brother. "Don't stand in the cold too long," he advised. "Snow's coming, they say."

"It's Wyoming," Ren replied. "We always have snow."

"That must be nice," Merrie said hesitantly. "We hardly ever have even a flurry where I come from."

Ren didn't reply. He glanced at Delsey. "I'll be in late. Just leave me some cold cuts in the fridge."

"I'll do that. You be careful with that horse," she added with affectionate concern. "He bit Davey yesterday."

"What horse?" Randall asked.

Ren's face tensed. "We had a new cowboy, one I took on faith because Tubbs hired him and said he was a good hand. He was out at the line cabin, where we didn't see him much. When I rode out there to ask him about some of the bred heifers, I found him passed out dead drunk, and the horse we'd given him as a saddle mount was bleeding from deep cuts he'd put in him, God knows with what. I beat the hell out of him before I called the authorities and they took him away. He's being prosecuted for cruelty to animals. I told them I'd be happy to testify," he added coldly.

Merrie wrapped her arms tightly around herself and shivered. That brought back painful memories of what she'd endured from her father. Lashings, beatings, all her young life. She was only twenty-two and she'd never been on a date, never been kissed, never had any friends…

Her father was so rich that everyone in the area was afraid of him, so the girls—Merrie and her older sister, Sari—had never told anyone what went on in the beautiful mansion in Comanche Wells, Texas.

"Cold?" Randall asked softly as she shivered.

She shook her head. "My father...hurt a horse like that once."

"Did you turn him in?" Ren asked curtly.

She swallowed. Hard. "People were too scared of him. It wouldn't have done any good. The trainer just made sure the horses were never out when he went to the stables."

"You live on a ranch?" Ren asked.

She nodded. "Not nearly as big as this one. We just had...have...horses."

"Well, you won't go near this one. Hurricane is the most dangerous animal on the place. He took a hunk out of one cowboy's arm and barely missed killing another who tried to get a bridle off him. He won't let anybody touch him."

"The bridle's still on?" Randall asked worriedly.

"Yes." Ren grimaced. "His head's rubbed raw by it. The cowboy probably dragged him around with it. We'll try again to get the vet to sedate him." He shook his head. "Can't hold him still long enough for the man to get a needle in him. He knows a guy at the forest service who has a tranquilizer gun. He's trying to borrow one."

"Poor thing," Merrie said softly. "A man who'll do that to a horse will do it to people," she added, her eyes lowered as she remembered her father.

Ren studied her curiously. "In fact, the sheriff thinks he had a poster on the man Tubbs hired." He looked at Randall. "Next time, I'll do the hiring," he said with a faint upturn of his mouth. "Tubbs has no judgment about people."

"She does," Randall said, hugging Merrie close to his side. "She paints."

"A lot of people paint," Ren said dismissively. He checked his watch again. "Have a safe flight," he told his brother.

"Thanks," Randall said. He smiled. "Stay out of trouble."

Ren shrugged. "Not my fault," he replied. "The man insulted my cattle."

"The Billings police were very unhappy with you," Randall persisted.

Ren chuckled. "Yes, they were. They made me take a brief anger management course. Then I went to a conference in Montana and another guy insulted my cattle." He sighed. "Guess I'll stay out of Billings until the police forget what I look like."

Randall shook his head. Ren winked at him and walked out the door without a word to Merrie. His spurs jingled as he walked. They sounded like bells to Merrie, who smiled at Randall.

"He'll be all right," he assured her. "He's just uneasy around people he doesn't know. Right?" he asked Delsey.

She drew in a breath. "He's awful around people he doesn't know. I hope you've got grit, young lady," she added with a smile. "He'll test you."

"I've lived through hard times," Merrie said with a warm smile. "I'll just keep out of his way."

"Not a bad idea," Delsey said with a laugh. "Especially with winter coming on and snow forecasted. It's hard on cattle and cowboys when it gets deep."

"I love snow," Merrie said wistfully.

"You wouldn't if you'd ever lived through a Wyoming winter," Delsey assured her.

She just grinned.

"Well, I've got to go, too," Randall said. He kissed Merrie on the cheek. "You be careful. Stay away from the stables, and don't let Ren bother you." He hesitated. "If he gets too bad, just text me and I'll take you home. Okay?"

She felt a chill of premonition when he said that, but she managed a smile. "Okay." She hugged him. "Thanks, Randall."

"You're my friend," he teased. "No worries. You'll be fine here. Take care."

"You, too," she said.

"Drive slowly," Delsey said, shaking a finger at him. "No more speeding tickets!"

"Dreamer," he chided. He winked at her as he left.

DELSEY SHOWED MERRIE to her room. "I'll have one of the boys bring your luggage up. It's still sitting in the hall where Randall left it." She paused. "Don't let Ren upset you," she added gently. "He's hard on people he doesn't know. Especially women. He had a bad experience. It's made him cold."

"I won't bother him," Merrie promised. "I brought my sketchbooks and my knitting. I'll keep busy."

"Good. If you need anything, I'm usually in the kitchen or somewhere in the house. There are helpers who come on certain days to help me with the heavy stuff. I'm feeling my age a little, but Ren likes the way I cook," she said with a laugh.

Merrie drew in a long breath. "Our housekeeper, Mandy, taught me to cook. She even taught me how to cut up a chicken and field dress game." She laughed softly. "I love being in the kitchen, too."

"I'll let you help, after you've been here a bit." Her wise dark eyes searched Merrie's. "It's a stalker, isn't it? Randall told me."

Merrie hesitated. "I don't want to put anyone in harm's way…"

"Ren has this place protected like it was Fort Knox," Delsey told her. "Nobody gets in here without security clearance. Did you notice the cameras at the front gate when you came in?" Merrie nodded. She continued. "We even have facial recognition software. It tracks people."

"Wow," Merrie said softly.

"Sadly, it didn't work on the cowboy who beat that poor horse." She winced. "Hurricane was the sweetest gelding on the place. It breaks my heart to see what that man did to him." She drew in a breath. "If he keeps this up, they'll have to put him down." She bit her lip, then forced a smile. "Well, I'll leave you to unpack." She looked out the door and peered over the banister. "Brady!" she called. "Can you bring those bags up here?"

"Sure thing, Miss Delsey," the cowboy said with a long drawl.

He brought the bags up the staircase to Merrie's room.

"Thanks," she said softly, with a smile.

Brady tipped his hat. He was Delsey's age, but was wiry and tough and apparently very strong. He grinned at Merrie. "You Mr. Randall's friend that come to stay awhile?" he asked.

"Yes, I am. I'm Merrie. Nice to meet you, Brady."

"Nice to meet you, too, miss." He turned to Delsey. "Willis wants to know if you'll make the men a cake."

"I will," Delsey replied. "What kind do they want?"

"Chocolate, with that white frosting you make."

"I'll start on it right now." She turned to Merrie. "Have you had lunch?"

"Yes, thanks," Merrie told her. "Randall got me a cheeseburger and fries on the way here."

"Okay, then. Supper's at seven. Ren keeps late hours. Sometimes he doesn't even show up for supper. Like tonight. He told me to leave cold cuts in the fridge, which means he probably won't get home until bedtime."

"Ranching is hard on schedules," Brady said with a chuckle. "Especially for boss man. He has to be everywhere before the bad weather coming."

"I called that contractor," Delsey added to Brady. "If you see Ren, tell him the man's coming tomorrow morning to see what work needs doing."

"I'll tell him." He tipped his hat again. "See you girls later."

Merrie grinned. Delsey just laughed.

"He's nice," Merrie said.

"They mostly are. But we have a few who work security here," she added solemnly. "One of them is dangerous. He came to us from Iraq, where he'd been training policemen. We don't know much about him. He keeps to himself most of the time when he's not watching the livestock."

"Who is he?" Merrie asked curiously.

"They call him J.C. Nobody knows what the initials stand for."

"I'll stay out of his way," Merrie promised. She stretched. The gold chain around her neck chafed a little. She pulled out the pretty filigree gold cross she wore and dangled it on her sweatshirt.

Delsey grimaced. She wanted to warn the girl, but she didn't want to make her more nervous than she already was. Ren wouldn't like that cross. It would prod him, like waving a flag at a bull. But maybe he wouldn't see it.

She smiled at Merrie and left her alone to unpack.

MERRIE CAME DOWN for supper, silently hoping Ren wouldn't be at the table. She really didn't want to antagonize him any more than she had by just walking into his house.

"It's a big place," Merrie commented as she ate the delicious beef stew and homemade rolls Delsey had made.

"Very big. It's too much for me to keep by myself,

which is why we have others come in to help out," she said with a laugh. "Most of them are wives of the men who already work for us. It's a way for them to make a little more money to supplement their husbands' incomes. Some of them keep chickens and sell eggs. Others raise garden crops and sell the excess in summer. We have a good life here."

"The house is so beautiful," Merrie said softly.

Delsey frowned slightly. "You're the first woman Randall brought here who ever said that."

"But, why?"

Delsey shrugged. "Well, it's rustic, isn't it?" She looked toward the living room with its big chairs and long sofa, all done in burgundy leather with cushions that had a Native American look. The rugs on the floor were the same. There were crossed swords above the mantel and an antique rifle perched on a stand.

"It looks like him," Merrie said absently. "It's sturdy and quiet and comforting."

Delsey was lost for words. She knew that the girl was talking about Ren, but she was surprised that she was so astute. Sturdy and quiet and comforting. She just hoped Merrie wasn't in for too big a surprise when Ren disapproved of something she said or did.

REN CAME IN very late. Merrie had gone downstairs, still in her jeans and sweatshirt, to ask Delsey about an extra blanket. It was kept cold in the house and she was used to warmer temperatures in Texas.

She stopped on the staircase when Ren spotted her, and his hard face grew even harder. He was looking pointedly at the front of her sweatshirt. For a minute she wondered if she was wearing something with writing on it. Then she remembered, it was just gray and plain. She swallowed hard. Surely he wasn't looking at her chest!

"Why the hell do you wear that?" he asked shortly.

She was taken aback by the venom in the question. "I... I like sweatshirts," she began.

"Not the sweatshirt. That thing!" He pointed to her cross.

She recalled Randall saying something about Ren's feelings on religion. It hadn't registered at the time, but it did now. She put her hand protectively over the cross.

"I'm a person of faith," she said in a faint tone.

"Faith." His eyes glittered at her. "Crutches for a sick, uneducated world," he scoffed. "Superstition. Useless!"

She drew in a sharp breath. "Mr. Colter," she began.

"Take that damned thing off, or hide it. I don't want to see it in my house again. Do you understand?"

He was like her father. He spoke and it was like thunder. He frightened her. She tucked the cross under the sweatshirt with shaking hands.

"And if you're looking for something to eat, we don't have à la carte food after supper time. You eat at the table with us, or you don't eat. Am I clear?"

She swallowed down the fear. "Yes, sir," she said, her voice as shaky as her legs.

"What are you doing down here in the dark?"

"I... I wanted to get a blanket," she stammered. "It's cold in my room."

"We don't run a sauna here," he said icily. "Even on a ranch this size, we conserve heat. There are blankets in your damned closet. Why don't you look before you start bothering other people about trifles?"

She backed away from him. He was much scarier than she'd first thought. That posture, that icy look on his face, the fury in his eyes made her want to run. She'd rarely been around men. Mostly at art classes, and the men who took art were gentle and kind. This man was a lone wolf, not even housebroken. He made her shake when he spoke. Her first impression of him, of a handsome, kind man, took a nosedive. He was the devil in a pair of faded blue jeans.

"That's it," he chided. "Run away, little girl."

She shot back up the staircase. She never even looked back when she got into her room. As an afterthought, she locked the door.

SARI HAD SAID that Merrie could call her, but she was afraid to. Even though she had six throwaway phones, she was afraid that one of them could be traced if she used it. The man who was after her would be wily. Paul Fiore, Sari's husband, worked for the FBI. They were trying to find the man who'd been paid by the son of their father's former lover to kill Merrie. The man he'd hired to kill Sari had been caught, and turned out to be their chauffeur. The man he'd hired for Merrie was far more dangerous.

Timothy Leeds had planned to kill both of Darwin Grayling's daughters, to hurt the man who'd killed his mother in cold blood. But Darwin had died suddenly, and Timmy had been too drunk to know who he'd hired to do the job. He was horrified at his own actions. He'd been grieving for his mother, furious at Darwin and wanting to get even, to hurt him. But Darwin had died just after Timmy made his deals. He'd taken cash, the money his mother had left him, and paid men to do murder. He was sitting in jail, waiting to be arraigned. He'd turned state's evidence, but there was no way to get around the fact that his intent had been to kill two innocent women. Intent was the thing in law. Merrie should know. Her older sister, Sari, was an assistant district attorney in Jacobsville, Texas.

She wondered what Sari would think of this taciturn, antagonistic rancher who was offended by a simple cross, a symbol of Merrie's faith. That faith had carried her and her sister through some incredible sorrows. Their father had beaten them both, kept them like prisoners in the mansion where they lived, made them afraid of men. He was a killer, and he'd been involved in laundering money for organized crime. If he'd lived, he'd have gone to prison for life, despite his wealth.

That wealth had almost cost Sari a husband. Paul Fiore was the only member of his entire family who hadn't gone into crime for a living. Paul had been with the FBI for a long time, with a brief few years as head of security for the Grayling properties. Now he was assigned to the FBI office in San Antonio. Sari had concocted a story whereby Darwin Grayling had left a hundred million dollars to Paul—half the amount Sari had received from their mother's two secret bank accounts that she'd left to the girls in her will. Each was given two hundred million, and it had almost sent Paul running. He didn't want people to think he'd married Sari for her money. But now he and Sari were very happily married, and Merrie was happy for them. She and her sister had some terrible scars, mental and physical, at their father's hand.

She sat on her bed, still shivering a little from the rancher's anger. She wondered if she was going to be able to stand it here. Ren Colter scared her.

SHE DID SLEEP, FINALLY. She went downstairs a little late for breakfast, hoping Ren would already be gone. But he was just getting up from the table.

He glared at her. "We keep regular hours here for meals," he told her curtly. "If you come sashaying down late, you don't eat."

"But, Mr. Ren..." Delsey protested.

"Rules aren't broken here," Ren returned. He looked at Merrie, who was stiff as a board. "You heard me. Delsey will tell you what hours mealtimes are. Don't be late again."

He shoved his hat down over his eyes, shouldered into his heavy coat and went out without another single word.

Merrie was fighting back tears.

"Oh, honey, I'm sorry," Delsey said. She drew the girl close and rocked her while she cried. "He's just getting over a broken engagement, and he's bitter. He wasn't like this before. He's basically a kind man..."

"He said my cross was stupid and I wasn't to let it show again," she sobbed. "What kind of man is he?"

Delsey rocked her some more and sighed. "It's a long story. He went to a famous college up north on a scholarship and a professor there changed his mind about religion. He was an excellent student, but when he came home, he was suddenly antireligion. He sounded off to his mother about her Christmas tree and her faith, and had her running away in tears. Then he overheard her telling Randall that Ren was as cold and heartless as his father, whom she'd divorced. She was proud of Randall, because he was a better son. Ren just left. He's never spoken to his mother again."

Merrie pulled back and looked at the older woman through red eyes. "She divorced his father?"

She nodded. She handed Merrie tissues to dry her eyes with. "His father owned this ranch, but it was a hard life. His mother had very expensive tastes, so the story goes, and Randall's father wanted her. So she ran away with him."

Merrie grimaced. "It's a huge ranch now."

"Yes, it is. But it was small and in debt when Ren showed up at the door just after that Christmas. He and his father began to work together to build up a breeding herd. Ren knew business, with his Harvard business degree, and his father knew cattle." She smiled. "It took fifteen years, but they diversified into oil and mining, as well as cattle, and they built a small empire here. Ren's very proud of it. His father was, too. He died two years ago." She sighed. "Ren wouldn't even let his mother come to the funeral. He's still bitter about what he heard her say. He won't speak to her at all."

"It isn't human, to hold a grudge like that," Merrie

said quietly. "He seems such a cold man," she added softly.

"There's a kind man under all that ice. It's just that he's been frozen for a long time."

"He scares me to death," Merrie confessed.

"He won't hurt you," Delsey said quietly. "You have to stand up to him, honey. A man like that will walk all over you if you let him."

"I've lived almost twenty-three years with a man like that," Merrie told her. "He..." She swallowed and her arms folded over her chest. "He was brutal to us, especially after our mother died. He wanted sons. He got us. So he made us pay for it. We couldn't even date. He wouldn't let us have friends. We still can't drive a car. I've never even been kissed. How's that for a stifled environment?" she asked with a hollow laugh. "The only concession he made was that we were allowed to go to church. You have no idea how important faith was to us when we were growing up. It was all that kept us going." She fingered the cross under her sweatshirt. "My mother gave me this cross. And I'm not taking it off."

Delsey smiled. "That's the spirit. You tell him."

"Sorry. I'm not a lemming," Merrie teased.

Delsey laughed. "You're a tonic, you know."

Merrie looked wistfully at biscuits and sausage and eggs. "I guess I'll be on time at lunch," she said.

"He's gone. Sit down and eat."

Merrie sat at the table, her eyes worriedly glancing at the door.

"Stay there," Delsey said. She went and looked out

the front door. Ren was going down the hill toward
the barn in his big red SUV. Snow had started to fall
lightly.

She went back to the kitchen. "He's gone to the barn.
After that, he'll ride out to the line cabins and check
on the livestock. Snow's starting to fall."

"It is?" Merrie was excited.

"Eat first," Delsey said with a laugh. "Then you can
go play in the snow."

She hesitated with her fork over the eggs. "Thanks,
Delsey."

"It's no problem. Really."

Merrie sighed with pleasure and dug into breakfast.
Afterward, she slipped on a light jacket and her boots.
She was sorry she hadn't packed a coat. They never
had snow in Comanche Wells in autumn. They rarely
even had it in winter.

"Child, you need something heavier than that!"
Delsey fussed.

"I'll be fine. I don't mind the cold so much if there's
snow." She laughed. "If I get too cold, I'll just come
back inside."

"All right, but be careful where you go, okay?"

"I will."

SHE STARTED WALKING around the house and down the
path that led to some huge outbuildings with adjacent
corrals. There was even a pole barn with bench seats.
Inside it, a man was working a horse with a length of
rope, tossing it lightly at the prancing animal. It was

black and beautiful, like silk all over. It reminded her of home and her family's stable of horses.

She played in the thick flakes of falling snow, laughing as she danced. It was so incredibly beautiful. She caught her breath, watching it freeze as it left her mouth, enjoying the cold, white landscape and the mountains beyond. She wanted to paint it. She loved her home in Texas, but this view was exquisite. She committed it to memory to sketch later.

She was curious about the poor horse that had been beaten. She could empathize with it, because she knew how that felt. She had deep scars on her back from her father's belt, when she'd tried to save her poor sister from a worse beating. Her father had turned his wrath on her instead.

She shivered, remembering the terror she and Sari had felt when he came at them. He wouldn't even let a local physician treat them, for fear he'd be arrested. He got an unlicensed doctor on his payroll to stitch the girls up and treat them. There was no question of plastic surgery. They had to live with the scars.

Not now, of course. Sari and Merrie were both worth two hundred million each. They'd gone shopping just before poor Sari ran away to the Bahamas to get over Paul's rejection. But Merrie had bought sweats and pajamas and very plain clothing. She still couldn't force herself to buy modern things, like crop tops and low-cut pants. She didn't want to look as if she was hungry for male attention.

Her eyes were drawn to a huge building with two big doors at its front and a corral adjoining it, with doors that opened into the building. The area was cross-fenced, so that each animal had a slice of pasture. That had to be the stables. She wandered closer, hoping not to run into any of Ren's men. She wanted to see the poor horse. She knew they'd stop her. Ren would have left orders about it, she was sure.

She waited in the shadows until two men came out.

"We can grab a cup of coffee and come back in thirty minutes," one told the other. "The mare isn't going to foal tonight, would be my bet, but we have to stay with her."

"Let's don't be gone long," the other one said on a sigh. "Boss has been in a terrible temper lately."

"He should have known that woman was nothing but trouble," the first one scoffed. "She wrapped him up like a late Christmas present and kept him off balance until he bought her that ring."

"Don't mention Christmas around him," the other man muttered. "Almost got slugged for it myself last December."

"He doesn't believe in that stuff," the first man sighed. "Well, to each his own, but I love Christmas and I'm putting up a tree month after next. He can just close his eyes when he drives by my cabin, because the damned thing is going in the window."

The other man laughed. "Living dangerously."

"Why not? He pays good wages, but I'm getting tired of walking on eggshells around him. The man's temper gets worse by the day, you know?"

"Think of all those benefits. Even retirement. You

really want to give that up because the boss is in a snit?
He'll get over it."

"Hasn't got over it in six months, has he?"

"It takes time. Let's get that coffee."

"Vet's coming tomorrow to check on the mare.
Maybe he got that tranquilizer gun for Hurricane.
Damned shame, what happened to him."

"Not as bad as what happened to the man who did
it," the other man said, wincing. "Boss turned him
every way but loose. I never saw so many bruises, and
he was a big man. Bigger than the boss, even."

"The boss was in the army reserves. His unit was
called up and he went overseas. He was captain of some
company, not sure which, but they were in the thick of
the fighting. He changed afterward, I hear."

"He's been through a lot. Guess he's entitled to a
bad temper occasionally."

"I didn't mind seeing him lose it with that damned
cowboy who beat Hurricane. Damn, it was sweet to
watch! The man never landed a single punch on the
boss."

"Sheriff noticed all the bruises. He said he guessed
the man was so drunk he fell down the stairs headfirst."

His companion burst out laughing. "Yeah. Good
thing he likes the boss, ain't it?"

"Good thing."

They walked on. Merrie, who'd been listening, grimaced. Ren had been through hard times, too. She was
sad for him. But that didn't make her less afraid of him.

She opened the stable door and stepped inside.
It was cool, but comfortable. She walked down the

bricked aisle carefully. There were several horses inside. But she knew immediately which one was Hurricane.

He was coal black with a beautiful, tangled mane. He pitched his head when he saw Merrie and stamped his feet. Then he neighed. She saw the bridle. It was far too tight. She could see blood under it. She winced. There were visible lashes down his sides, near his tail. Deep cuts.

"Poor baby," she said softly. "Oh, poor, poor baby!"

He pricked his ears up and listened.

She went a step closer. "What did he do to you?" she whispered. She moved another step closer. "Poor boy. Poor thing."

He shook his mane. He looked at her closely and moved, just a step.

She spotted some horse treats in a nearby bag. She picked up two of them, putting one in her pocket. She held one in her palm, so that the horse couldn't nip her fingers, and slowly moved it toward him. If he was that dangerous, it would be difficult even for a cowboy to feed or water him. She saw a trough in the back of the stall. It seemed to contain water. But the feed tray was inside the stall, and it was empty. He must be starved. She moved all the way to the gate, one step at a time.

CHAPTER TWO

HER FATHER HAD taken a whip to one of the Thorough-breds once, when Merrie was in high school. She'd gone to see him after her father left the ranch on a European business trip with that Leeds woman. The trainer had talked to the horse softly, but it wouldn't let him near it. Merrie had braved its nervous prancing and gone right up to it. The horse had responded to her immediately, to the trainer's delight. After that, Merrie had been its caretaker. At least, as long as her father wasn't around. He'd killed a dog she loved. He might have done the same to a horse that she'd shown attention to. Sari and she had never understood why their father hated them so. Probably, it was payback. He was getting even with their late mother, through them, for cutting him out of the bulk of her family wealth.

"Have you had anything to eat, baby?" she asked Hurricane in a whisper as she moved her hand closer to the big horse. "Are you hungry? Poor baby. Poor, poor baby!"

He moved closer to the fence. He shook his mane again.

She went closer and sent her breath toward his nostrils, something she'd watched their trainer do with horses he was breaking back home. She blew gently into the big horse's nostrils. Her father's Thoroughbreds had been off-limits to the girls when they were growing up, or she might have learned more about horses. The injured Thoroughbred had been the only one of her father's horses that she had access to. Although there were saddle mounts that the girls had permission to ride, they were careful not to pay too much attention to them when their father was around.

"I won't hurt you," she whispered. Her face was drawn and still. "I know how you feel. You know that, don't you, baby?"

He moved closer, looking at her. She held the treat out in her palm.

"Aren't you hungry?" she asked softly.

He shook his mane and then, suddenly, lowered his head. But it wasn't to attack her. He took the treat from her palm and wolfed it down. He looked at her again, quizzically.

"One more," she said. She pulled the second treat from her pocket, held it out on her palm. Again, his head lowered and he took the treat gently from it with his lips. He wolfed that down, too.

"Sweet boy," she said softly. She held out her hand.

He hesitated only for a minute before he moved closer and lowered his head toward hers. She pulled him down by his neck and laid her head against the side of his. "Oh, you poor, poor thing," she whispered, her voice breaking. "Poor horse!"

He moved his head against her, almost like a caress. She didn't see the two returned cowboys in the back of the stable, gaping at her. There was Hurricane, laying his head against her. They were spellbound.

She touched the bridle. Hurricane hesitated at first. But then he stilled. She reached up and unbuckled the halter. Very carefully, she took it away from his head and slipped it off. She grimaced at the bloody places there and on his body.

"Sweet boy," she whispered as she put the bridle aside. She reached her hand up and stroked him gently. "Sweet, sweet boy." She laid her forehead against his with a long, heavy sigh.

After a minute he lifted his head and looked at her and whinnied.

"You need medicine on those cuts, don't you," she said softly.

"And you need therapy," Ren Colter said coldly from behind her. "You were told to stay away from that horse!"

Hurricane jumped and moved back from the gate. He shook his mane and snorted.

Merrie turned with the halter in her hand. She walked toward Ren and pushed it toward him.

He stared at it, and her, with utter shock. "How did you get that off?"

"He let me," she said simply. "Do you have medicine I can put on the cuts?"

"He'll kill you if you walk into that stall with him," Ren snapped. "He's injured two cowboys already."

"He won't hurt me," she said quietly.

He started to speak. But then he looked at the horse.

Hurricane wasn't stamping and running at the gate, as he had before. He was simply looking at them.

"You're sure of that?" he asked in a quiet undertone.

She looked up at him with quiet, sad pale blue eyes. "Sort of," she said. "Of course, if I'm wrong and he kills me, you can always stand over my grave and say you told me so."

The sarcasm pricked his temper. "You think you know how a horse feels?" he asked sarcastically.

She shivered a little, even though it wasn't that cold in the stable. She didn't want to discuss anything personal with that cold, hard man. "He hasn't attacked me, has he?"

He hesitated, but only briefly. He turned to the two cowboys who'd been standing there while Merrie worked magic on the dangerous animal. "Do we have some of that salve the doctor left?"

"Uh, yes," one man stammered. He went to get it and handed it to Merrie. "Ma'am," he said, taking off his hat, "I ain't never seen nothing like that. You sure have got a way with animals."

She smiled. "Thanks," she said shyly.

Ren's dark eyes narrowed. "If he starts toward you, you run," he said firmly.

"I will. But, he won't hurt me."

They moved back, out of the horse's line of sight. Ren was concerned. He didn't want his brother's girlfriend killed on his ranch. But she did seem to have a rapport with the horse. It was uncanny.

She opened the gate and moved into the stall, with firm purpose in her step and no sign of fear.

"Sweet boy," she whispered, blowing in his nostrils again. "Will you let me help you? I won't hurt you. I promise."

He shifted restlessly, but he made no move to attack her as she reached up and put some of the salve very delicately on the bad places on his head. From there she moved to his injured flanks, wincing at the cuts. She put salve on those, too, but she could tell they needed stitching. It was no wonder that he was still in this condition. He'd injured anyone who came near him. He was afraid of men, because a man had hurt him. Women, on the other hand, were not his enemies.

She finished her work, smoothed her hand over his mane and laid her head against his neck. "Brave, sweet boy," she whispered. "What a wonderful horse you are, Hurricane."

He moved his head against her. She patted him one more time and left the stall, securing the lock. She smiled at the horse and told him goodbye before she walked back down the aisle where the men were.

"The cuts on his flank really need stitching, I think," she said softly. "But he's afraid of men. A man hurt him. Women didn't." She looked up at Ren. "Do you have a female vet anywhere within driving distance?"

Ren started. She was right. The horse hated men. "There's one over in Powell, I think. I could send one of the boys to bring her here."

"He'll probably let her stitch him up."

"You can come out and work your witchcraft on him to get her in the stall, can't you?" Ren asked sarcastically.

She drew in a breath and turned away. She didn't bother to answer him as she left.

He stared after her with mixed feelings. He hated women. But this one…she was different. All the same, he wasn't letting her close enough to bite, even if that wild horse would.

"You shouldn't be so harsh with her, Mr. Ren," the older cowboy said quietly. "Looks to me like she's had some of that at home already."

He glared at the cowboy, who tipped his hat, turned and lit a shuck out of the stable.

MERRIE WENT TO her room. She wouldn't cry. She wouldn't! That Wyoming bad man wasn't going to upset her.

She pulled out her drawing pad and her pencils and went to work on a study of Hurricane. He was so beautiful. Black as night. Soft as silk. She was drawn to him, because he was like her. He'd been through the wars, too.

It took a long time to finish the drawing. She colored it with pastel pencils, delicately. When she finished, she had an awesome portrait of Hurricane. She smiled as she put it in the case with her other drawings. She'd have to do one of Ren, she decided. But she'd have to make a decision about whether to put just horns or horns and a forked tail on the subject of the picture.

WHEN SHE GOT DOWNSTAIRS, she was late again for supper. But this time Ren was there and he wouldn't let Delsey put anything on the table.

"You know the rules," Ren said harshly. "If you don't get to the table on time, you don't eat!"

She didn't want to tell him that she'd been drawing his horse and had gotten lost in her work. She didn't want to fight. She'd had so many years of fighting. It was easier to just conform.

"All right," she said in her soft, quiet voice.

He glared at her. He hated her beauty. He hated the way she knuckled under. He wanted a fight, and he couldn't start one.

He turned away from the table and pulled off his belt. It was a new one and he'd cinched it too tight. He doubled it, pulled it together and snapped it.

Merrie gasped and ran into the kitchen, hiding behind Delsey and shaking all over.

"What the hell…?" Ren exclaimed.

He walked into the kitchen with the belt still in his hand, and Merrie screamed.

"Put that thing down!" Delsey said quickly. She pulled Merrie into her arms and held her close, rocking her while she sobbed.

Belatedly, Ren realized that the belt had upset her when he snapped it. Frowning, he took it back into the living room and tossed it into his chair. He went back into the kitchen.

"She thought you were going to hit her with it," Delsey said.

Merrie was still shaking, sobbing. It brought back horrible memories of her father and his uncontrollable temper. He'd hit her and hit her…

"I've never hit a woman in my life," he said in the

softest tone she'd heard from him. "Not even under provocation. I would never raise my hand to you. Never."

She bit her lower lip. She couldn't quite look at him. "O-okay," she stammered.

He looked torn. Her reaction to the belt was unsettling. Someone had used one on her. He began to understand why the damaged horse had responded to her. She was damaged, too.

"Get her something to eat," he told Delsey gently. "Anything she wants."

"Yes, Mr. Ren," she replied. She smiled at him.

Merrie didn't speak. She was still shaking.

He left the two women alone and went into his study. It had been years since he'd had even a drink of the scotch whiskey he kept in the cabinet. But he poured a small measure and downed it. It troubled him, seeing Merrie's reaction to the belt. Despite his unwelcoming attitude, he didn't like seeing her frightened. He liked even less knowing that he'd frightened her.

"HE'D NEVER STRIKE YOU," Delsey assured Merrie as she put ham and bread and mayonnaise on the table. "Here. Let me make you a sandwich. You'll feel better."

"My father...always snapped the belt like that, just before he used it on us." She drew in a shuddering breath. "He's gone, now. My sister and I should feel sorrow, but all we can feel is relief. It was like being freed from prison." She looked at Delsey. "He wouldn't even buy us clothes unless he picked them out. We couldn't date, we couldn't have friends over, we couldn't go to anyone else's home…" She lowered her eyes. "He was so paranoid that he had us followed everywhere we went."

"You poor child," Delsey said, touching her hair. "You're safe here. Mr. Ren may sound like a lion, but he would never hurt you."

She swallowed. "Okay."

"Now sit down here. Would you like some milk?"

"Oh, yes. Please."

Delsey made her a sandwich and a glass of milk, and busied herself with the dinner dishes while she ate.

"Thanks," she said when she finished. She took her plate and glass to the sink.

Delsey hugged her. "Don't worry. Things work out, even when you don't think they will."

She smiled and hugged the older woman back. "I'll try. Thanks."

"No problem. You go to bed and sleep. You'll be fine in the morning."

"Good night."

"You, too."

BUT IT WASN'T a good night, and she wasn't fine. She woke up screaming in the middle of the night. Her father was standing over her with his belt. It had blood all over it. He was yelling as he brought it down on her back with all his strength behind it…

"Wake up, damn it!"

She felt hard hands on her arms, pulling her up, felt whiskey-scented breath on her face. But the hands weren't hurting her. They were warm and they felt good on the bare skin. She opened her eyes.

Ren was sitting on the bed, wearing flannel pajama bottoms and nothing else. His broad chest, hair-roughened, was beautiful. She thought how she'd love to paint him like that. He was the most gorgeous man she'd ever seen. But she didn't dare let it show, how she felt. She lifted her eyes to his and winced.

"I'm sorry," she whispered. "I had a nightmare."

His big hands smoothed down her arms. "About what?"

"Something in the past," she said evasively. "Long ago," she lied.

He drew in a long breath. "It was the belt, wasn't it?"

She hesitated, but finally she nodded. "I can't stand to hear a belt snapped like that. Daddy always…" She stopped.

"Your father hit you with a belt?"

She nodded.

"So did mine, when I was a kid. I used to have welts on the backs of my legs. I was a reckless boy, always into something I shouldn't be. Dad got impatient."

She didn't want to tell him the truth, about the scars on her poor back. She didn't want him to see them. She always wore nightgowns with a high neckline, so that no part of her back showed.

He touched her cheek, pushed back the disheveled platinum hair that had come loose from the braid she wore it in. "Don't you take it down at night?" he asked curiously.

The feel of his hand on her face made her feel odd

things. She felt trembly all over when he brushed her cheek like that. Her heart kicked into gear, unsettling her.

"No, I have to put it up when I sleep," she said. "It gets in my face. I really should cut it. But it's been long all my life."

"It would be a crime to cut hair this beautiful," he said quietly.

She looked up into his eyes and couldn't look away. Neither could he. His breath came quickly. He brushed his fingers along her cheek, down to the bow shape of her pretty mouth. They lingered there, teasing the soft flesh, making her feel liquid, melting. She wanted to push close to him, feel him hold her. She wanted to tempt his mouth down to hers and see what a kiss felt like. She was hungry for something…

Incredibly, his head started to bend. She felt his whiskey-scented breath in her mouth. She drew in her own breath as she looked at his sensuous lips and wondered how they were going to feel grinding hungrily into hers.

His hand slid to the back of her neck and began to pull, ever so gently. She felt her lips parting, her body throbbing, as his mouth came closer, closer, closer…

"What happened?" Delsey asked from the doorway.

Ren drew back from Merrie, glaring at her as if he was angry. He got to his feet quickly. "She had a nightmare," he said shortly. He turned away, grateful that his pajamas were loose. "She's all right. I'm going back to bed."

"Are you all right, dear?" Delsey asked. She was

wearing a cotton nightgown and a long cotton robe. She looked like an angel.

"I'm fine…now," Merrie said breathlessly. "Just a nightmare. I'm so sorry I woke everybody up."

"I wasn't asleep," Delsey confessed. "I was watching a movie on my iPad."

"You can do that?" Merrie asked excitedly. "How?" Ren left them talking and went back to his bedroom. As an afterthought, he slammed the door. That woman was really a witch. He was reeling just from touching her mouth. He wasn't going to be led into that sweet trap a second time. If she was in the market for a rich husband, Randall could have her. She was Randall's girl, anyway, wasn't she?

He turned off the lights and climbed into bed, surprised at his own vulnerability.

MERRIE DELIBERATELY SLEPT LATE so that she wouldn't have to sit at the table with Ren at breakfast. It was cowardly, but she worried that he'd be out for blood. He'd almost kissed her the night before. But he was going to hate himself for that weakness, and it would be open season on Merrie if she gave him the opportunity.

She poked her head into the kitchen, breathing a sigh of relief when she didn't see him.

Delsey was putting away the dishes. She grimaced when she saw Merrie.

"I know. I came late," Merrie said softly. "It's okay. I don't eat much, anyway."

The older woman looked hunted. Merrie went close

and hugged her. "Thanks for saving me last night. I hope I didn't get you in trouble with the boss."

Delsey hugged her back. "Not so much. I've been around since he was in college. I guess he's used to me." She drew away with a sigh. "He was topping cotton this morning," she added, using an old Southern term for someone being furiously angry.

Merrie laughed softly. "That's very Southern sounding," she commented.

"I was born in Eufaula, Alabama," Delsey said surprisingly. "I married a cowboy who was traveling through town with his boss on a cattle-buying trip. Met him in a café and went back to Wyoming with him three days later. We were married for twenty-five years before he had a heart attack. I stayed on working for Mr. Ren's father after he died."

"I'm sorry."

She smiled. "It was a long time ago. I still miss him. I wish we could have had children, but that wasn't in the cards."

"I would like children, I think," Merrie said sadly. "I'm just not sure about marriage. My poor mother," she said softly. "I don't think she had a single happy day with my father. She lived for Sari and me. Until…" She closed up like a flower and smiled. "Did they get the female vet to come over from Powell?" she asked.

"Yes, they did," she replied. "Mr. Ren was on his way to the stables."

"He said they might call me to use some witchcraft on Hurricane so he'd let the vet in the stall with him," Merrie murmured.

"He says a lot of things he doesn't really mean," Delsey said softly. "Mr. Ren's had a hard life. His father mostly ignored him. Then his mother divorced him to run away with Mr. Randall's father, and she made Ren go along. He didn't want to. He wasn't crazy about his dad, but he loved this ranch."

"How old was he?" Merrie asked.

"He was ten years old. Mr. Ren's father went crazy after they left. He got drunk and stayed drunk for years. The ranch was falling apart by the time Mr. Ren graduated and came back here. He sobered up his dad, reorganized the ranch and started making improvements. He let the land stand for loans to improve pasture and fencing, to buy seed bulls, to upgrade the equipment and refurbish the stables and the barn…" She laughed as she finished putting up dishes. "He was like a whirlwind. The ranch got out of the red two years after he started. Fifteen years later, he has an empire here. His dad lived long enough to see a prosperous future, but not long enough to enjoy it."

"That's sad."

"It was. Mr. Ren's mother wanted to come to the funeral, but he refused to let her near the place."

Merrie caught her breath. "Why?"

"They've had some problems," Desley said. "Mr. Ren overheard her say something that hurt him real bad. I told you about that. He just left. Never even said goodbye. Hitchhiked out here to his dad, moved in and started to work. He's like that," she added. "He doesn't say what he's going to do. He just does it."

"He's scary, in a way," Merrie said.

"Lots of people are, until you get to know them," Delsey told her gently. "He's not a violent man…"

"…told you to get the damned rope on him first!" Ren was raging outside the window. "Now look what you've done, you idiot! I ought to lay you out on the ground, Grandy!"

Merrie held her breath as Ren stormed in the back door, half carrying a man with blood all over one arm.

"Oh, dear," Delsey said. "Grandy, what in the world?"

"Clean him up, would you, Delsey?" Ren asked, putting the man in a chair. "Probably needs stitches. I'll get Tubbs up here to drive him into town to the doctor." He glanced at Merrie coldly. "If you faint, don't do it in here. I've got enough problems."

"How did it happen?" Delsey asked, while Merrie stood just staring at the bleeding man.

"He was trying to rope a horse. Horse reared up and threw him into a sheet of tin."

"Was it Hurricane?" Merrie asked worriedly.

"Yes, it was Hurricane," he shot at her angrily.

She moved closer to him. "Couldn't I help?"

He hesitated. He didn't want her near the horse. He was furious at her because he'd been weak the night before. He didn't want her around, didn't want her near him. She was Randall's girl…

"You might let her try before anybody else gets hurt, Mr. Ren," Delsey intervened.

"Hell!" He tilted his hat low over his eyes. "All right. Come on."

Delsey washed the deep cut on Grandy's arm. "Cut a vein, I think," she told Ren.

"Tubbs is on his way. Wrap a towel around it," Ren told her.

"Sorry, Ren," Grandy said sheepishly.

Ren just glared at him. He opened the door, let Merrie out and followed her.

She'd grabbed her light jacket. It was freezing cold outside and flurries of snow touched her face. A dusting of it was on the ground from the day before. She hadn't had time to really enjoy it. She lifted her face to it and smiled, her eyes closed.

Ren glanced at her, and an unfamiliar tenderness tugged at his cold heart. She was like a child, he thought. She took pleasure in the simplest things.

"Your jacket's too thin for a Wyoming autumn," he said, fighting down the feelings she provoked in him.

"It rarely gets much below freezing in South Texas," she replied, almost running to keep up with his long strides. "This is the heaviest coat I own."

"Tell Delsey to take you to town and get a warmer one. I have an account at Jolpe's. It's a chain department store." He didn't add that it was one of the real high-end shops. It catered to movie stars who came to Jackson Hole, which wasn't too far away.

"I'll do that. Thanks." She was going to spend her own money, but he could think what he liked.

"Randall would take you himself, if he was here," he added deliberately. He had to keep reminding himself that she belonged to his stepbrother.

"Of course he would."

They walked into the stables, down the stone walkway to the stall where Hurricane was kept. The female vet, middle-aged, with blond hair and blue eyes, glanced at them as they approached.

She grimaced. "I can't get the stupid tranquilizer gun to work. I should have asked Kells with Game and Fish to show me again how to use it..."

While she was talking, Merrie went right up to the gate of the stall and held her hand out. It contained one of two treats she'd taken from a nearby bag.

She opened her hand, the treat on her palm, and offered it to the nervous gelding.

"Hi, sweetheart. Remember me?" she asked softly, smiling.

Apparently he did, because he came right up to the gate and tossed his mane, whinnying softly.

"That's a sweet boy," she said, watching him nibble the treat. She smoothed her bare hand over his head, between his eyes. "What a sweet boy!"

The vet, mesmerized, just stared at her. "He just knocked one of the cowboys into that pile of tin in the aisle," she pointed out, indicating a small refuse pile from some repairs.

"She has a way with horses, apparently," Ren said curtly. "Can you keep him diverted while Dr. Branch gets in the pen with him?"

"Of course I can," Merrie said. She smoothed her hand over the horse's ears, calming him.

The vet took advantage of the lull to go into the stall and examine the cuts. "I can use a local on these," she said. "If you can just keep him busy..."

"I can do that," Merrie assured her.

She talked to Hurricane, smoothing her hand over

his face, his ears, his cheek, all the while talking to him. When he felt the needle he started to shift, but Merrie drew him back and laid her forehead against his, talking to him again. He calmed. The vet began to put in the stitches, working efficiently. It didn't take long.

Dr. Branch came out of the stall with a long sigh. "That's some bedside manner you've got there, Miss...?"

"Grayling," Merrie said. "My name is Meredith, but everybody calls me Merrie," she added, with a smile.

"Merrie, then. Thanks for the help."

"I didn't mind. I love horses."

"That one certainly seems to like you," Dr. Branch said. She shook her head. "I couldn't get the stupid tranquilizer gun to work. I guess I need more training with it," she said with a laugh.

"Will he be all right now?" Merrie asked, because she was worried. Some of the cuts had been very deep.

"I gave him an antibiotic," she replied. "If there's any obvious infection around the cuts, I may need to come back and see him. You know the signs, I'm sure," she said to Ren.

"I know them all too well. Thanks for coming, Doc."

"My pleasure." She picked up her bag, smiled at Merrie and walked back down the aisle.

"I thought he'd have to be put down," Ren commented.

"He's not a bad horse. He's just been exposed to a bad man," Merrie replied. She was still smoothing the horse's forehead. "He's so beautiful. I drew a portrait of him," she added softly.

"Did you?" He sounded disinterested. "He'll settle down now. I have work to do."

"Am I being evicted?" she asked, eyebrows raised.

"For the time being, yes."

She sighed, nuzzled Hurricane's face with her own and left him. He whinnied when she got halfway down the stall. She turned and smiled at him. "I'll come back again."

He tossed his head.

"Don't tell me you can talk to horses, too," he scoffed.

"I don't know," she said honestly. "Daddy never let us near the stables when he was home."

He scowled, looking down at her. "What sort of horses did he keep?"

Thoroughbreds, but she wasn't telling him that. She liked being just plain Merrie. "Quarter horses," she lied. "He sold them all over the world."

"But you weren't allowed to ride them?"

"Not the registered ones, no. He didn't trust us with them."

"Why?"

She grimaced. "He thought we might injure one, I guess. He kept a few saddle horses for guests. We got to ride those. They were old and swaybacked, but at least we learned how to ride."

He raised an eyebrow. There was a big difference between riding a quarter horse and a swayback, he thought privately. He wondered if she was bragging, and her father hadn't had more than one or two horses. Surely, her clothes were an indication that she and her family didn't have much money. All her attire seemed to consist of gray sweatpants and sweatshirts, most of which had either writing or logos on them.

Her boots, at least, were proper ones. No designer footwear there, he mused, looking down at her small feet. She had on boots that had seen hard wear. They looked a lot like his own, except that hers hadn't been subjected to smelly substances and too much water.

"The vet seemed nice," she commented.

"She was. Nice, and quite smart. Her husband is also a vet. They specialize in large-animal calls."

"Out here, I guess they'd have to," she commented, looking around at the long, beautiful pastures that led off to sharp, jagged white peaks in the distance. "Is that the Rocky Mountains?" she asked.

"No. Those are the Teton Mountains. We're closer to Jackson Hole than we are to Yellowstone."

"I don't know much about the territory out here," she confessed. "I've never been out of south Texas in my life."

He scowled. "Never?"

"Daddy didn't want us out of his sight," she said simply.

Daddy sounded like a paranoid schizophrenic. But he wasn't going to say it out loud.

They walked into the kitchen. Delsey had stopped the bleeding temporarily with a large towel, under which bandages could be seen. A tall, good-looking cowboy with blue eyes and black hair was standing beside Grandy. He looked up when Merrie walked in, and his eyes twinkled.

"It is she. The witch woman!" he teased.

Merrie's eyebrows met her hairline. "Excuse me?"

"Your fame has preceded you, my lady," the man said, making her a sweeping bow. "I expected choirs of cherubs singing praises…"

She felt her forehead. "I don't think I have a fever," she murmured.

"He does Shakespeare at our local playhouse," Delsey said, rolling her eyes. "That's Rory Tubbs, Merrie, although none of us ever use his first name," she introduced them. "He's playing King Lear."

"Not King Lear," he muttered. "Macbeth!"

"I always get those two confused," the older woman conceded. "There you go, Grandy. You'll live until Tubbs can get you to the doc."

"Hurricane didn't kill you, then?" Grandy asked Merrie.

She smiled. "No. He's a sweet horse."

"You'd think so," Grandy muttered. "He didn't pitch you headfirst into a pile of tin, now, did he?"

She laughed softly. "No, he didn't. I hope you'll be all right," she added gently.

Grandy actually flushed. He got up and grabbed his hat, nodding at her before he put it on. "I'll be fine. Nothing but a cut," he murmured.

"A big cut, but he'll still be fine," Tubbs added with a flash of white teeth. He tipped his hat. "See you again, fair maiden."

She smiled.

"Don't die," Ren told Grandy. "I can't afford to lose you."

Grandy grinned at him. "Hard to kill a weed, boss." He grimaced. "Next time, I'll listen."

"Next time, you'd better," Ren said. His eyes smiled at the older man, even if his mouth didn't. It was impossible to miss the very real affection Ren had for his men.

"I always listen, don't I, boss?" Tubbs asked. "And I can drive in six feet of snow and ice." He buffed his nails on his coat. "I'm irreplaceable."

"I can do that myself," Ren shot back. "Don't get cocky."

Tubbs chuckled and herded Grandy out the back door toward the waiting pickup truck.

"Don't flirt with the men," Ren said icily.

She gaped at him. "I smiled at him!"

"Don't smile at them, either," he added belligerently.

She just stood there, uncertain and undecided.

"Oh, hell," he muttered. He turned on his heel and went back out the door. He slammed it behind him, rattling the elaborate glass pane at the top of it.

"He'll break that one day," Delsey said with a sigh. She shook her head. "No pleasing him today, is there?"

"Is he always like this with women?" she wanted to know.

She fought for the right words. "Well, not with older women," she qualified.

"Maybe I can age ten years or something," Merrie said under her breath.

Delsey laughed. "You really do have something special in you, if you could get that wild horse to let the vet treat him."

"He's been hurt," Merrie said. "He's just scared."

"Maybe. But if I were a man, I wouldn't go in the pen with him."

Merrie laughed. "Neither would I," she confessed.

"Want a sausage biscuit?" Delsey asked, peering around her toward the door, just in case Mr. Ren was somewhere nearby.

"I'd love one, thanks, and some coffee. I'll sneak them up to my room while he's away."

"I promise you, he isn't usually this unreasonable," Delsey began.

"I just rub him the wrong way. Some people are like that. It's okay." She smiled reassuringly. "I won't tell him you fed me," she added.

Delsey laughed. "Well, not right away," she replied.

CHAPTER THREE

MERRIE FINISHED A preliminary sketch of Ren, one she planned to turn into a portrait of him later. He really was a striking man, she thought, studying it. But there was something more than just looks there. He was strong and independent and deliberate in the way he went about things. It was all there, in her sketch.

She was so glad that Hurricane had received the care he needed. The vet really knew what she was doing. She'd go back out and check on him tomorrow. Meanwhile, she worked on sketching Ren's portrait. She loved the hard lines of his face, the incredible masculinity that radiated from him. He brimmed with authority, but not like her father had. Her father had been cruel and domineering. Ren tended to dominate, too, but not in a cruel way.

Delsey had told her that Ren almost never had a drink. But she was sure he'd had whiskey on his breath when he came to see her after her nightmare. He'd looked guilty and haunted after he'd snapped the belt and she'd run away from him. So there was kindness there, inside him. He just didn't let it show. He was like a wolf who'd put his paw in a fire and drew it back at once, resolving never to go near fire again. Some woman had hurt him badly, Delsey had said. She didn't think he was the kind of man who went through women in droves, like his brother, Randall. She liked Randall very much as a friend, but she'd never have wanted him for a boyfriend. He was flighty and he loved women. He never stuck with one for longer than a few weeks, and she was sure he'd never been in love. One day, she thought with laughter, he'd meet his match.

She put a campfire and a wolf in the background of Ren's portrait. It seemed to suit. She added lodgepole pines for a backdrop. She drew him in the shepherd's coat and the wide-brimmed hat he wore around the ranch. He looked very lifelike, as if he could walk off the page of the sketchbook.

She wished she had her paints and canvases, but those were back in Texas. She'd hesitated to use her cell phones, even though Paul had assured her they couldn't be traced. And it wasn't as if she could have her painting supplies sent up here, not without the risk of having someone notice where they were going. Paul had worried about the man Timmy Leeds had hired to kill Merrie. He'd sounded very professional, and Paul mentioned that he'd been in the business for many years. Men who weren't competent got weeded out fast.

Here, in Wyoming, she could forget for hours at a time that she was being hunted. She gave a thought to Ren and Delsey, and prayed that she wasn't putting them in harm's way just by living in the house with them. But, then, Randall had assured her that Ren had state-of-the-art surveillance and very capable bodyguards on the place. He'd also assured her that Ren knew exactly why she was here. It relieved her a little.

She remembered that Ren had told her to go shopping for a coat. She'd have to do that. Maybe there was an art supply store in town. Wait, what about Amazon? She could have kicked herself for not thinking of it sooner. She had an account, with her brand-new credit card backing it up.

She pulled out her cell phone, loaded the app and started shopping for supplies. It didn't take long to find everything she needed. Now she just had to find a room to paint in. She'd ask Ren.

But not today, she decided. He was bound to be in a snarly mood when he came in from working around the ranch. It amazed her how much there was to do on a ranch this size. There were buildings that had to be repaired, stalls in both the barn and stable that had to be scrubbed and filled with fresh hay, tack that had to be mended, machines that had to be worked on—it was a never-ending process.

Then there were the cattle. In bad weather, cowboys paid even closer attention to them. The herds were checked several times a day by cowboys, who were expected to be out working no matter how bad the weather got.

Most of the outbuildings, Delsey had told her, were made of steel. It was durable, and even snow that packed several feet in winter couldn't collapse the roofs. There were lean-tos out in the sweeping fenced pastures, for the cattle to shelter in when the weather got rough, and those were also made of steel, with sloping roofs. Heated water troughs were everywhere. The men carried hay out to the cattle when snow got deep. It was placed in troughs with grates, so there wasn't so much waste as the cattle ate. There were many corrals where horses were worked. Some were used to contain animals when they were due to be branded, tagged, castrated and inoculated. Those had loading chutes. Animals were herded down them either to trays used to work the calves, or to loading docks where the beef steers were loaded en route to other pastures or buyers.

Merrie had read about spring roundup on ranches, and she really would have loved to see the process. But it was October. No roundup was going on now. Instead, she found a DVD that showed the process on Skyhorn, the name of Ren's big ranch.

While he was out, she put it in the DVD player, gathered up her knitting basket and settled back to watch the men work.

She was knee-deep into knitting a hat and watching Ren talking to a reporter about how branding was done when she heard a door open. She thought it was Delsey and paid no attention, until she heard a deep voice behind her.

"What the hell are you doing?" Ren asked curtly.

She jumped, and looked up from her knitting with red cheeks. "Sorry. Was it okay if I use the DVD player?"

He scowled as he noticed her subject matter. He swept off his hat and wiped his forehead on his sleeve. "I'd forgotten about that," he murmured. "A reporter for a local station was doing a story about ranches and wanted to interview me. I don't usually do them, but he was known for fairness in journalism."

Her eyes asked the question.

He dropped into the leather armchair that nobody else was supposed to sit in and stared at her. "We get a lot of people who want to shut down the beef industry entirely." He shrugged. "Opinions are like...well, everybody has one," he said, amending what he'd been about to let out.

"I guess so," she said. "The cattle industry may be an artificial use of land, but buffalo and other ruminants have been around for a very long time. Animal gases may contribute to climate change, but I'd put nuclear testing and volcanic eruptions at the top of any list I made about gases in the atmosphere."

He raised one dark eyebrow. His attention was drawn to the interview she was watching. They were using the branding iron on the steers.

"That doesn't bother you?" he asked.

She shook her head. "I know about branding. Some people said freeze branding was better, but it sheds off with the coat. A burned brand lasts forever." She glanced at him. "I even know what a running iron is. But I didn't learn that from the video," she said, nodding toward the screen. "I love to read Zane Grey novels. I guess I have every book he ever wrote."

"Me, too," he confessed. "What's your favorite?"

"The Light of Western Stars," she said. "You know, the hero was loosely based on a real person, Red Lopez, who fought on the Arizona border during the Mexican War in 1910."

Both his eyebrows went up. "You know your history."

"I would have studied it," she said. She lowered her eyes to her knitting. "But I was tired of people shadowing me. Daddy wouldn't let us leave the house unless somebody was with us. I took art classes at our local community college instead of doing a degree."

"Why did he have people following you?"

"He was afraid we might meet a boy and try to go out with him," she said on a hollow laugh. "This nice cowboy asked me out once, when I was sixteen. I'd met him in school. His sister was in my class. He worked on a ranch. He was just a little older than me." She shifted on the sofa. "Daddy found out. The cowboy suddenly left for Arizona." She lowered her eyes back to the hat in her lap that she was knitting while Ren gaped at her.

"Why didn't he want you dating?"

She bit her lower lip. "He had very definite ideas about what sort of men he wanted us to marry, and when."

"Then how did you meet my brother?" he asked curtly.

She went back to her knitting. She didn't answer him.

He leaned forward. "How?"

She let out a shallow breath. "He had a good friend who was in my art class. I'd seen him around town when he was visiting, and when he came to see the exhibit at our college, we started talking." She smiled. "He wasn't scared of Daddy. Just the same, I could never invite him to the house, and I had to make sure we were always in a crowd at college when I talked to him. Daddy was…not quite normal."

He'd already figured that out. "Your sister is married, though?"

Randall must have told him that. "Yes. Just recently. Paul's a senior agent with the FBI in San Antonio. He used to work for Daddy, long ago." She stopped. She didn't want to talk about her father or his fortune.

"What does your sister do?"

She smiled. "She's an assistant district attorney in Jacobs County."

"Didn't you want to have a profession? Some way to earn a living?"

She didn't want to talk about that, especially. "I hope to do that with my art, one day," she said. She looked up into a faintly disappointed face. She knew he thought she had no ambition. It hurt. But she wasn't telling him anything more about Graylings. Not yet. "That reminds me," she said softly. "Is there a room I could use to paint in? I have paints and canvases coming. I don't want to make a mess…"

"There's a studio," he said. "It belonged to…my father's wife." He never called her his mother. "She used it for painting. There's a drop cloth in there, as well."

"Thanks," she told him. She wondered if Ren had loved his mother, before their sad parting. She'd have to ask Randall. She wouldn't dare ask Ren. He was already fuming about something; perhaps a bad memory of the woman. She was certain that he wouldn't have referred to his mother at all if she hadn't asked the question about the studio.

He waved away the gratitude. His eyes went to the

quick, efficient movement of her hands. "What are you making?"

"Hats," she said with a smile. "I make dozens and give them away, to children I meet on the street, to old people in the waiting room when I have dentist appointments. I gave some to a woman who helps Mandy in the house, who works with an outreach program as a volunteer." She hesitated. "I mostly do it when I'm watching television."

"You make hats?" Delsey asked from the kitchen. She came into the living room, stirring something she was making in a bowl. "Could you make me one?" she asked. "I'm forever going in and out to take trash, and my head gets cold even when I put on a coat."

"Sure. You can have this one when it's finished." She held it up. It was green and gold and tan.

"I like that!"

She laughed. "Thanks."

"I'll just finish getting this cake ready to go in the oven. Apple pound cake, Mr. Ren, with vanilla frosting."

"Something to look forward to tonight," he said, and smiled at her.

"It'll be ready by then." She went back into the kitchen.

"I thought you'd be squeamish," Ren remarked as Merrie's attention went back to the screen.

"I like cattle," she said sheepishly. "I don't know much about them. There are ranches all around the house where Sari and I grew up. Most of the people in Jacobs County either run cattle or work on ranches."

"Sari?"

She laughed softly. "Her name is really Isabel, but only Paul calls her that. To the rest of us, she's Sari."

"Are you like her?"

"Oh, no," she replied. "Sari's redheaded and has really blue eyes. Mine are sort of a washed-out version of hers. And she's very smart. She graduated in the top of her class from college and law school."

He cocked his head and studied her. She was pretty and sweet. Smart? He didn't care if a woman was smart or not. He liked Merrie. Even though he really didn't want to.

He got to his feet, slapping his work gloves into his hand. "You can come back for spring roundup," he mused. "I'll take you out and you can see the process firsthand."

"You'd do that for me?" she exclaimed, her face radiating joy. "Oh, I'd love to see it!"

He smiled faintly. "Okay." He turned toward the kitchen. "Delsey, I'll be back late tonight. Fred and I have to ride out to the line cabins and check on the men."

"All right. It's going to snow kittens and you're already sniffling. Don't stand out in the cold."

"Stop worrying," he muttered. "I'm fine."

"You don't sound fine," she shot back. "You sound stuffed up."

"I'm going now," he replied. "See you later."

"Okay. Go kill yourself and see if I care!" she called back.

He just laughed. He glanced at Merrie, tipped his hat and went out the door. It was really coming down outside. Snow seemed to come often in autumn here in Wyoming. Merrie wondered if the weather was always like that.

MERRIE WAS ON TIME for supper. She and Delsey ate a nice stew with biscuits, then Merrie went up to her room to sketch some more. She'd gone to bed when she heard Ren's footsteps come up the stairs. Odd how slow they sounded. His step was always quick and confident. Probably he was just tired, she thought. She closed her eyes and went back to sleep.

The next morning, she was on time for breakfast, but Ren wasn't sitting at the table, as he usually was.

Delsey frowned as she put things on the table. "Not like him to be late. I'm going up to check on him."

"I hope he's all right," Merrie said.

"Warned him about being out in that snow when he was already feeling bad. He never listens." She was still muttering as she went out the door and up the staircase.

Delsey was back very soon. She went directly to the phone in the living room, picked it up and dialed.

She told someone Ren's symptoms, then nodded. "Yes, I'll have Tubbs drive him right into town. Thanks, Sylvia."

She hung up. Then she called down to the bunkhouse, asked for Tubbs and had him come up to the house.

"Ren's sick?" Merrie asked, worriedly.

"Yes. He sounds as if he's breathing water," Delsey said worriedly. "He almost never gets sick, but there's that virus that was going around, and he won't take care of himself. Out in the freezing cold and wind for hours…" She stopped. "Go eat, child. He'll be all right. He's tough."

Merrie managed a smile. She felt sad. When Ren walked in the door, the house came to life. It was an odd thing to feel about a man she barely knew and didn't really like. But he seemed to fill the house up with color just by being in it.

MINUTES LATER, DELSEY propped him up with her shoulder and helped him walk down the staircase. His face was a pasty white, and he looked terrible. When he coughed, the congestion was audible.

"I'm all right," he was protesting.

"You're not all right. Merrie, can you hold on to him for me while I see if Tubbs is out there? I think I hear the truck…"

"Of course." Merrie took Delsey's place under Ren's arm and felt the hard muscular body closer than she ever had before. He was warm and strong, and smelled of fir trees. She liked the feeling she got, being near him like this. It was something she'd never experienced.

Ren liked the softness of her young body. He liked the feel of her. He liked it too much, he thought to himself. He moved restlessly. He felt really sick.

"It's okay," Merrie said softly. "The doctor will give you something, and you'll get better."

"I've got work to do…!"

"It will get done when it gets done," she said firmly. "You can't work if you're dead, now, can you?"

He looked down into her soft pale blue eyes. "Pest," he muttered.

She grinned up at him. "Certifiable."

He managed a laugh, but it made him cough.

Delsey motioned to them. "Tubbs is right outside. Come on, Mr. Ren." She looked out the door. "Tubbs, come help, he's heavy!"

"Yes, ma'am!"

Tubbs came shooting in the door, grinned at Merrie and took Ren under the arm. "Come on, boss man. You can't die. We'll all have to go looking for work and we'll never find anybody else who'll yell at us and threaten to soak our blankets in vinegar."

"Tubbs…" Ren began irritably.

"On the other hand, if you die, I want that nice watch you have, the one with all the dials," Tubbs continued.

Surprisingly, Ren burst out laughing, which caused another coughing fit.

"In you go, boss man. You're not dying today." He waved to the women, got in beside Ren and drove away.

Merrie went back inside the house with Delsey, rubbing her arms because it was bitterly cold outside.

"You need a winter coat," Delsey said firmly.

"I'll go shopping. But not today." Merrie laughed. She followed Delsey into the kitchen. "He'll be okay, won't he?" she added, worried and not able to hide it.

Delsey suppressed a smile. "He'll be fine. Dr. Fellows will make sure of it. He delivered Ren."

She cocked her head. "How long ago?" she wondered.

"Almost thirty-seven years," Delsey replied. "He was born December 6."

"I see." He was older than she'd thought. Thirty-six, to her twenty-two. Well, she'd be twenty-three in November. It was still fourteen years. She supposed a mature man like that would think of her as just a child. It depressed her. She wondered why. He was hot-tempered, irritable, impatient, overbearing... Well, she had to finish that knitting, and adding to the adjectives would take a long time.

REN CAME HOME LATER, with Tubbs still supporting him.

"We have medicine and orders from the doctor," Tubbs said, helping Ren up the staircase. "I expect him to take the first and ignore the second."

"You can bet on it," Ren muttered.

Tubbs just laughed.

After he got Ren settled, he came back down the staircase. He tipped his hat to the women. "I have to go ride the fence line and look for breaks."

"Button that coat," Delsey said firmly. "One sick man is enough."

Tubbs grinned at her. "I never get sick." He glanced at Merrie and started to speak.

"Out," Delsey said, because she had a feeling he wanted to ask Merrie out. Ren wouldn't like it.

He made a face. "You're as bad as he is," he remarked, nodding up the staircase.

"Where do you think I learned it from?" Delsey returned, and she grinned.

"Ah, well, fair maiden, there's always tomorrow," Tubbs said, and made Merrie a sweeping bow before he left. "Parting is such sweet sorrow!" he added on his way out.

Merrie looked after him, but not with any real interest. She turned back to Delsey. "Will Ren take the medicine, you think?"

"I would bet money that he sticks it in his medicine cabinet and closes the door," Delsey replied. "It's what he did the last time, and he ended up right back in Dr. Fellows's office."

Merrie hesitated. "Does he wear pajamas?" she asked, flushing.

"Ah. I see." Delsey smiled gently. "He wears the bottoms," she said. "Think you can get the medicine in him?"

"I got medicine in an outlaw horse once," Merrie replied.

Delsey smiled gently. "Let me heat up some soup for him, and we'll both take it up."

"Great!" Merrie said.

Delsey kept her thoughts to herself. It was a relief, however, to notice that dashing Tubbs hadn't made an impression on the young woman. The boss looked at Merrie in a way he hadn't looked at a woman since that she-cat took him for the ride of his life. It was a start.

Ren was in bed with the covers pulled up to his waist, looking miserable, when Delsey and Merrie walked in.

"I just need rest," he muttered, glaring at them. "Not mothering!"

"Nobody's mothering you," Merrie promised. "Where's the medicine?"

He glared at her.

"In the medicine cabinet, I'll bet," Delsey told her.

"Traitor!" Ren shot at her.

Merrie walked into his bathroom and opened the medicine cabinet. There were two prescriptions. One was an antibiotic, one was a powerful cough syrup.

She carried them both triumphantly back into the bedroom and started to open the antibiotic.

"Is that the cough syrup?" Delsey asked, reaching for it. She had a spoon in her hand. She read the directions, poured some into a spoon and pushed it toward Ren's defiantly closed mouth.

"Open up, or I'll roll you in a towel and shove it into you," Merrie said forcefully.

The words, and the tone, caused him to burst out laughing. He opened his mouth, and Delsey spooned the cough syrup in.

"Very nice," Merrie said. She held a pill in her hand. "This one, too," she said.

He stared up at her. "You wouldn't dare," he said.

"Delsey, have you got a really big towel and two strong men...?"

"Hell." He opened his mouth and glared at Merrie as she put the pill on his tongue.

He swallowed it down with some of the milk Delsey had brought him.

"Milk causes more mucus, you know," Merrie commented.

"It's all he'll drink when he's sick." Delsey sighed as she put the tray with legs over him and set the soup and spoon and napkin on it.

"He needs to drink lots of water, to thin the secretions so he can cough up the mucus," Merrie added.

"I'm right here," Ren muttered. "I can hear both of you."

They both stared at him.

He grimaced and picked up his soup spoon. "All right, you had your way. Now get out of here and let me eat my soup in peace."

"It's not soup. It's oyster stew. Your favorite," Delsey added with a warm smile.

He made a face at her, but then he smiled. "Okay. Thanks."

"You get better. If you need anything, use the intercom," Delsey added, indicating the unit on his bedside table.

"I won't. But thanks." He included Merrie in that. "Don't think that threat about the towel made any difference," he added firmly.

She grinned at him. "Liar," she said mischievously.

He just chuckled.

THAT NIGHT, MERRIE went in to see Ren before she went to bed. She was still fully dressed. She didn't want to be seen by a man in just pajamas and a robe, even if it was a modern world.

She knocked lightly and peered in the door. "Doing okay?" she asked.

He glared at her. "Close the door, from the outside," he said icily.

"Yes, sir." She closed it, wincing at his angry tone, and went down the hall to her own room.

He was so unpredictable. One day he was almost nice to her, the next he snapped her head off. She looked at herself in the mirror and realized the cause of his sudden irritation. Her cross was visible around her neck, outside the sweatshirt she was wearing.

She fingered it gently. Her mother had given it to her when she was a little girl. She'd changed the gold chain many times over the years, but the cross remained the same. It was something from her mother, her childhood, something priceless. Ren didn't have to like it. But she wasn't taking it off.

His coldness hurt her. She wondered why. He was just Randall's brother. He wasn't even nice most of the time. Ah, well, she thought, she wasn't going to be here long anyway. No use wasting thoughts on a man who'd probably pay to see her breaded and deep-fried.

IT TOOK HIM two days to get up enough strength to leave his bed. He was a little unsteady on his feet when he came down to breakfast, but his bad attitude was back in full force.

He pulled out a chair and glared at the women. "I don't need babying, in case you had that in mind. I feel fine."

Merrie stared at him. "Okay."

"Okay," Delsey agreed.

He popped his napkin out and folded it in his lap on top of his immaculate jeans and chaps. The spurs on his boots made a jingling sound when he moved his feet under the table.

"Is that sausage?" he asked suddenly, pointing his fork at the platter next to the bacon and eggs.

"Yes. Merrie likes it."

"I hate sausage," he said curtly.

"I love it," Merrie replied, just to irritate him. She gave him a long, steady look. "It just makes me feel good, thinking of pork being shoved through a sausage grinder."

His eyebrows went up. It was the way she said it, eyeing him the whole time. "I would not fit in a sausage grinder," he said abruptly.

She sighed. "Pity," she said, with a blithe smile.

He choked back a laugh and reached for the coffeepot.

SHE WALKED OUTSIDE before he left, enjoying the previous night's fall of new snow. It lay like a blanket over the hills and mountains in the distance. She wrapped her arms around herself, because it was below freezing and her coat was more decorative than functional.

"I thought I told you to go to town and buy a coat," Ren muttered as he came outside, sliding his hat over his brow.

"There hasn't been time," she replied.

"I'll have Delsey drive you in tomorrow," he said. His eyes gave the old coat a speaking glance. "Don't you own a decent winter coat?"

She flushed and lowered her eyes. "We had a very strict clothing allowance when Daddy was alive," she said with stinging pride. "He thought coats were a waste of money. He only gave us enough money to buy jackets, but I found this coat on sale."

"I'm surprised they weren't giving it away for free," he said haughtily.

She frowned at him. "Not everybody is rich, Mr. Colter," she said shortly. "Most people in the world just do the best they can with what they have."

He lifted an eyebrow and slid his eyes over what he could see of her trim figure. "How old are you?" he asked suddenly.

"Twenty-two," she returned.

His eyes darkened. Too young, he was thinking. Years too young. Twenty-two to his thirty-six. She was striking. It wasn't so much beauty, although she had that, as poise and grace. She moved like some graceful fawn, barely leaving traces of her footsteps when she walked.

"You're just a kid," he said quietly, thinking out loud.

"It's the mileage," she said suddenly.

He frowned. "What?"

"It's the mileage. Some people are old at twenty and some are young at eighty. It's the mileage."

"I see." He cocked his head and studied her openly. "You aren't old enough to have much mileage, just the same."

She smiled. "I don't let it show. It takes a lot fewer muscles to smile than it does to frown."

He cocked his hat low over his brow. "Don't expect to see many smiles around here in winter."

"Not true," she said pertly. "Delsey smiles all the time. So does Tubbs."

At the mention of the younger man's name, he froze over. "Tubbs is here to work, not to make calf's eyes at you," he said, his tone biting. "Don't encourage him. He likes blondes."

"I haven't encouraged anybody," she protested.

"See that you don't." His smile was colder than the snow around them. "After all, you're Randall's...friend, aren't you?" he added, a note of contempt in his tone.

"Yes," she said, not understanding. "Randall's my friend."

"You remember that."

He turned and marched off toward the truck, where one of the men was waiting for him. "Tell Delsey I'll be late," he called over his shoulder. "We're going quail hunting."

He was gone before she could even answer.

"Well, he's in some great shape to go out hunting," Delsey said irritably as she puttered around the kitchen. "Hunkered down in a snowbank waiting to spook a covey of quail! He'll catch his death!"

"He really doesn't listen to reason."

Delsey laughed. "No. He doesn't."

CHAPTER FOUR

THAT NIGHT, DELSEY had gone up to bed when Ren came in with a bag of partridges. He put them in the kitchen sink.

"Just leave them there," he said when he noticed Merrie watching television in the living room. "Delsey can deal with them in the morning. Good night."

"Good night," she called after him.

Well, at least he was speaking to her, Merrie thought wistfully. She finished watching her program, then turned the television off.

She was about to switch the light off in the kitchen when she remembered the partridges in the sink. It would be a shame to leave them there all night and expect poor Delsey to dress them even before she could start breakfast the next morning.

She pulled up a trash can and went to work. It didn't take long. She had them dressed and in baggies in the fridge. She dealt with the refuse, taking it outside to the garbage can, so the men could haul it off to the county landfill. They took a load most days.

She went to bed, feeling a sense of accomplishment. It was a rare feeling for a woman who'd hardly ever lived, except in the shadow of a tyrant.

SHE WENT DOWNSTAIRS to breakfast. Voices came up the staircase.

"I left them right there in the damned sink!" Ren growled. "I can't think what became of them."

"They're in the fridge," Merrie said.

He glared at her. "You don't put dead birds…"

"Ren?" Delsey held up the Ziplock bags with the dressed partridges in them.

He frowned. His eyes snapped back to Merrie with a question in them.

"Mandy taught me how," she said simply. "She's our housekeeper, back home, although she's more like a mother. She thought we needed to know how to do more than just cook. She even taught us how to dress chickens."

Ren was fascinated. She didn't seem the sort of woman who'd take to such a basic sort of occupation. She looked fragile, citified, as if she'd faint at the sight of blood. But Grandy's wound hadn't sent her swooning. She'd watched tapes of branding without flinching. Now, here she was field dressing game. He wasn't sure he'd ever known a woman besides Delsey who could do that. He tried to picture Angie, in her Paris gowns, soiling her hands with bird feathers in a sink.

"If it bothers you that much, I can glue the feathers back on," Merrie began outrageously.

He hid the smile the words engendered. "Full of surprises, aren't you, Miss Grayling?"

"Just one or two, Mr. Colter." She frowned. "Colter. There was a mountain man, Jim Bridger's protégé, they said, named John Colter. I heard a song about him on an old album my mother had."

"Yes. He discovered fumeroles and hot springs on the Shoshone River near Cody, as the story goes," Ren related as they sat down to breakfast. "They nicknamed it Colter's Hell, although most people thought he was spinning a tall tale until they actually saw it."

"I've never been there," Merrie said.

"Yellowstone National Park is near there. It's beautiful," Delsey remarked. "Pass the strawberry preserves, there's a dear."

Merrie handed them to her. "It's a place I'd love to see. Yellowstone, and the Little Big Horn Battlefield, and the museum."

"More history," Ren remarked.

Merrie smiled softly. "I live on YouTube. I've been on tours of all those places, but I'd love to see them in person one day. Especially the battlefield. Mama said that one of our relatives actually was in the fight."

"In the cavalry?" he asked.

She cleared her throat. "Not exactly."

He paused in the act of lifting the spoon from his coffee cup and stared at her.

"My great-great-great-grandfather was a full-blooded Oglala Lakota."

His eyebrows arched as he studied her closely.

"I know, I don't look it. But my mother's father had black hair and eyes and very dark skin. It was from her father's side that we got our blood."

Ren pursed his lips and chuckled. "One of my ancestors was Northern Cheyenne."

"They fought the Lakota," she mused.

"Tooth and nail. Well, usually, except at the Little Bighorn, when they joined together to fight Custer and his men."

She ate a spoonful of Delsey's delicious scrambled eggs. "How's Hurricane?" she asked.

He gave her a cold glance. It still rankled that she'd been able to do something with a horse that he couldn't. "Healing," was all he said.

She just nodded. He made his antagonism for her so obvious. It was uncomfortable.

He finished breakfast, threw down the last swallow of his coffee and got to his feet.

"Wear a muffler," Delsey said without looking up.

"Oh, for God's sake," he bit off.

"Wear a muffler," she repeated. "You're still not well."

He muttered something about overprotective mother hens. But he got a scarf and wrapped it around his neck before he put on his coat and hat.

Delsey got up and fetched a big thermos. "Hot coffee. It'll keep your insides warm."

"My insides are already warm." He grimaced, bent and kissed her wrinkled cheek. "Thanks," he said gruffly.

Merrie didn't lift her eyes until he was out the door and gone. She sipped coffee with a wistful glance at Delsey. "I set him off just by being in the house." She sighed. "He really dislikes me."

"It wouldn't matter who you were, child," Delsey said with a smile. "That she-cat razed his pride, made him a laughingstock on social forums online." She shook her head. "She was vindictive. None of what she said about him was true, but it was almost impossible to counter it."

"Yes, it is." She wondered what the woman had said about Ren. He was proud. It must have hurt his feelings very badly to be ridiculed in a way he couldn't fight.

There was the sound of a big truck out front, followed by a door slamming and a knock at the door.

Delsey went to answer it, and she stared blankly at the parcel service driver. "You sure that's for here?" she asked him with a grin.

"If there's a Miss Grayling here, it is," he replied, putting a stack of boxes just inside the front door. A flutter of snowflakes entered with them.

"It's my art supplies!" Merrie enthused. "Oh, thank you!"

"That's all art supplies?" Delsey asked, shaking her head. "What'd you do, order live models?"

The parcel driver chuckled, waved and left.

"It's an easel and some canvases and a lot of paints," Merrie replied. "I was afraid to ask Sari to send my supplies out here from Texas. I didn't want anybody to trace them."

"Oh, yes," Delsey agreed, remembering. "That stalker."

Merrie frowned. Well, perhaps Ren hadn't felt comfortable telling Delsey the truth. It didn't matter. Surely the FBI was hot on the trail of the contract killer by now.

"So I thought it would be better to order them from here," Merrie added. "Do you have a pair of scissors?"

"Something better." She grinned, went into the kitchen and came back with a knife in a leather pouch. "Ren gave it to me for my birthday. It's made by the same people who made the skeet gun he uses in competition."

"He shoots?"

She nodded. She bent to open the packages. "Not so much these days. Mostly he hunts elk or deer or partridge. Business is so complex here that he doesn't get a lot of time off."

"The men stay very busy."

"That's ranching, honey," Delsey said. "There's always something."

"It was that way at our ranch, too," Merrie confessed. "But we only had horses. No cattle. I don't know much about them yet, but I'll learn. YouTube is great!"

Delsey gave her a droll look. "Ren is better. Why don't you ask him to take you around and show you how he manages cattle?"

She sighed. "He'd point me to the path that leads down to the stables and tell me to help myself," she said with a wistful smile. "He doesn't want me around. Randall must have known that, before he brought me here. I should have stayed in Comanche Wells."

Delsey touched her hair gently. "No. You should be here, where you're safe. Ren will come around. You'll see. Now let's get these things into the studio."

THEY MOVED THE art supplies into the room that Merrie was using for a studio. "Did his mother really paint?" she asked.

Delsey nodded. "Yes. His father never remarried. He loved his ex-wife until the day he died."

Merrie's lips parted. "Ren didn't say that his mother painted, did he?"

Delsey winced. "He never talks about her. Never calls her. She sends cards and letters—well, she used to—and he sends them right back, unopened. I don't think he's even seen her since he graduated from college and came here." She shook her head. "It's sad. His mother was a nice person, from what Randall says about her, and she grieves for Ren."

Merrie didn't know what to say. She drew in a long breath. "Our mother was like spring itself," she commented, idly touching the unassembled easel in its box. "She loved us so much. She was always doing things with us, taking us places, loving us. After she died, life was a nightmare."

Delsey didn't pry, but she was openly curious. "What did she die of?"

Merrie bit her lower lip. "We think our father killed her. Please don't tell him," she said, nodding toward the door with a worried expression, indicating that she meant Ren. "Our father was violent. Paranoid. She died of a concussion, but one of our local doctors thought it was murder. He tried to do an autopsy, but he was suddenly called out of town, and Daddy paid somebody to do it while he was gone and classify it as an accidental death."

"Why didn't the doctor protest?"

"Because Daddy made threats to the people in charge." She shivered and wrapped her arms around herself. "You can't imagine the fear he instilled in people. He had something on every single person who worked for him—even Mandy. Mandy had a brother who was in the mob up north. Daddy threatened to have her brother sent to prison. He knew people who could plant evidence. Everybody in Comanche Wells, where we live, was scared of him. Even people in Jacobsville were. He terrorized the whole community."

"You had people in law enforcement…"

"Who had families," Merrie said gently. "If you threaten someone's child, it makes an impression. He was very good at intimidation." She didn't add that he was richer than just about anybody in that part of Texas.

"My goodness," Delsey said worriedly. She studied the younger woman and read the lingering fear. "Well, he can't hurt you anymore."

"No." Merrie let out a soft laugh. "We can finally leave towels on the floor. The rugs don't have to be straight. The bed doesn't have to be inspected to make sure it's made right. We can have disorder, for the first time in our lives. I even have mismatched towels in my bathroom." She grimaced. "He used the belt on me once for doing that."

"Mr. Ren's father used a belt on him, too, he said."

"Not like mine did, I imagine, with the belt buckle. It was a heavy one, too, made of metal. I have…scars." She swallowed and moved away. "That's all in the past now. He can't hurt us anymore."

"I'm sorry. It must have been a very rough childhood."

"Worse. We couldn't go to parties or learn to dance or drive, we couldn't go on dates. My goodness, I'm twenty-two years old and I've never even been kissed!"

Delsey was shocked. "But you're Randall's girl-friend…"

"No, I am not," she said firmly. "I'm Randall's friend, and that's all." She smiled. "You see, he's one of those men who likes lots of women. He doesn't love them, he just uses them, and when he's bored, he goes and finds another one. Sari and I went to church. We were taught that women don't play around before marriage. Actually, we were taught that men shouldn't, either. That children came of love between two people, in marriage, and that children deserved two parents to raise them." She gave Delsey a sheepish look. "That doesn't get us far with modern people. So we keep to ourselves."

"Child, there are a lot of people who still feel that way. It's just that they're shouted down and made to feel inferior because they have those beliefs. It's a test, of a sort. If we believe in something, we shouldn't have to defend those beliefs." She laughed. "Isn't it funny how some people say we need to respect the opinions and beliefs of other people, and then they go to town on us for being religious? They don't respect the beliefs of anybody except themselves, and they don't really believe in anything past having a good time and doing whatever they please. Rules are for fools."

"I really like you," Merrie said softly, and smiled. "You're like our Mandy, back home. She's been with us since we were very small. After Mama died, she sort of became our mother, if you know what I mean."

"Sort of like me and Ren." Delsey laughed. "I love Randall, too, but he isn't around much. He does most of the marketing and showing for the Black Angus pure-bred seed bulls that our Skyhorn Ranch is famous for. He's gone most of the year."

"He's good with people," Merrie said. "I liked him the first time I saw him. But he wasn't the sort of man I could ever get interested in. I'm no party girl."

"Did he think you were?" she asked.

"I'm not sure. He flirted with me, but I don't know how to flirt. I tried to go on a date one time, with a cowboy I knew. Daddy found out. He had the cowboy chased clean out of the state, threatened him with an old felony charge he'd been acquitted of." She swallowed. The memory was harsh. "Then he knocked me down the stairs and…" She stopped. "I never tried to go out with anybody again."

"Oh, child," Delsey said softly. "I'm so sorry!"

"So I wasn't really comfortable with the idea of going places with Randall. I didn't tell him much, but I let him know that it was dangerous for me to date anybody, and that we were too different to be involved with each other. But I told him I'd love to be his friend." She smiled. "That worked out much better. He's very nice."

Delsey, looking at her, could understand why Randall might have wanted to get involved with her. She was pretty and sweet and kind. But Randall could never settle for just one woman. He was too flighty. Ren, on the other hand, was certain that Merrie was like Randall's other girlfriends who came here. Most of them came on to Ren. They were glittery women who had modern attitudes about sex. Delsey didn't approve, but it wasn't her place to say anything. If one of Randall's women ended up in Ren's bed, it didn't concern her. They knew the score. She frowned. She hoped Ren wasn't putting Merrie in that category. There could be consequences. He wasn't around the woman enough to know her background, and Randall hadn't been forthcoming about her. It was a recipe for disaster.

Well, that wasn't a problem that needed solving today. Delsey continued to help Merrie put her canvases and paints and accessories away, including the fine brushes she used.

"What are you painting?" Delsey asked, looking pointedly at the sketchbook on the easel.

"Promise you won't tell him?" Merrie asked worriedly.

"I promise."

She pulled up the cloth she'd draped over an old canvas she'd found and displayed the contents. The painting was only a sketch right now. She'd found a leftover canvas in the room and used it to sketch her subject while she'd waited for her art supplies to arrive. Since she had neither paint nor drawing pencils, she'd used a soft lead #2 pencil to do the preliminary outline.

Even so, the image was so realistic it could have walked off the canvas. Delsey actually gasped.

"You said you painted a little," Delsey exclaimed. "This isn't... It's magnificent!" she said, lost for the right words.

Merrie smiled. "Thanks. I've always loved to draw. Sari said that we might buy…" She almost said "an art supply store," but she caught herself. She didn't want to give away her monied background. It usually intimidated people. "That we might be able to exhibit my work at the local art store."

"Art store, nothing," Delsey scoffed. She looked at the sketch with soft eyes. "You captured that look on his face that I could never understand."

"It's sorrow," Merrie said quietly. "He's alone, inside himself. He can't get out, or let anyone else in. He's strong, and tender, and brimming over with love. But he doesn't really trust women. Or like them very much." She turned to Delsey, who seemed surprised at her perception of Ren. "How did he get mixed up with that woman you told me about?"

Delsey bit her lower lip. "Angie? She was one of Randall's girls. He brought her here to visit. She knew that Ren had more money than Randall inherited from his father, so she went after Ren. She was always wrapped around him, playing up to him. He's a lonely man, for the most part, and she was aggressive physically. If you want my opinion, she made him so hungry that he got engaged to her in desperation. Then he found her with two of his business associates at a party. Apparently the three of them were romantically involved. Ren took the ring off her finger and flushed it down the toilet, with her watching."

"Poor Ren."

"She even spread lies about Ren online. We know a man who works for local rancher Mallory Kirk—Red

Davis. Red's a wonder. He can hack anything. The FBI tried to hire him, but he likes cattle better than people, so he refused. He did some work for Mallory's brother, when his girlfriend was targeted by her vicious stepfather with obscene Photoshopped pictures online. He got rid of every trace. He did the same for Ren. Angie was arrested and prosecuted for what she did to him. She got off with probation, but she never put a word out about him again. Still, it's made him bitter. That was months ago. He's still brooding about it."

"I noticed."

"He's not generally a mean person. I'm sorry that he's been so hard on you. If you'd met under different circumstances, he might have reacted differently."

"In other words, if Randall hadn't brought me here."

"Exactly. You're the first woman Randall has brought here since Angie. That probably helped set him off."

Merrie sighed. Just her luck, to be attracted to a man who had a false impression of her because of Randall. She was only just realizing why Ren resented her presence here.

"I probably should go back home," she said, thinking out loud.

"He's not mad at you," Delsey countered. "Besides, aren't you trying to get away from that man who's stalking you?"

Merrie turned, frowning. She was putting these people in danger just by being in the house with them. Delsey was so like Mandy back home; sweet and kind and loving. "There are things you don't know about me," she began.

The sound of the phone ringing downstairs interrupted them.

"Oh, goodness, I'll have to get that. I told Ren we should have phones upstairs and he said it was a waste of money," she muttered on the way downstairs. "It isn't his poor old legs that get worn out running up and down stairs to answer phones!"

Merrie chuckled to herself. She looked at the sketch of Ren on the canvas. It captured the very essence of the man himself. It was, she decided, going to be the best painting she'd ever done.

She worked on it tirelessly for a week, reworking it until she had it just the way she wanted it. When it was finished, she turned it to face the wall, just in case he walked in, and started painting one of Hurricane.

She was late to supper one night, and Ren was inflexible about house rules again, so she didn't get to eat. She had a sandwich in the small cooler in her room that Delsey had provided. She washed it down with a bottle of spring water, also from Delsey. She hoped Ren wouldn't discover her stash of food. He probably wouldn't approve. And it wasn't as if she hadn't become accustomed to rigid rules of behavior back home. She'd just hoped it wouldn't be like that someplace else. Maybe everybody was like her father and Ren, wanting things just so and refusing to change.

She tiptoed back down to her art studio after she finished the sandwich, wearing her nightgown and a thick white cotton robe that covered every inch of her except for her bare feet. She'd forgotten to pack slippers.

The door to the studio was ajar. She opened it, and there was Ren, gaping at the portrait of Hurricane that she'd just finished.

He heard her come in and turned. He was wearing jeans and a long-sleeved red flannel shirt with a black checkerboard pattern. His feet were in socks, not boots. His hair was mussed, as if he'd brushed it back in irritation.

"You did this?" he asked, amazement in his whole look.

"Well...yes," she confessed, flushing. She hoped he hadn't looked at the other canvas. She glanced at it, relieved to see that it was still turned to the wall.

"You said you could draw a little," he persisted.

She shrugged. "Just a little."

"This is gallery-quality art," he said, trying to formulate thoughts. He'd been shocked when he saw what his houseguest could do with paint and canvas. He'd never known anyone who could paint like this. And he'd rarely seen a painting done with more skill or insight. The horse on the canvas had faint scars on its head and neck and back. The eyes, though, were what made it. If a horse had a soul, this one did. The look in its eyes made him feel odd. It was the look of a human who'd been badly beaten, not an animal.

"Thanks," she said belatedly.

"Have you done anything else?" He was looking at the portrait turned to the wall.

"That one's just started. It's not ready to be seen," she protested weakly.

He cocked his head. "Sketches, then?"

She hesitated. Then she moved to the cabinet where her sketch pads and extra canvases were stored. She pulled out the biggest sketchbook and reluctantly handed it to him.

He sat down in one of the room's padded chairs and started looking. The subjects entranced him. There was Delsey, immortalized with a pencil, showing the inner beauty in a way he'd never actually seen before. There were his men, old and young alike, captured on the paper. There was his prize bull, Colter's Pride 6443, in his shiny black glory, so lifelike that he could have walked off the page.

All the sketches told a story. He saw pride, grief, pain, resignation, amusement and sorrow in her subjects, saw their past and present in the eyes that were so very expressive.

"My God," he said finally, and it was in a reverent, soft tone. He looked up. "This is why you keep missing meals," he guessed.

She shrugged. "I get lost in my work," she said. "A line is out of place, or there isn't enough shadow, or I've got one eye that doesn't really match the other. So I draw and erase and change until I get it right." She smiled sadly. "Sari used to say that I'd be carried off by a tornado one day with my brush in my hand, staring at a canvas." She laughed. "She's probably right. I lose track of time when I'm working."

He cocked his head. Her night attire was strange.

He remembered the nightmare she'd had, remembered how he'd felt as he looked at her. She was Randall's girl. Randall had made that clear in a couple of phone calls during the time she'd been here. *This one isn't like Angie*, he'd teased, *so hands off. Merrie's mine.*

Merrie. He wanted to call her Meredith, since it suited her more than that juvenile version of her name that his brother used. Randall had told him her full name. His eyes slid over the thick cotton bathrobe that covered her from her neck down to her bare ankles. He smiled at her bare feet.

"It's too cold in the house to go walking around without shoes," he chided. "You'll catch cold, like I did."

She moved her toes restlessly. "I'm not cold."

"You don't have any slippers," he translated.

"I'll go shopping online."

"I told you, I have an account in town at a local store. Delsey will drive you there. Get a coat. And some slippers." He pursed his lips. "Buy an evening gown, too. Something pretty. With shoes and an evening bag to match. And whatever you need to go under it." His eyes narrowed with curiosity about what she looked like under that thick robe.

She pulled the robe tighter. "Why an evening gown?"

"There's a party. I don't want to go, but if I don't, there'll be more gossip. Angie's going to be there," he added coldly.

Angie, Merrie recalled from conversations with Delsey, was the woman who'd cheated on him. "A party?"

"Yes." He stared at her with suddenly cold eyes. "You can dance, can't you?"

"No," she said wistfully.

His eyes widened. "You can't dance?" he exclaimed.

She flushed. "Daddy wouldn't let us go on dates," she said. "I've watched people doing it on TV, and Sari and I danced a cha-cha together just once…" Her voice trailed away, and she winced.

He moved forward in his chair. "Just once?"

"Daddy caught us. He believed dancing was wrong…" She swallowed. "No, I don't dance."

"I can teach you."

She looked up into his soft, black eyes and felt herself melting inside. "You can?"

He nodded. His eyes slid down her body. "Why do you wear a housecoat that covers you up like an elderly woman?"

"I've never been around men when I was dressed for bed," she replied. She shifted uncomfortably. "When I had the nightmare, that was the first time anybody except Sari or Mandy ever saw me in bed."

He was eyeing her closely. She was good, he thought. She played the innocent with a real flair. But she was Randall's girl, and Randall didn't date girls who didn't put out. So she was just like Angie, only even better at acting the part.

"I should go on up," Merrie said, not liking the way he looked at her.

He tore his gaze away from her and looked back at the portrait on the easel. "I meant what I said about your talent," he said quietly. "You should be exhibiting."

She smiled. "I might, later on. I could never dare do it when Daddy was alive. He hated the very idea of us doing anything that drew attention to him. He was...a very private person."

"Sounds like he was a lunatic," Ren said flatly, "and he should have been sitting in a jail cell. What the hell is wrong with the community you live in? Don't people care about what happens to their neighbors? Hell, I punched a guy two years ago for hitting on my wrangler's twelve-year-old daughter. I fired him to boot. It wasn't my problem, but I made it my problem. We take care of our own in small communities. At least, here in Wyoming we do."

She drew in a long, slow breath. "You don't know how it was," she said finally. "Daddy had friends in the mob. He could use them for all sorts of terrible things. People were afraid of him. Even people in positions of power. Not so much now, of course. We're a hotbed of retired mercenaries and former military, and Eb Scott runs an internationally known counterterrorism school a few miles down the road from our house. He loaned us two of his guys when someone tried to kill Sari."

He made a sound deep in his throat. "Someone tried to kill Sari?"

"Morris. He was one of Daddy's guys who'd do anything for money. This woman's son hired him to kill my sister."

He was shocked. "Why would he want to kill your sister?"

She frowned. "Didn't Randall tell you why he asked me to stay here, on the ranch?" she asked worriedly.

"He said you were being stalked by a rejected admirer," he said, and his eyes told her that he found that almost unbelievable. She was pretty, but she wasn't a beauty.

Merrie sighed. "My father…killed a woman. She turned him in to the FBI because he was involved in money laundering. Her son was, is, unbalanced. He loved his mother very much. She left him a lot of money, money that the Feds couldn't touch. He thought Daddy must love us both terribly because he was so overprotective, so he put out contracts on both of us."

Ren just gaped at her. Obviously he hadn't been told anything.

"Morris had worked for Daddy for a long time and he knew us. When he shot at Sari, he missed. The second time he did it, Paul, Sari's husband now, recognized the tire track pattern of the car where the shells were found. It was a car from our garage. So Morris was arrested and we thought that was the end of it."

His face was hard. "Go on."

She grimaced. "But Paul found out that Morris was only hired for Sari. For me, he went to Brooklyn and hired someone well-known in mob circles for success as a cleaner. The woman's son thought I was the youngest, so I was more precious to Daddy than Sari was. Paul said the man had been in the business for almost two decades, and he had an impeccable reputation for killing people. He's after me now."

Ren sat back in the chair, just staring at her with troubled black eyes.

"I'm sorry," Merrie said. "I thought Randall had told you the truth. I shouldn't be here. You're all in danger. I should go…"

"No."

She was shocked by his simple reply.

"I have state-of-the-art security here," he continued. "We have eyes all over the ranch, at every single gate. We have recognition software to filter everyone who comes on the place. We have infrared cameras everywhere." He drew in a breath. "My bulls are worth millions. I don't take chances with their safety. But it also means you'll be safe here. Damn my brother for hiding the truth!" he cursed. "I wouldn't have sent you home."

She bit her lower lip, hard. She fought tears. "Thanks. It isn't that we don't have protection at home, we do. Plus two of Eb Scott's guys moved into the house and Sari defied Daddy and told him they weren't leaving. He left in a huff, but he was arrested soon after and had to make bail." She shook her head, smiling sadly. "He planned on marrying off Sari to a Middle Eastern prince. So that he'd have millions for his defense attorneys. His ill-gotten gains were confiscated by the Feds, you see."

"What did she say to that?"

"That she wasn't going. He'd locked her in the den with him. We were worried, but he promised he just wanted to talk to her. Then we heard him snap the belt." She closed her eyes and shivered, oblivious to the pained look of the man near her, who was eaten up with guilt for frightening her with his own belt early in their acquaintance.

"Our bodyguards heard her scream and broke into the office. Sari's arm was bleeding where he hit her with the belt. Daddy was sitting in a chair where he fell, stone dead."

"Good grief!"

She stuck her hands in the pockets of her robe. "Sari said she'd killed him. Paul assured her that she hadn't. The autopsy found evidence of heavy drug use and a lesion in his brain. The combination produced a heart attack. But we had to watch Sari for a couple of days. She locked herself in her room. Paul had to fly back from Brooklyn, because he was the only person she'd listen to." She smiled. "She'd loved him for years and years. He went away suddenly. He'd given Daddy a ridiculous reason for leaving, you see. He said that he was married—actually he was a widower—and that Sari had flirted with him, like young girls do. Daddy accepted his resignation, and gave him severance pay. Then after he was gone, Daddy called Sari into his office…"

Ren leaned forward. What he was learning about his houseguest made him furious on her behalf. He was sorry her father was dead, because he'd have liked to have a physical discussion with him about using a belt on a woman.

"What did he do?" he asked quietly.

"He almost beat her to death," Merrie said unsteadily. "I heard her screaming. Mandy had been sent off on a long shopping holiday by Daddy, so she wouldn't know what he did to us. I ran into the office and tried to stop him, but he turned on me." She closed her eyes against the painful memory. "He had a doctor on his payroll, one who'd lost his medical license. He stitched the wounds and gave us antibiotics to take and took care of us while we healed. When Mandy came back, we didn't dare tell her. Daddy said he'd killed people and got away with it, and how would we feel if something happened to Mandy? So we pretended that it never happened."

Ren sat back in the chair with his legs crossed. He couldn't believe a man could be that cruel to his children. And the dead woman's son must have hated Grayling with a passion to hire hit men to go after his daughters.

"Didn't the man who hired the killers know that Grayling was dead?"

"He found it out after he hired the man to kill me. Great timing, wasn't it? They said he collapsed and started crying. He's done everything he could to help them catch the guy. He's in jail, waiting for trial. Even the cooperation won't keep him from serving time."

"And it shouldn't," Ren said coldly. "What a damned cowardly thing to do."

"Daddy killed his mother," she said simply. "He got drunk and hired people to get even with him." She shook her head. "I still can't believe it's happening. It's like watching an old movie about gangsters on television."

"It must seem that way to you." He got up from the

chair and stood in front of her. "I promise, you'll be safe here."

She looked up into his black eyes and felt her stomach drop to the floor. He was so handsome. She thought she'd never tire of looking at him.

"Oh! Death will find me, long before I tire of watching you," she said absently as she looked at him. She flushed from chin to forehead when that slipped out.

CHAPTER FIVE

REN ACTUALLY LOOKED AMUSED. "Are you quoting Rupert Brooke? He died in 1915, so the poem was published after he died in World War I."

She smiled shyly. "It's a beautiful poem. I didn't mean to blurt it out…"

He moved a step closer and touched her long, soft blond hair. "Do you remember the last line of that poem?"

"Yes. I didn't mean…"

"And turn, and toss your brown, delightful head amusedly, among the ancient Dead," he quoted.

"Well, if I didn't watch people, I couldn't paint them," she said, flustered.

His eyes slid sideways, to the painting turned to the wall. "Come on, coward. Show it to me," he teased.

She ground her teeth together. He made her nervous. She was unsure of herself and he was…he was flirting with her. Wasn't that flirting? She'd had only Randall do that with her. No, that cowboy of Ren's, what was his name? Tubbs. Yes, Tubbs had flirted with her. She didn't know how to handle it.

Reluctantly she picked up the canvas, turned it

around and placed it on the second easel in the room. She stepped back and let him look at the portrait.

It was him, immortalized in oils, sitting in front of a campfire, his hat pulled low over his eyes. He was looking toward the fire, holding his big beautifully masculine hands toward it. Beside him lay a scrolled-barrel skeet gun and a knife in a fringed leather sheath, of a soft tan color. In the background were tall lodgepole pines, and in the distance, a teepee, barely visible on the horizon.

Ren was almost too stunned to speak. The painting showed the man, not the persona he showed to the world. Everything he felt was there, in his eyes: the despair, the grief, the buried hatred, but also the strength and solidness and authority that radiated from him.

"I've never seen anything like it," he said finally. "It's… I can't even find the words." He turned to her. "You can name your own price for that."

She shook her head. "I give them away. I don't sell them."

"You should sell them," he persisted. "Nobody in the world can turn down money in these hard times."

"I have all I need." It was true. She wasn't telling him, but she had two hundred million in a Swiss bank account.

She was a conundrum. Ren wanted her and hated himself for it. She was Randall's. She had to be experienced. But when he got close to her, she backed away, as if he frightened her. Was it an act? He was going to find out, very soon.

"It's a gift," Merrie said. She handed the canvas to

him. She hated to part with it, because she'd done it for herself. She couldn't admit that.

"Thank you," he said formally. "You're sure you won't accept a check?"

"I'm sure."

"All right. The one you're doing of Delsey…"

"I'm going to give it to her," she interrupted with a grin. "She's so nice. I don't know how I'd have managed without her."

"Yes. The small cooler in your room that you keep stocked with sandwiches and bottled water…?" he teased.

She flushed. "Oh, gosh, I didn't think you'd know!"

"I know everything that goes on around here. I'm the boss." He drew in a breath. "Oh, hell, be as late as you like for meals. I'll tell Delsey. There's no way to rein in artists. It would be like herding cats!"

She laughed helplessly. "I'll try harder," she said.

He shrugged. "No problem. Good night." He looked back at her with something in his black eyes that kept her awake for a long time afterward.

THE NEXT MORNING at breakfast, Ren asked her to ride out with him, to see the ranch.

"Gosh, you mean it?" Merrie exclaimed.

"I mean it," he said, trying not to show how her enthusiasm touched him.

She grinned and dug into her breakfast. Delsey, watching, hid a smile.

Ren frowned when she came out in her usual light-weight coat. She had on one of her little knitted hats, in shades of yellow and blue and pink, to keep her head warm. Her long blond hair flowed from it like silk. "It's snowing, and the temperature is well below freezing," he pointed out. "You're going to freeze in that."

"Oh, no, I'll be fine!" she protested, frightened that he might change his mind if he thought she might get sick from the cold. "Really!"

He was debating, and she saw it in his face.

She moved a little closer to him, her pale blue eyes intent on his tanned face. "I'll be fine. I promise."

Her voice sent echoes of pleasure through his body. Since Angie, he hadn't even looked at a woman. But Meredith made him feel younger, optimistic; things he hadn't felt in many years.

"Really," she repeated.

He drew in an exasperated breath and pulled his hat low over his eyes. "All right. But if you get sick, I'll never let you forget it. Got that?"

She just grinned.

HE PUT HER on one of the older saddle horses, a palomino he called Sand. He rode a black gelding, a beautiful shiny horse that looked much like Hurricane. She mentioned that.

He chuckled. "He should look like him, he's Hurricane's brother. He's just four years old."

"He's beautiful."

"Catch up," he called as his horse moved ahead down the long path that led past the barn and stables, with their adjoining corrals.

She coaxed her mount to go faster. She loved to

ride. It was a shame that she'd never had the opportunity to do much of it. Her father hadn't liked either of his daughters to go out on the ranch, where there were men working.

"How big is the ranch?" she asked, idly lifting her face to the soft snowflakes that were raining down.

"Thousands of acres," he said.

"Our little place is only a couple of hundred acres," she commented. She didn't add that their little place ran some of the most famous Thoroughbreds in the world.

"You couldn't run many head of cattle there, could you?" he asked idly.

"Daddy had horses. He never liked cattle."

He glanced back at her with a wry grin. "I like horses because they're necessary to work cattle. Drives Tubbs nuts when I say that. He's in love with every horse on the place." He grimaced. "He's still kicking himself for hiring the man who beat Hurricane."

"Anybody can slip once in a while," she said. "It's hard to see what's inside a person by just looking."

He pulled up his horse and studied her. "*You* can."

She flushed. "I always thought it went with painting. You can't paint what you don't see."

He searched her pale eyes as snowflakes passed between them. "You should be exhibiting in galleries."

She smiled. "Thanks. I might do that, when I get back home."

Home. He felt uncomfortable at the thought of her leaving. Then he had to remind himself, again, that she was Randall's girl. He turned the horse and started off again.

Merrie followed along behind him on the trail, feeling a little uncomfortable at the way he looked at her. He couldn't seem to make up his mind whether he liked her or not. She wished she knew more about men.

He took her through the big barn to show her the prize bulls he kept. "They have heating and air-conditioning, and one cowboy stays with them most of the time. They're worth a fortune."

"They sure are pretty," she said.

He smiled. "I think so. We breed for superior bloodlines, for conformation, weaning weight, birth weight and weight gain ratios. I took several courses in genetics when I first came back here to stay with my father. He had the practical know-how, but it took a little science to move us up the chain of purebred sires."

"Where are the cows?" she asked innocently.

He chuckled. "Out in the pastures. We don't put the bulls on them until they're ready to be bred, to drop spring calves. That happens in August, so our calf crop will drop in April, when the lush grass is just coming up. Of course, we have to hope that the weather doesn't do something crazy, like it's doing right now." He indicated the heavy snow falling outside the barn. "This is late October, but the temperature is unusually low, and that snow is getting deep fast."

"It's so beautiful." She sighed wistfully. "We're lucky if we get an inch of snow every ten years back home."

"We get sick of it some years," he mused. "We have to carry hay out to the far pastures if snow gets deep enough. Have to make sure we break the ice in the water troughs so the cattle can drink. Have to have men check the herd two or three times a day. That time doubles when we've got pregnant cows or, especially, heifers. Some of them have to be brought up near the barn, in case they have trouble calving."

"It sounds very complicated."

"It is. Complicated, and beautiful." He looked around him. "I lived in Boston for four years while I went to college. Hated every minute that I wasn't in class or studying."

"I guess I'd have liked college. But I didn't really have a career in mind like my sister did. She wanted to be a district attorney from the time she was a teenager." She sighed. "I did get so sick of watching endless *Perry Mason* reruns with her," she laughed.

"You said she was an assistant district attorney."

"Yes. She just took her bar exam a few months ago. Passed it on the first try, too. Plenty of her classmates didn't. I was so proud of her." She wrapped her arms around herself. "Daddy actually went to her graduation. He was away on business when I graduated from high school."

He leaned against one of the gates, his arms folded over his sheepskin jacket. "I remember my graduation day," he mused. "None of my family came, but my classmates and I treed a local bar afterward."

"Sari's classmates had a big party. Of course she couldn't go. Daddy got furious when she even mentioned it…" Her voice trailed away. "One of her classmates was moving in with her boyfriend. Daddy called her a slut and dragged us away from her. People stared at us like we were from the ice age."

"He didn't think people should live together?"

"Only if they were married." She looked up. "Mama took us to church. It was the only place outside of shopping with Daddy that we were ever allowed to go. We were raised with an old-fashioned morality. We took a lot of heat for it in school." She touched her sweater, where the small cross lay underneath. "Religion was all we had. It kept us going through some hard times, when Daddy lost his temper." She sighed. "It's so nice to be someplace where I'm not watched every single minute of the day."

"Why did your father have you watched?" he asked, curious.

"So we wouldn't get involved with men," she said simply. "Sari said Daddy told Paul that he didn't want his daughter marrying some grubby little lawman." She winced. "Paul had been with the FBI. He was the only member of his family who wasn't involved with the mob. He was very proud. It hurt him, to have Daddy say such a thing. As if he had no worth, because he'd been in law enforcement."

"He didn't approve of your sister getting involved with him?"

"He didn't know, or they never could have," she replied. "Paul loved her so much. More than anything in the world. He broke up with her because of money... well, because of Daddy," she amended, not wanting to tell him the whole truth. "She went off to the Bahamas to try to get over Paul, and got caught in a hurricane.

Paul and Mandy, our housekeeper, flew down there to look for Sari." She shivered. "Paul used his FBI credentials to get to the disaster scene. He found a body with red hair. He thought it was Sari. Mandy said she'd never seen him cry." She stopped and swallowed. "They went back to Nassau to arrange to fly the body home, and there was Sari, drenched but alive getting off a sailing ship that had rescued her and some of the other tourists on the tour. It was a wonderful homecoming."

"They're married now?"

She laughed. "Oh, yes. Paul was going to be noble, but Mandy said Sari locked him in a bedroom with her. They were married less than a week later."

He chuckled. "She sounds like a character."

"She is. My best friend, as well as my big sister."

"I never had siblings, until my mother married Randall's father," he said, pain just slightly visible in his hard features. "He was well-to-do, so mother finally had everything she ever wanted. I haven't spoken to her in years, but I loved Randall," he said, his voice softening. "We're not full brothers, but that never mattered. I'd do anything for him."

"He speaks the same way about you," she replied.

"Hey, boss!" one of the hands called. "Snow's getting pretty deep. Want me to hitch up the sledge and start hauling hay to the south pasture?"

"Good idea, Bandy," Ren called back. "Call some of the part-timers in, if you have to."

"I will."

"Your men are nice," she said.

He chuckled as he shouldered away from the fence.

"They're competent, or they wouldn't work here, nice or not. We'd better get going, before the snow gets any deeper."

She was afraid he was going to cancel the tour. She beamed when she realized that he wasn't.

He turned away from the sweet, shy look on her face. He wondered about her. She didn't seem to fit a pattern at all.

THEY RODE THROUGH the lodgepole pines to a small stream, its banks thick with snow, that ran through the property. It was like a silver ribbon in the snowy landscape.

"I just can't get over how shallow the streams and rivers are out here," she remarked. "Back home, even streams are pretty deep in places."

"A lot of things are different out here in Wyoming. We had a cowboy lost in a blizzard once. Took us two days to find him, and he wasn't alive by the time we did. He didn't follow the cardinal rule."

"Which is?" she asked, genuinely curious.

"Stay put. It's best to stay on a trail or path or road, if you're near one. But you never keep walking. It's suicide."

"I'll remember," she said. "What kind of trees are those?" she asked, indicating some hardwoods near the stream.

"Cottonwoods," he told her, smiling. "Old-timers used to scrape the sap from them and eat it like ice cream."

"Wow!"

He chuckled at her enthusiasm. "Are you always that excited to learn new things?"

"Always," she replied. "I read a lot about the Inuit, up in Alaska. They have over fifty words for snow."

"We have just a few words for it, and none of them are repeatable in mixed company," he said, tongue in cheek.

It took her a minute to get what he was saying. When she did, she burst out laughing.

He pulled his hat lower over his eyes. "The boys usually have a campfire out near the first line cabin. We'll go that far and then turn back. Snow's getting deep, and I'll have things to do."

"Okay." She was looking forward to seeing a real campfire. She hoped the one she'd put in Ren's painting was realistic. She'd seen them in movies, but never in real life.

THE LINE CABIN was small, made of rough wood. There were three cowboys sitting around a big bonfire. One was making coffee. Another was frying what looked like bacon and eggs.

"Hey, boss!" the youngest cowboy said, smiling. "Damned stove stopped working, so we're roughing it."

"I'll have Grandy come out and see about fixing it tomorrow," Ren promised. "Got enough coffee for two more?"

"Sure do. Bacon and eggs, too."

"We just had breakfast, but thanks," Ren replied.

He dismounted and helped Merrie down.

She grimaced as she tried to walk.

"Legs sore?" Ren teased. "Riding takes some getting used to."

"I noticed," she said with a laugh. "I haven't ridden a horse in months."

"Wish we could say that," one of the other cowboys commented wistfully.

"This is Meredith," Ren introduced her. "She's a friend of Randall's. She's staying with us for a while."

He introduced the cowboys to her. One, a tall and rangy one, was named Willis. He was the ranch foreman. The rest of the men greeted her enthusiastically. One got her a cup of coffee, another offered her a camp stool. She sat down and sipped coffee while Ren asked them about predators that had been seen nearby.

She almost dozed off. Ren called her name. He had his horse by the reins.

"The boys and I are going to ride down to the fence line for just a couple of minutes to look at a sick heifer. Will you be all right until I get back?"

"Of course," she said, holding out her hands to the warmth of the bonfire. She smiled. "I'll wait right here."

"See that you do." He vaulted into the saddle. "Won't be long." He turned his horse and caught up to the others.

Merrie watched them until they were out of sight. The snow was beautiful. The campfire was so warm. She closed her eyes and smiled. Then she heard it. A long, echoing howl. It sounded like a wolf, and very close by.

She stood up, her heart racing. The howl came

again. It sounded closer. She looked around nervously. She had no weapon. She'd read about wolves. Wouldn't they attack lone people sometimes?

The howl grew louder and closer. Merrie panicked. She'd promised not to move, but there was a wolf and it sounded as if it was coming closer, right into the camp. She felt fear like a sickness in her gut. If she'd only had a weapon!

She got up from the camp stool and moved away from the howling, back down into the shelter of the lodgepole pines. Perhaps if the wolf couldn't see her, it would leave. Her heart raced like a ticking watch as she kept backing into the woods.

She didn't mean to go far, but the snow suddenly picked up and turned everything white around her. She couldn't see a foot in front of her. She hoped she was going the right way, to try to get back to camp. Ren would be back soon. Surely he'd see the wolf and make it leave!

The snow fell harder. It blinded her as she walked. In less than five minutes, she was hopelessly lost. And that howling was closer than she'd realized.

She recalled what Ren had told her about the cowboy who got lost in a blizzard and was found dead. She also remembered what he'd said to do. Don't keep walking. Stay put. Keep on a path or a trail.

She looked around and grimaced. There wasn't either. She was in a small clearing near a stream. She didn't have a cell phone with her, or any matches. She couldn't make a fire. She was freezing cold, because she didn't have gloves and she'd had to hold on to tree trunks to get away from the howling thing.

Great, she thought. *I'll freeze to death, and it's my own fault. Nobody will ever find me. I'll be covered up with snow and lost in the wilderness. Why didn't I stay put?*

She sat down at the trunk of the tree and wrapped her arms tight around herself. "Stupid, stupid," she muttered to herself. All because something howled. It was still howling, only it sounded closer. She had nothing that could be used as a weapon. There was a big limb nearby, but she couldn't budge it. The whole limb was frozen. That made her hands even colder, and numb.

The snow was coming down in bucket loads. Ren was probably going crazy trying to find her. He was going to be so mad…!

The sudden sound of a gunshot startled her. She jumped to her feet, shivering. Then it dawned on her. It was a signal.

"I'm here!" she called. "I'm down here!"

There were voices. One was deep and very angry. She winced as Ren came into view, moving down the hill as if the snow wasn't even there.

He came to a stop in front of her and stood with his hands on his hips, glaring down at her with black eyes that absolutely glittered.

"Oh, Ren!" She threw herself against him and held on for dear life. "I'm sorry. I'm sorry! I did a stupid thing. I heard a wolf howling and it sounded so close. I got scared and I just didn't think. I'm sorry!"

He let out the breath he'd been holding and jerked her close, inside his open jacket, enveloping her in his strong arms. He rocked her, loving the feel of her soft body against him, drinking in the scent of honeysuckle that still clung to her hair. It had been a long time since any woman had made him feel protective, possessive.

"It's all right," he said at her ear, his voice like velvet. "I only meant to be gone for a minute or two. We lost track of time."

"The howling scared me," she confessed sheepishly. She loved being held by him. She felt safer than she'd ever been in her life, right now. She closed her eyes with a soft sigh and listened to Ren's heart beat under her ear.

"We have wolves on the place," he said. "One of them, however, is a pet. That's what you heard," he added with a soft chuckle.

"A pet?" She lifted her head and looked up into his black eyes at close range. Very close range. She felt swollen all over because of the way he was staring at her.

"It lives in the cabin with Willis, when he's out here with the nighthawks."

"Oh." Her eyes were searching his. They fell involuntarily to his chiseled mouth. She'd never been kissed in her life, but she wanted to be. She'd never wanted anything so much. "Nighthawks?"

Ren intercepted that look and understood it better than she realized. He was tempted. Very tempted. But she was Randall's girl, and the snow was about to cover them up. He took her by the waist and moved her back away from him.

"Nighthawks. The men who watch over the various herds at night, from line cabins like this one, when we have bad weather. We have to go back to the house now," he said. "You must be frozen in that flimsy coat."

"My hands are cold, too," she said. She grimaced. "No gloves."

"You're going shopping tomorrow, snow or no snow," he replied. "I'll have Tubbs drive you and Delsey to town. She's got the card for the account."

"Oh, but I could…"

"You'll do as you're told," he mused, smiling at her consternation. "You won't win an argument with me. Give it up."

"Okay. Thanks," she said softly, her pale eyes adoring on his hard face.

His body clenched. He liked the way she was with him. He hated his brother. He didn't know what he wanted anymore. He felt like a man walking headlong into quicksand.

"While you're at it, buy an evening dress."

"An evening dress?" she asked absently.

They mounted up. He led the way back up the trail.

"I told you. There's a party for a friend of mine who's moved into a new house with his wife. You can go with me. They'll have a band and hors d'oeuvres. You can dance, can't you?"

She swallowed. "No," she said miserably. "I've never even been to a party in my life, except birthday ones when Sari and I were very small and our mother was still alive."

He frowned. "You really can't dance?"

She grimaced. "No. So I guess I won't need the dress…"

"I can teach you to dance," he said quietly. "It's not that difficult."

Her face lost its tautness. She smiled. "I'd like very much to go with you," she said. "If your friend wouldn't mind. I don't know anybody here."

"He won't mind."

"Okay."

He thought about teaching her to dance. He thought about teaching her a lot of things. His body got hotter and hotter with images that flittered through his mind as they reached the house. If she was telling the truth, he'd enjoy teaching her. That brought him back to reality. Angie had pretended to be innocent, too.

He glanced at Meredith, who was beaming at him. Was she the real deal, or was she like Randall's other women?

He was going to have to find out, sooner or later. And if she wasn't the real deal, then he might be saving his brother from more heartache. That was it. He was taking her out for a noble reason. To see if she was what she pretended to be.

They left their mounts at the stable. He walked her to the back door.

"Stay inside," he said firmly.

"Okay, boss," she replied with a faint smile. "Sorry about all the trouble."

He shrugged. "Rescuing Eastern tenderfeet is what we do around here. In between the winter headaches, at least."

"I never got to meet the pet wolf."

"When the weather clears I'll introduce you," he said. "Get a heavy winter coat. And a dress. Something pretty."

She grinned. "I'll get something gorgeous, so I won't let you down."

"Let me down?" he asked.

"I wouldn't want to embarrass you in front of your friends," she added. "I don't have much fashion sense. I'm glad you're letting Delsey go with me. She'll know what I should buy."

He felt odd inside. She didn't want to embarrass him? Angie had gloried in embarrassing him, everywhere they went. She loved to stir up trouble. There was a good chance that she was going to be at this party, and he'd thought about staying home, just to save his pride.

But he could take Meredith with him. Show Angie that she wasn't difficult to replace. He studied Meredith's pert figure and smiled. She'd look stunning in an evening gown, with her hair and makeup done properly. She was very pretty.

"Have your hair done, while you're at it."

Her eyebrows arched. "Have it cut?" she faltered.

"Good Lord, no!" he exclaimed. "It would be a crime to cut hair like that," he added, his eyes more expressive than he meant them to be as they lingered on her soft, pale blond hair that fell to her waist in back.

"Oh."

"Have them teach you how to style it. To go with the evening gown. And get some makeup if you don't have any."

"I have powder and lipstick. That's all I ever wear," she said. "I don't like a lot of makeup."

He pursed his lips, and his black eyes twinkled. "It puts a man off, too."

"Puts him off?"

"I look really bad wearing a woman's lipstick."

She flushed to her throat. She couldn't even find words. She turned and ran.

Ren looked after her with a puzzled expression. She was incredibly shy. And that didn't seem like an act.

He wondered as he went back outside whether she could really be so innocent. Her father had been over-protective—paranoid, to his mind. She hadn't been allowed around men. She'd been hit with a belt for trying to date a boy. That was what she'd said. But she was Randall's girl, so how did that fit?

Randall was a sweet man, and Ren truly loved him as a brother. But Randall was a ladies' man who changed his women like he changed his socks. He slept with them until the newness wore off, then he went hunting again.

But Meredith didn't have the look of a sophisticated woman. She didn't act like one, either. Perhaps her attitude was put on, but she wore that cross and refused to take it off, even knowing that Ren didn't like it. A woman who was religious would have morals of steel, and principles to match.

He went back to work and put Meredith out of his mind while he organized the men and left for the outlying pastures.

MERRIE WAS OVERWHELMED. "He wants to take me to a party," she told Delsey with barely contained excitement. "He wants you to go shopping with me tomorrow and get a dress!"

Delsey shook her head. "Well, I never." She laughed. "He hasn't even talked about going on a date since Angie cheated on him."

"He doesn't talk about her, does he?"

She shook her head while she worked around the kitchen. "She really hurt him. He's never been a playboy, not like Randall. He's deep, and he keeps to himself. Not that he's totally innocent," she said with a laugh. "They still tell tales about him when he was a young man and new to wealth. But even then, he was choosy. And he wants to take you to a party!"

"You have to help me find the right sort of dress. I don't want to embarrass him."

"Honey, you're not the kind of woman who'd embarrass any man. You're very pretty, but it's what's inside that makes the difference. You have a kind heart. That's rare in this world."

Merrie smiled. "Thanks, Delsey."

"We'll find something beautiful but conservative."

"My thoughts exactly!"

"And a winter coat."

Merrie grimaced. "It's going to be such a waste. I won't need it in Texas."

"You're not going back right away, are you?"

That reminded her of the reason she was here, and it made her uneasy. "No. Not right away," she confessed.

"Then it will get plenty of use," Delsey said, smiling. "Now help me with the salad. Ren's going to be starving when he gets in tonight."

"I thought he'd be furious at me," Merrie said absently. "I got lost in the woods." She laughed. "I heard what sounded like a wolf howling, and Ren and the men were nowhere in sight. They'd gone to look at a sick animal. So, like an idiot, I ran away from the sound of the wolf and got lost. But Ren found me. I've never been so relieved in my life. And he didn't even yell at me."

Delsey was watching her animated face, and drawing conclusions. Ren would have yelled at most any woman who'd done something so foolish. But he hadn't been angry at Merrie. Ren never showed much emotion. However, Delsey would have bet her egg money that he was feeling something new with their houseguest.

The only thing that worried her was that he thought Merrie was Randall's girlfriend, and that way of thinking could have consequences if he acted on it. If he thought Merrie was like Randall's other girlfriends, the ones who usually came on to him, and if he treated her like one of them...

Well, surely he could see how innocent she was. Even Delsey could see it. No, he wouldn't do anything to upset the girl. He was raised to be a gentleman, however far he'd strayed from his upbringing and the education he'd gotten from that smart college he'd attended. He'd treat Merrie like the lady she was. She was sure of it. Merrie was over the moon. She had a date with the handsomest man she'd ever met, and like Cinderella, she was going to the ball! She'd have an elegant gown and she and Ren would dance and dance.

CHAPTER SIX

MERRIE STARED OUT the window at the snow, which was so white that it lit up the night sky. Ren was out there, somewhere, with his men, checking on the cattle. It was a huge ranch. Delsey had shown her a map of the entire area. There were a lot of purebred cattle, and they had to be watched carefully in the cold and the snow.

She hoped that Ren was warm, and that he didn't have a relapse from his bronchitis. At least he had Delsey to take care of him.

He was so handsome. Merrie thought that she'd never tire of looking at him. Then she remembered the poem she'd blurted out, and his reaction to it, and she blushed some more. Well, he was gorgeous. That was a fact.

She wondered if he had an ulterior motive for asking her to go to the party with him. That woman, Angie, was going to be there. He wouldn't want to go alone, especially after the vicious things she'd said about him. His pride wouldn't have let him.

On the other hand, Merrie would make sure that stupid woman didn't hurt him again. She was going to protect him, whether or not she had the right.

SHE'D BEEN CERTAIN that Ren would never want to take her out on the ranch again, not after she'd gotten lost and had everyone in an uproar. But the next morning, he made sure Delsey drove her into town to get a warmer coat and some proper boots. And, of course, the evening gown they'd discussed. Odd, she thought he'd mentioned having Tubbs drive them when he'd spoken of it. But it was just Merrie and Delsey.

"He doesn't have to buy me things," Merrie protested when they were in one of the ranch's big SUVs, headed toward Catelow.

Delsey chuckled. "No, he doesn't. But it's his money, isn't it? Let him spend it, if he wants to." She glanced at her young companion. "It's been a long time since Ren was concerned about the well-being of a woman."

"Did he love that other woman, the one who cheated on him?" she asked quietly.

"He thought he did," she agreed. "But it wasn't love. He bought her things because she asked for them, and she'd worked him up until he was crazy to have her. That isn't the same as what he's doing now." She turned her head toward Merrie. "He's concerned about you, about keeping you warm and safe. Never would have occurred to him to feel protective about that she-cat."

"Oh." She felt unsettled. She shifted restlessly in her seat. "He's a very masculine man," she said. "I feel safe when I'm with him. But he needs looking after, too," she added softly. "He doesn't take care of himself."

Delsey didn't say a word. Her expression did, but she was careful not to let Merrie see it. Both of them were nurturing people, with the right partners. Delsey was sure that there were happier times ahead for them both. But she wasn't going to comment on it, and risk alienating the sweet young woman in the vehicle with her.

"Is it much farther?" Merrie asked as they wound around through the lodgepole pines.

"Just up ahead," she said.

And there was Catelow, covered in snow, looking like any small town in any northern state in the country. Except there were huge jagged mountains in the distance, their sharp peaks covered with snow. It was a perfect setting. There were houses dotted around in the outskirts, and a beautiful church with a tall spire, looking right at home there.

"The church is beautiful," Merrie noted.

"Isn't it?" she agreed. "It's the Methodist church. I was baptized there when I was just a child. So were both my parents. Mr. Ren's father and mother went there when he was very small." She made a face. "That fancy college ruined him," she muttered. "He came out of it not knowing who he was anymore."

"Sometimes that happens," she agreed. "Not my sister, though." She smiled. "Sari had ideals and beliefs that dynamite couldn't budge. We went to the Methodist church from the time we were toddlers. When people made fun of Sari in college, she just told them exactly what she thought. Even if they didn't agree with her, they respected her for standing up for what she believed."

"Rare courage, in this day and time," Delsey said sadly.

"Do they have Christmas parades here?" she wondered aloud.

She chuckled. "Catelow hasn't changed much in the past hundred years, and I don't think it ever will. Yes, we have parades. We have decorations. We have Christmas trees everywhere, and Santa Claus appears at the local department store to see the children every December."

"That sounds like home," Merrie said. "We live in Comanche Wells, which is tiny. But Jacobsville, down the road, is our county seat, and we have beautiful decorations every year for Christmas. Parades and parties and caroling. Some people dress up like they did back in Charles Dickens's day in the oldest part of town, and tourists come from miles around to see them. We have decorations crisscrossing the street. It's magic." She sighed. "We have a nine-foot tree every year at the house," she added. "Daddy was never home at Christmas, which meant we could celebrate it. Mandy had the cowboys put us up a tree and we decorated it and gave each other little presents. I learned to knit so that I could have things to give." She grimaced. "Daddy wouldn't even let us have an allowance, or work part-time to earn money."

"Your father doesn't sound very nice."

"He was terrifying," Merrie confessed. "I wish we'd had a father like other people do, one who loved us and wanted to do things with us." She leaned her head back against the seat. "When he died, we were sorry, but it was like being set free from prison."

"I'm sorry it was so hard for you."

She smiled. "You're the nicest person, Delsey," she said sincerely.

JOLPE'S WAS AN odd fit for a small Western town. It would have suited Beverly Hills or Manhattan just as easily. It seemed to cater to the richest patrons, because you could buy anything from diamonds to evening gowns to the latest ski gear.

Merrie, who'd been in only midrange stores in San Antonio, even after their father's death, was fascinated.

"Coats," Delsey said. She smiled. "You pick out whatever you want, honey. I've got Ren's black card in my pocket."

"That's very kind of you, and him, but I pay my own way," Merrie said softly.

"Child…"

Merrie patted her on the shoulder. "I'll get something nice, I promise."

Delsey just sighed. "He'll kill me."

Merrie laughed softly. "He won't know."

Delsey looked worried. But she gave in. "All right, then. I'm going next door to the coffee shop."

"I'll come find you when I'm through."

The older woman hesitated again, but the determination in Merrie's face defeated her. She just smiled and accepted defeat.

MERRIE FOUND A gorgeous black wool coat with a mink collar. It suited her blond fairness and gave her a sophistication she'd never had. She loved it at first sight. It wasn't exactly the thing to wear out on the ranch, but it would pair well with an evening gown. Even the saleslady said so. She bought it, and then found a shearling coat similar to Ren's that she could wear when they went riding.

Then she wandered into the evening wear department, where a kindly older woman asked if she could help.

"Yes," Merrie said quietly. "I have scars on my back, and I need a couture gown that won't let them show."

The older woman looked at her sympathetically. "Let me show you what I have," she said softly. "It's an odd sort of gown. We haven't had anyone interested in it, because it's not traditional." She stared at Merrie and smiled. "But I think it might suit you. Let's see."

It was an Asian-inspired dress, probably the most expensive gown in the store. It was cherry red, with black frog buttons that led up to a high neckline. The skirt had discreet slits on both sides and fell to her ankles. It was exotic and shouldn't have suited her. But it did.

Looking in the mirror, Merrie felt like a fairy princess come to life. She almost gasped at the difference the dress made in her appearance.

When she came out of the dressing room, the saleslady was fascinated. "Yes," she said, nodding. "I thought it might suit you." She smiled. "My dear, you'll be the talk of the town in that. It's the most expensive model we carry, though…" she added worriedly, because she'd seen Merrie wearing clothing that was obviously off-the-rack.

Merrie smiled. "I can assure you that nothing in the store is beyond my pocket. It's all right."

"I'm very sorry…"

"Not necessary. I'm still getting used to having money." She laughed softly, and it brightened her eyes and made her look beautiful. "I'll take it," she added.

The saleslady beamed.

MERRIE PAID FOR her coats and dress with her own gold card. She added a pair of designer boots and some new jeans and sweaters to the pile. She felt more exhilarated than she had in years. She couldn't wait for Ren to see her in the dress. She wasn't even going to let Delsey see it until the night of the party. She was going to shock people. It felt great.

They were driving back to the ranch when Merrie had a twinge of fear. She'd used her credit card. What if the man who was stalking her looked at such things? What if he could track her through her credit card or through her Amazon purchases?

She suddenly felt sick. She should have been more careful. Ren knew why she was here, but Delsey didn't. She glanced at Delsey with concern on her face. The older woman had become family to her in the time she'd been at the ranch. She didn't want anything to happen to her.

Delsey misinterpreted the look. "You did get something nice, didn't you? For the party, I mean?" she worried.

"I got something beautiful," she replied. "Don't worry. I have some money of my own. I inherited it from my mother. That's what I used for the gown, and my coats."

"Coats?"

"I got two," she confessed sheepishly. "One to wear when Ren takes me out riding and the other to wear with my lovely new dress."

"All right, then." Delsey smiled but she was worried. She wondered if their houseguest knew much about high society and the brutal way women who traveled in those circles could act toward women who didn't have dress sense, or who wore cheap clothing. They'd eat poor Merrie alive if she showed up in an off-the-rack gown, and Ren would blame Delsey for not insisting on going in with her and paying for her things.

On the other hand, Merrie was an artist, so perhaps she'd know how to dress properly for fancy parties. Delsey certainly hoped she did.

WHEN THEY GOT back home, Delsey helped carry the bags upstairs. There were several of them.

"Thanks," Merrie said.

"No problem. Now I've got to get downstairs and start baking my ham." She laughed. "Ren loves it. I had Tubbs pick me up one at the store yesterday. I'm making scalloped potatoes and asparagus to go with it. And a chocolate cake for dessert."

"My stomach is growling already!" Merrie enthused.

"Don't be late coming down to dinner," Delsey teased.

"I won't. I promise!"

Merrie hung up her beautiful gown and the two coats she'd purchased. She was still worried about her stalker.

She picked up one of her throwaway phones and called Sari.

It took three rings before her sister picked up. "Sari, it's me," Merrie said.

"Oh, honey, I've been so worried!" Sari exclaimed. "You haven't called, you haven't written... Is it bad up there?"

"No, no, it's fine." Merrie laughed. "I was afraid to use the phone, that's all. Has anything happened?"

"We don't have a clue where the killer is," Sari said sadly. "But Paul's working overtime trying to track him. So is Eb Scott."

"I did a stupid thing," Merrie began.

"What?"

"I used my credit card in Catelow," she said. "There's a party that Ren wants me to go to with him, and I didn't have a dress..."

"He's taking you to a party?" Sari exclaimed. "Really?"

"It's not like that," Merrie said quietly. "Randall didn't tell him why I was really here, so I did. He said I'd be safer here than anywhere else. He's abrasive. But he's sort of nice," she faltered. "Anyway, I used the credit card. Did I mess up?"

"He doesn't know where you are. I'm almost certain of it. But I'll tell Paul, just in case, okay?"

"And I ordered supplies from Amazon," she added sheepishly. "I had to have paints and canvases and I knew you couldn't send them to me without giving away my address up here..."

"It will be all right. We have another ally, helping us hunt the contract man."

"We do? Who?"

She laughed. "You'll never guess."

"Tell me!"

"Paul's cousin Mikey."

"The mob boss? Really?"

"Really. He's got a soft heart, apparently, and he's fond of Paul. He said he'd do some checking on his end and see what he could turn up."

"Wow. I feel really special now."

"Apparently you are special, if the Wyoming iceman likes you," Sari teased.

"He's not bad. He's just been hurt. Wounded animals strike out."

"You see deep inside people, baby," Sari said softly. "You always did. I miss you so much. We've hardly ever been apart."

"I know. I miss you, too, and Mandy and Paul." She sighed. "I guess I can't come home anytime soon, huh?"

"Well, you could, you know that. We still have the Avengers around," she teased, referencing Rogers and Barton. "But you're safer up in Wyoming for the moment."

"I suppose so. I'm getting a lot of painting done. I've done two canvases already."

"Oh? What of?"

"A horse that was maltreated by a cowboy. He'll let me near him, but he attacked some of the men who came around."

"That's you," Sari said gently. "Wild things always came close to you, even birds. What else?"

"I painted Ren."

"Ah."

Merrie flushed and was glad her sister couldn't see. "It's not like that," she protested. "I swear. He's been nice to me, sort of."

"Ah."

"Will you stop saying that?"

There was soft laugh. "Okay. Listen, we gave you six throwaway phones. Couldn't you call more often? We can afford to buy a lot more of them, you know."

"All right, then, I'll call once a week. How's that?"

"Excellent. And I want to hear about the party. When is it?"

"Soon, but I'm not sure exactly when. I got this beautiful gown," she added. "It's exotic and expensive, and I look very different in it."

"Put your hair up, too, when you wear it," Sari suggested. "It will make you look more sophisticated."

Merrie laughed. "I'm not sophisticated. But you're probably right. I've got some of those glittery red rhinestone clips in my bags. I'll use them. They'll go with the dress."

"You'll look lovely. Take pictures."

"You bet!"

"Call me again soon."

"I promise I will," she said. "Hug Mandy and Paul for me. I love you."

"I love you, too, baby. I'll talk to you soon."

"Okay. Bye."

She hung up. She missed her sister. It had been hardest being separated from Sari, because they'd always been together. She still worried about using her credit card. She hoped the contract killer wasn't monitoring it. From what Paul had let slip about the man, she knew that he was meticulous. He'd find out everything he could about her, about her habits, before he struck. He'd plan it like a battle campaign.

She'd never thought that she'd be a target, even when she knew what her father was really doing to make money. She hadn't thought that anyone would come after her, or Sari, because of their father. She no longer had those illusions. Timmy Leeds had wanted to kill both women to hurt Darwin Grayling. But he hadn't known that Darwin was already dead by the time he hired contract killers. Or that he thought his daughters were worthless, good only for getting more money when he married them to millionaires.

It was a good thing that they'd captured Morris so quickly. He was hired for Sari, and now he was behind bars. But Leeds got someone very special for Merrie, because she was the youngest and he thought it would hurt her father more to lose her.

Little had he known that Darwin Grayling didn't care for his daughters. He kept them chaste because he could sell them to the highest bidder to marry that way. It pained her to recall that Darwin had tried to make Sari fly to the Middle East to marry a prince who would finance Darwin's defense against money laundering charges and murder. Their father had never wanted them. He'd only planned to use them to get richer.

She would never understand why money was so important to some people. It was nice to have a little spending money, and to be able to pay bills. But other than that, what use was it? You surely couldn't take it with you when you died.

That brought back to mind how much she was really worth. She hadn't told Ren, and she knew that Randall hadn't. Ren thought she was poor. She could see it in his eyes when he looked at her clothing. He probably thought she was a gold digger. He might even think she'd set her cap for him.

That was worrying. She knew that Angie had been Randall's girl, but she'd gone after Ren when she realized that he was richer than his brother. Delsey had hinted that Ren amused himself with Randall's women who came to stay at the ranch. They were mostly sophisticated and worldly, and didn't mind becoming a diversion for the reclusive rancher.

But Merrie wasn't like that. She knew nothing about men. Would Ren know that? Or would he deem her as fair game because he thought she was Randall's woman?

Surely he realized that she didn't know much about men. Or did he? Well, she told herself firmly, if he ever made a real pass at her, the truth would reveal itself.

REN TOOK HER out with him the next day, over to where men were fixing a big break in the fence that faced the highway. It was still snowing, but not as much as the day she'd gotten lost.

He crossed his arms over his saddle horn and smiled at her. "We have fences down a lot. Trees fall on them." He indicated a large tree limb that had broken off a towering pine and was lying across the broken fence. "Sometimes cattle break through them, if they're spooked. Other times, we have accidents with heavy equipment."

"Accidents?"

He pulled his hat lower over his eyes. "Tubbs is a disaster on a Bobcat," he said with a heavy sigh. "Great at wrangling horses. Driving equipment not so much. He ran a Bobcat right through a fence and took the poles on both sides with him."

She smothered a laugh. "Oh, dear."

"So we spent the morning fixing the fence. And the Bobcat," he added. "He took the fence with him right into a lagoon." He made a terrible face. "The men set records for new cusswords that day."

"You have a lagoon here?" she asked, wide-eyed. "Like the ones in the movies, with palm trees…" Her voice slowed as he stared at her.

"Lagoons," he emphasized. "They're full of cattle waste. Liquid fertilizer," he clarified.

Her lips fell apart. "And Tubbs drove a bobcat into one? The poor animal!"

"Animal?"

"Yes. You said it was a bobcat," she faltered.

He rolled his eyes. "Eastern tenderfoot," he mused.

"A Bobcat is a piece of heavy equipment. We use it to dig ditches and push down trees, things like that."

"Oh, gosh," she ground out. "I guess I don't know much about ranches."

"But you live on one," he pointed out.

"Yes, but we were never allowed outside when the men were working. Just to go riding, and Paul had to go with us. We were kept clear of anything that involved the horses. We had to sneak around even to see them in the stables!"

He thought that her father was paranoid. But didn't say it.

She glanced at his expression. "I always loved horses," she confessed. "The trainer was so kind. When Daddy wasn't around, he'd let Sari and me play with the colts. They were so sweet. So were the mares. But the stallions…gosh, they made Hurricane look tame."

"Quarter horse breeding stock?" he asked.

She hesitated for a second. "Well, yes."

"We breed quarter horses, too, and train them. Well, Tubbs trains most of them. He has two cowboys who help him."

"Is that why you have so many round corrals?"

"Yes. I don't like corners," he said with a chuckle.

"Why?"

"A rider who's inexperienced can get himself attacked if he backs a horse into a corner and doesn't give him an escape route," he explained. "We had a man bitten just last week for trying to box one of the horses up to catch him." He shook his head. "He de-

cided that cowboying was a lot harder than it looked,
and said he was going back to driving a truck."

She laughed softly. "All our corrals had corners,"
she said. "But our trainer was awesome. He was never
kicked or bitten, even by the stallions. He had this incredible patience with the animals," she added softly.
"He said you never taught a horse anything by hitting
him or whipping him or using spurs on him."

"He's right. We use gentle methods on all our
horses." His face hardened. "Except Hurricane. I
should have hit that man harder before I fired him."

"He's healing, though," she said. "And now the vet
can get in with him and I don't have to run interfer-
ence for her."

He raised an eyebrow.

She flushed. "Well, I did sneak out there a couple
of times, just to see how he was doing. Nobody knew,"
she added quickly, to protect Grandy, who'd let her in.

He gave her a sardonic look. "Grandy knew, Meredith," he said in his deep, soft voice.

She grimaced, although her heart jumped to hear
him speak her full name in that deep, soft tone.

"It's all right," he said with a resigned sigh. "We've
already agreed that trying to rein in artists is like trying to herd cats. Just be careful," he added. "Any animal can be dangerous. Especially horses. They can be
spooked by the oddest things. A paper rattling. A plastic bag blowing past them. A loud sound."

"I know," she replied. "We had a horse get loose
from the trainer and come right inside the kitchen
because a car backfired on the highway," she added,

laughing. "It was a good thing that he was just a colt. But Mandy had to have the kitchen refloored. We never told Daddy." She repressed a shiver. "He'd have had the colt killed."

"What?" he exploded.

She winced. "He had a violent temper. If a horse looked threatening, or if one came too close and he saw it as a threat…" She broke off and wrapped herself closer in her coat, trying to break off the memories.

"Your father had issues," he said flatly.

"Yes," she replied sadly. "He was unbalanced, and we never knew. The autopsy revealed a lesion in his brain. The medical examiner said that his drug use was what finally killed him. His heart gave out." She looked up at him. "Sari and I never even smoked marijuana, but our father was addicted to heroin. They said his habit cost him thousands of dollars a day. That's one reason why he was doing…illegal things to get more money."

He drew in a long, irritated breath. "We don't tolerate drug use here," he said. "We hired on one cowboy with a habit and caught him in the act. He was offered the choice between rehab and jail. He went to rehab."

"What happened to him?"

He smiled. "He turned into the best cattle foreman we ever had. Now he keeps an eye on the younger hires."

"That was nice of you."

"I'm not a bad man," he said. He glanced at her and raised an eyebrow. "You remember that."

"Okay."

His eyes were twinkling. So were hers. He looked up. "We'd best be getting on if I'm going to show you the line cabins."

"Okay!"

He laughed at her enthusiasm. "Exciting new things to see and explore?" he teased.

"Everything is new up here," she said, following alongside him. "It's so...vast," she said finally, looking around. "Can you imagine how the mountain men felt when they saw the mountains and the endless valleys? Especially if they saw it in winter, with snow lying on it like a soft blanket."

"It's beautiful," he agreed. "People come out here to live so they can breathe. You can ride for miles and never see another person. Antelope and buffalo and moose come up to the outer pastures. Even bears, occasionally. It's a hunter's paradise."

"I'd hate to shoot anything," she murmured.

He chuckled. "That's how I feel about it. We issue a few hunting leases, but only when the deer population outgrows the predators. I don't mind a nice venison stew myself, but I've never killed just to be killing."

She approved. He had a hard exterior, but a soft center. The more she learned about him, she liked. The cold man of her first few days here had been eclipsed by this kind, interesting man who was working his way into her heart.

THE LINE CABINS were spaced out. Each was in an area where cattle were kept, so that someone was always watching, protecting, making sure the herds were healthy and out of danger. She learned that Ren had a livestock foreman and another man who just watched over the purebred bulls. There was a farrier, who shoed horses, another man who tamed horses for the remuda, one who kept all the horse trailers and cattle trailers in repair. The entire operation was a vast responsibility.

"We had a heifer get her foot stuck in a fence once," he said. "She would have frozen to death if Lucky, who stays in that cabin, hadn't been around. Another went into labor and had to have her calf pulled. Still another was attacked by a wolf."

"What do you do about wolves?" she asked. "I've heard that you can't kill them."

"We contact the USDA's Wildlife Service. They take out wolves on behalf of Fish and Wildlife if there's a proven need. But I try to live with them," he replied. "They're majestic, part of the realm of nature. We scare them off, if we can. If that doesn't work, and we start losing a lot of our calf crop, we have to call the authorities."

"That's sad." She turned her attention skyward and gasped. "A raven!"

He looked up. "Yes, we have them here all the time. They're carrion feeders. They serve a purpose, like the wolves who keep down the rabbit population."

She glanced at him. "He's just over there," she pointed. "Could we go and see him?"

He got lost in those soft gray eyes, so much so that he almost forgot what she'd asked.

"Of course," he said. "But he'll fly away the minute we get close."

"That's all right. I just want a closer look."

He turned his horse and led the way. The raven was sitting on a rock. He lifted his head and stared at them, and started to move.

"Please don't," Merrie said softly. She got down off her horse and moved just a little closer. "Beautiful fellow," she purred.

The raven seemed equally fascinated with her. He hopped a step closer, then stood there looking at Merrie.

She stopped when she was an arm's length away, her artist's eyes capturing every line and curve of him. "I'm going to paint you, pretty bird," she told him, smiling. "You're so majestic!"

He made a raucous sound, ruffled his wings, and suddenly took to the air. He circled a couple of times before he flew off.

"Well, that's one for the books," Ren said, riding closer. "I've never seen one let a person get that close."

"I love birds," she said, remounting her horse. "I like to paint them. Although we don't have ravens where I live. Just crows. But they're very similar."

"They are."

"Will I ever get to meet the wolf?" she asked suddenly, remembering the one that was kept as a pet was in one of these line cabins with Ren's foreman, Willis.

He chuckled. "Okay. Come along."

CHAPTER SEVEN

THE WOLF WAS named Snowpaw. He was big and silver and he had yellow eyes. But he was missing a leg.

"Oh, the poor thing," she said softly.

Willis, the tall, rangy ranch foreman who owned him, just smiled sadly. "We had a neighbor who liked to set bear traps in the woods. Nasty, terrible things that can mangle an animal before it kills him, and they aren't limited to bears. Anything can get caught in them. Snowpaw did. I pulled him out, but it was impossible to turn him loose. So I got a license as a wildlife rehabilitator from the wildlife folks and they let me keep him. In my spare time, I take him to schools to show children that wolves aren't the vicious, mindless animals they're sometimes portrayed as."

"He's so beautiful," she said gently, leaning forward in her chair.

Snowpaw cocked his head and studied her for a minute. Then he got up and loped his way to her, laying his head in her lap.

"You sweet boy," she cooed, smoothing her fingers through the fur between his ears.

Willis was gaping at her. So was Ren.

"What?" she asked, still stroking the wolf.

"My girlfriend came to visit and he sat in the corner and snarled at her the whole time," Willis said. "He even growled at my mother!"

"A raven just sat on a rock for her and let her look at him from an arm's length away," Ren said, with a faint pride in his tone as he smiled at her. "You already know about Hurricane."

She flushed. She hadn't realized that her care of the beaten horse would have become known to the other cowboys.

"We all know." Willis chuckled. His dark eyes smiled at Merrie. "You're a legend already, Miss Merrie."

She flushed even more. "I just love animals," she faltered.

"You should see the portrait she did of Hurricane," Ren told him. "She's one hell of an artist."

"Could you draw Snowpaw for me?" Willis asked, impressed. "Just a sketch. I'd pay you…"

"I don't charge for my work," she said, smiling. "And I'd love to do it. He's magnificent," she added, rubbing her forehead over the wolf's head.

The wolf moved closer.

Ren just shook his head. But he was smiling. And there was something in his black eyes, something new, something that made Merrie's heart race. She couldn't quite figure out what it was.

On the way back to the ranch, he stopped at a gate and frowned. He got down off his mount and checked the camera sitting on a post next to it. He pulled out his phone.

"Willis. Has anybody been out here checking cameras today? They haven't? The camera at the stable gate leading down to the line cabin is leaning. It looks to me as if it's been handled roughly. Tell J.C. and have him get down here and look at it, will you? I know, could have been a big bird or a gust of wind. I just want to double-check. Sure. Thanks."

He hung up the phone and put it back on his belt.

"You don't think someone tried to tamper with it, do you?" she asked worriedly.

"It's unlikely that an intruder would have gotten this far." He chuckled as he vaulted back into the saddle. "We're about six miles off the main highway at the house. This is a quarter of a mile from there."

She glanced at him. "I don't want to put you and Delsey in harm's way," she said. "I could leave…"

He stared at her over the saddle horn. The leather creaked as he moved. He'd never had anyone worry about his safety, except Delsey. He was surprised at how much he liked it. Angie had never pretended to care if something happened to him.

"I have state-of-the-art surveillance," he reminded her. "And some of the toughest ex-mercs in the country. You're safe here. So are we. Okay?"

She let out a breath. "Okay."

He started riding, waiting for her.

"Randall should have told you," she said. "About why I came here, I mean."

He shrugged. "He knew you'd be safe. He just told me you'd had a stalker and you needed a place to get away from him."

"That would truly be the day." She sighed. "Although I think I'd prefer that to what I have. Imagine a man sending a contract killer against two women because he wanted vengeance on their father. I still can hardly believe it."

HE WAS QUIET as they rode.

"Do you think Sari and I might turn out like that, because of our father?" she asked worriedly. "I mean, I've never even hurt a fly. I catch them and put them outside…"

"Did you know that horses are pretty savvy about people?" he interrupted. "Hurricane savaged one of my men. He wouldn't let any of us touch him. But he let you doctor his cuts. If there was something evil in you, do you really think he'd have reacted to you that way?"

She drew in a breath. "I guess not. It just bothers me."

"What do you know about the killer?"

"Paul—my brother-in-law—says he's unique in the business. He's been at it for a long time and he has a reputation. He's managed to stay out of prison by bribing or even killing witnesses to his crimes. He's so confident, Paul said, that he dresses himself very distinctly and wears a ring that would help anybody identify him." She shivered. "They say he never misses."

The thought of a bullet going into that sweet, gentle woman contracted his heart. She was unique. He'd never known anyone like her. She evoked protective instincts in him that he'd never felt.

"He won't get to you here," he told her. "I promise you, he won't."

She managed a smile. "Thanks."

"Cold?"

"Not really. I love this coat! It's so warm!"

He wondered that she didn't thank him for it. She was unfailingly polite. Perhaps she'd grown to expect things from men. She was very pretty. He felt the old doubts creeping in. She could be sweet and still be like Angie. People had good qualities and bad. She might not think of using men as a failing.

He was suspicious of her. She seemed like the genuine article, but he wasn't certain that everything about her wasn't some sort of act. Angie had been sweet at first, curling around him like a kitten. She'd pretended to be just what he needed.

Not that she was innocent, or that she even tried to give that impression. She was ready for whatever he wanted from the day they met. Randall's woman, but she wanted Ren, because he was richer.

His face hardened. Women loved his money. He was sick of the fawning, the coy looks, the come-hither glances. He'd been pursued for years, mostly by women his brother brought to the ranch as guests.

This one seemed different. But she was still Randall's woman. He hated that. He'd never thought of being the only man in a woman's life before, but as he grew older, he found that most women left him cold. He'd worked himself half to death and founded something of a ranching empire out here. But when he died, it would go to Randall. And Randall would put it on the market before the coffin was in the ground. He knew that with absolute certainty. His brother didn't have the attachment to it that Ren had.

"You're quiet," she said, bringing him out of his dark thoughts.

"I was thinking about the ranch," he said.

"Delsey told me about it," she said. "It's so big! I don't see how you ever would have enough men to work that many head of cattle, or to do all the things you have to do in winter to keep the livestock from freezing to death."

He glanced at her and smiled. "Did you watch that other DVD, the one we did of winter on the ranch?"

"Is there one?" she asked excitedly. "I didn't see it!"

"I'll find it for you when we get home." He chuckled. "It shows all the hard work we do to get ready for production sales in the spring."

"What's a production sale?" she asked.

"A big headache."

She laughed. "No. Really."

"It's when we sell off some of our herd sires, producing purebred cows, calves and yearlings. We offer them in cattle magazines, online, in trade papers, that sort of thing. Then people come in droves to the ranch and we serve barbecue and beans and entice buyers into the barn." He chuckled. "We do a big business. But I think the food may have something to do with it. Tubbs is a master chef. He cooks for the sale."

"Tubbs?" she exclaimed. "The Shakespeare cowboy?"

He roared. "I guess we'll have to tell him about his new nickname," he teased, smiling when she flushed.

"Yes, him. He acts in community plays when he has free time. There isn't a lot of it."

"I've noticed that. It's very hard work."

"It is. But I love it." He stopped his horse and looked around at acres and acres of land, leading into the horizon where the sharp peaks of the Tetons were just visible. There were round corrals all around the barn and into the many pastures. They were fenced and painted and well kept.

"It's an elegant ranch."

"Thanks. But what I love about it is the animals. I like tending to them."

She smiled. "I love animals, too. We weren't allowed to have them when we were growing up." She laughed. "Sari says she's getting a big dog and it's going to live in the house. Paul said he had a friend who knew dog recipes."

He chuckled. "He wouldn't really, would he?"

"No. He loves Sari. If she wanted the moon, he'd be looking for ways to build spaceships. It's that sort of relationship. A true love match. I've only ever read about them, but Sari actually found one."

"Your sister sounds nice."

"She is. She's smart, too," she added.

"You're smart about drawing," he replied, because there had been a note of envy in her soft voice. "You have a great talent."

She flushed. "Thanks."

"Going to paint the wolf?" he teased.

"Oh, yes. I'm going to start sketching as soon as we get home."

He liked the way she said the word *home*. It made him think of a fire in the fireplace and food on the table. That was new.

They rode up to the porch. She dismounted and grimaced.

"I'm going to walk bowlegged for days," she said with a laugh.

"No doubt. Legs sore?"

"Very!"

"Soak in the bathtub for a while," he suggested, taking her horse's reins. "I'll walk the boys back to the stable and put them up."

"Thanks."

He shrugged. He gave her a long, steady look that made her heart race like crazy, made her breath catch in her throat. His black eyes held hers without blinking until she thought she'd pass out at the intensity of the look they exchanged.

Ren finally ended it. He averted his eyes. "I'll get back to work."

"Thanks for the ride. And the wolf introduction. I'll never forget it."

"Neither will I." His voice was gruff. He turned and walked away.

She watched him, curious. He seemed to like her company, but then he'd turn away as if he hated himself for it. She wondered why as she went into the house.

REN HATED WHAT he was feeling for one of his brother's women. She had a soft heart. He couldn't tell her that he knew his brother never dated a woman who didn't give out. Meredith seemed so innocent, but she belonged to Randall, who wouldn't turn his eyes toward a virgin. It was a puzzle. He led the horses back to the barn and forcibly put the woman out of his mind.

MERRIE LOST HERSELF while doing the sketch of the wolf. She remembered every detail of him, from the way his fur grew between his ears to the slant of his yellow eyes, to the way his fur grew down his back and his long fluffy tail.

She didn't realize how long she'd been at it until there was a knock at the door and Delsey peeked around it.

"Time for supper," she said. "Ren's downstairs." She nodded toward the staircase, and gave Merrie a meaningful stare.

"Oh! Sorry, I got so lost in…!"

She stopped suddenly when Ren peered in the door over Delsey's head.

"Well?" he asked.

"I'm coming," she protested. "I was just…"

"The wolf. Let's see," he interrupted.

She laughed, relieved. She pulled her sketch pad from the bed coverlet, where she'd been sprawled, and displayed her work.

"Amazing," Ren said, captivated.

"It looks like a photograph," Delsey said, shaking her head. "Honey, you have an amazing talent. You really should be displaying in art shows."

"Thanks," Merrie said softly. "I love what I do. I'm going to do a painting. This is just the preliminary sketch. I penciled in the colors, so I wouldn't forget them."

"Willis is going to be on top of the world when he sees it." He chuckled. "He loves that wolf."

"It shows. He's a sweet animal."

"Sweet? That wolf? He snapped at me and almost took my hand off when I brought a meal to Willis the last time he got sick!" Delsey exclaimed.

"The wolf laid his head in her lap and let her pet him," Ren said, his black eyes soft on Merrie's face.

"Now I know you've got talents." Delsey laughed. "Taming wolves. Painting beautiful pictures." She shook her head. "And all I can do is cook."

"Baloney," Merrie scoffed. "You're a wonderful cook! Cooking is an art. You just watch those shows on TV. You'll see!"

"Delsey could win any competition she set her mind to," Ren agreed. "Are you coming down? Artists need feeding, too, you know."

"I'm coming!"

She put the sketchbook down and followed them downstairs.

DELSEY HAD OUTDONE HERSELF. Ham. Mashed potatoes. Green beans that she'd cooked and canned the previous summer. Homemade rolls. And to top it off, a chocolate pound cake.

"I'm so stuffed that I'll never make it up the stairs!" Merrie laughed. "Oh, what a meal!"

"Thanks," Delsey said. "I figured the two of you

would be tired and cold after spending most of the day out in the wind."

"It's snowing again," Ren said. "I guess we'll take the Jag to the party. It's got better traction in snow."

"The party?" Merrie asked.

"It's tomorrow night. Forgot the date, did we?" he teased.

"But, you never told me when it was going to be," she protested softly. "You just said I could go with you." She hesitated. "I can't dance, you know," she added worriedly. "Daddy wouldn't let us have music in the house, if he was home. Is dancing hard?"

"No. Well, I take that back," he amended. "Some dancing is hard. I can't do those impossible strange dances that some people like."

"Impossible strange dances?" she queried softly.

He almost got lost in her eyes. Then he smiled. "The newer ones. They show them in movies."

"Oh, those. I don't think I could do them. And some of them look quite vulgar," she added uncomfortably. "I'm sure I wouldn't feel comfortable dancing like that in public."

Delsey was beaming. Ren was smiling, but he had reservations. Maybe she was honest. But she was still Randall's girl.

"How has Randall been?" Ren asked suddenly as he finished his second cup of coffee.

"Randall? Well, I don't know," she said honestly. "I haven't talked to him since he brought me here."

He scowled. "Don't you have a cell phone?"

"I have six, actually," she said shyly. "Throwaway

phones. Paul said they asked him if he was a drug dealer when he bought them for me at Best Buy. It was a joke. He knows the clerk," she added, laughing. "Paul says drug dealers use that sort of phone, so it can't be traced. He knew I'd want to talk to Sari," she added. "We haven't ever been apart, except when she went to the Bahamas and almost died." She lifted her coffee cup. "And now, of course. I miss her."

"You can call her on the house phone anytime you like," Ren said.

"I know. But I wouldn't dare. Paul said there are ways to trace a call without going into a house where the phone is. The man might have somebody monitoring Sari's calls. If he sees a number he can check out... well, it might be bad."

"I'd forgotten about your stalker," Delsey said. "I hope they can stop him. It must be awful."

"It really is," she said. "The cake was wonderful, Delsey. I'm going to go work on my drawing for a while before I go to sleep. Ren," she added, "thanks for taking me to see the wolf. It really was awesome."

He smiled. "You're welcome, Meredith. Sleep well."

"You, too. And Delsey."

She left them and went upstairs, already lost in her drawing and the changes she had to make.

"MEN WHO STALK women should be locked up," Delsey muttered. "Especially a nice girl like Merrie."

Ren almost told her the truth. But Meredith hadn't corrected Delsey when she'd called the man a stalker. He wasn't going to, either. It would just worry the older woman, who was like a surrogate mother to him. He'd tell her when he had to.

"Yes," he agreed. "They should."

She glanced at him. "Your mother called."

He froze. "Did she?"

"I know you don't communicate with her, but she's had some sort of medical test, and she's worried. She wanted to talk to you."

His jaw was set in stone. "Did she?" he repeated.

She drew in a long breath. "After someone's gone, there're no more opportunities to mend broken fences. You know what I mean?"

He nodded. A short jerk of his head.

"I hated my father," she told him while she cleared away the dishes. "He left my mother for another woman and I never saw him again. Years later, his new wife walked out on him and my mother had died. I was living with a cousin and going to school. Dad called wanting to speak to me. I refused." She stacked the plates together. "He died two days later in a car wreck." She smiled sadly. "Maybe he wanted to apologize, or try to explain what he'd done. I won't ever know. He didn't leave a will or anything in writing. It's like a story that has a beginning and a middle, but no end. I'll always wonder what he wanted to say." She picked up the plates. "I lost my chance. You haven't lost yours, yet." With that, she walked back into the kitchen.

He went into the living room and sat down. He turned on the television to a news program, but he wasn't really paying attention to what they were saying. He was thinking about what Delsey had said.

He'd hated his mother for years, blamed her for what he'd overheard. She'd said that Ren was cold and cruel like his father, that he was nothing like Randall's sweet father, whom she'd loved with all her heart.

Ren had tried to tolerate her. He visited her home infrequently when he was in college, mainly to see his brother. He loved Randall. They were very different, but the younger man had a heart of pure gold. Ren had been happy to give him an interest in the ranch, to see him grow into a fine, solid businessman who was an asset to the ranch. The only thing about his brother that he really disliked was the way he used women.

Ren hadn't seen his mother since he'd walked out. He'd been in his last year of college. It had been Christmas. He'd hated the holiday ever since. He didn't tolerate it in his house. Delsey, of course, had a Christmas tree in her room. His cowboys celebrated, too, with colored lights on their small houses and presents for their children under the tree. He'd wanted to outlaw any celebrations on his ranch, but Delsey had reminded him that he didn't have the right to tell people what to believe. She'd been kind, but firm. Didn't he remember when his mother and father used to take him to church? she'd asked softly.

He did. He hated the memory. It was when they were a family. He'd sit in his dad's lap and "drive" the car down the long road to the house. His father held the steering wheel, of course. Those had been bright, happy days. So soon over.

He remembered his father yelling at his mother for being unfaithful with his best friend, sleeping with a man when she was still married to him. His father had gone almost mad with the pain. His mother had said she was sorry, but she loved the other man and she was leaving and taking Ren with her.

That had led to a vicious custody battle, but his mother had won. The judge had felt that a boy's place was with his mother. Ren had hated her for taking him away. He'd hated the other man, whom she'd married when the divorce was final.

Randall's father had been kind. Probably kinder than a rebellious ten-year-old deserved. He'd tolerated the icy glares, the sullen temper, the lack of words. Ren hadn't spoken a single word to him that wasn't forced out of him. His mother had despaired.

But then Randall had been born. And Ren had changed overnight. The baby fascinated him. He loved to look at him, to watch him. He was crazy about him from the beginning. He helped his mother with feedings, and he watched the baby while she shopped; he absolutely loved Randall.

That had continued as the baby grew into a toddler, and then a preschooler. Ren was in college by the time Randall was in elementary school, and when he graduated, Randall was in the audience with his mother and father. Ren's father wasn't there, because he didn't have the price of a bus ticket. But he'd phoned Ren, to express his pride.

That had brought back the memories, and they weren't good ones, of why he and his mother were living with Randall's dad. Ren's father had lost his whole family, all at one time. He'd grieved for years.

That Christmas, after graduating in the spring with his bachelor's degree, Ren had started work on his master's, paying for it with scholarships, because he had a brilliant mind. He was living in the dorm, and he'd come home just to see Randall, whose father had died two years previously.

And he'd overheard what his mother said, when he'd been sarcastic about the Christmas tree and the whole idea of celebrating the holiday. In college he'd been taught that God was a myth, a superstition that held people back from excelling in life. His gorgeous female physics professor had assured her class of that. Ren had a crush on her, so he believed everything she said.

He'd gone home, with that new idea fixed in his mind. Then his mother had talked about Christmas and she'd been so excited about a pageant her church had planned. He'd made fun of it—and her—for being ignorant enough to believe in superstition and myth instead of science. She'd burst into tears and gone running in the kitchen to Randall for comfort. Then she'd said things that destroyed any love Ren had left for her, things he'd overheard when he'd gone to apologize. She'd said that her second husband was kind and gentle, that Ren's father had been cold and cruel and unfeeling. Ren, she said, was just like her first husband. Randall was everything a true son should be.

Ren, devastated by what he'd heard, had gone out the door before they came out of the kitchen. He hadn't seen or spoken to his mother since. Stupid, he thought, to carry a grudge for that long. His mother might die. How would he feel if he waited too long, as Delsey had?

It was something to think about. But not tonight.
He turned up the sound on the TV and listened, as the
newscast explained what money laundering was, and
related it to a huge bust that had netted the government
millions of dollars in a recent investigation. A picture
of a man flashed on the screen, a Comanche Wells citi-
zen with a last name that Ren might have recognized.
But he was looking at a programming guide for something to watch when it went by, and when he raised his
head, they had moved on to another story.

He changed the channel to a murder mystery he'd
watched before and liked.

THE PHONE RANG. Ren pushed the pause button and
picked up the telephone.

"Hello?"

"Hi!" It was Randall.

He chuckled. "How are you?"

"Selling cattle. You'll be proud. How's my girl?"
he added.

Ren felt his body clench. "Your girl is fine. Did you
know that she could draw like a professional artist?"

"Yes, I did." He chuckled. "Isn't she awesome?
When she feeds birds outside, she has to shoo them
off the feeders. They aren't afraid of her." Ren knew
that because Merrie had told him.

"She drew a picture of Willis's wolf."

"Oh, you shouldn't have let her near Snowpaw. He's
got an attitude problem…"

"He laid his head in her lap and let her pet him."

"Good heavens!"

"She has a real talent with animals, too. Remember Hurricane?"

"Yes. I hope the man serves time," he added coldly.

"No doubt he will. We couldn't get near Hurricane even to get his bridle off. Your girl—" the words went through him like ice daggers "—walked right up to him and he let her remove it. I thought the boys were going to pass out. He threw one of them into a pile of tin. Had to have stitches."

"Tames wolves and paints beautiful portraits." Randall chuckled. "She's something, isn't she?"

"Yes."

Randall hesitated. He wanted to tell his brother that she wasn't like his other girls, that Merrie was special. But he didn't know how to bring it up without putting his brother on the defensive.

"Delsey said your mother called today," Ren said. He never said "my mother." He always said "your mother" when he spoke about her to Randall.

He sighed sadly. Ren was never going to relent. "Yes. She's not doing well. They found a growth on one of her breasts. They did a biopsy, to see if it's cancer. She doesn't know anything yet."

"I see."

Randall hesitated. He loved his brother. But in spite of everything, he loved his mother, too. He hated the distance between the only family he had in the world.

"Tell her," Ren said stiffly, "that I hope things turn out all right."

Randall's heart lifted. "I'll tell her," he promised.

Ren's attitude had changed very suddenly. He wondered if Merrie had something to do with it.

"Delsey said she refused to talk to her father. He died two days later. She said," he continued, "that it was wrong to let time run out and never try to mend fences. Maybe she's right."

Randall didn't say anything. He just waited for Ren to continue.

"I'll think about it," Ren said finally. "That's all I'm saying."

"Okay," his brother said softly. "That's fine, Ren."

"I'm taking Meredith to a party tomorrow night, because I don't want to go alone," he said, trying to sound indifferent. "You don't mind, do you?"

"Of course not," Randall replied. "Watch her around men, will you?"

"What do you mean?"

"It's hard to put into words. She's okay around the cowboys, I guess. Not so shy?"

"No. She gets along with all of them. Even Willis."

"She's different when it's men her age," Randall continued. "She gets all quiet and tries to hide behind me. She doesn't like men coming too close to her. So keep that in mind, will you? Any party that Angie's going to will have men who drink to excess. You know that already."

"I'll take care of her," Ren said curtly.

"Okay. Thanks. She's…special. You know?"

Ren's face hardened. "She's nice enough," was all he'd admit to his brother.

Randall hesitated again. "She's not like most of the women I bring to the ranch," he started to say.

"I know she belongs to you. Don't worry about it," Ren assured him.

"It's not quite like that," Randall said.

"Ren!" Delsey called from the staircase. "Willis called. There's a truck pulling up to the main gate. A big truck. The driver says he has a delivery."

"What sort of delivery?" Ren asked at once.

"Barrels."

"Barrels? Of what?"

"Beats me. Willis doesn't know, either. He's headed for the gate."

"Tell him to stop right now. Randall, I have to go. I'll speak to you later."

"Okay. Take care."

"You, too."

He hung up. "I'll get my jacket. Tell Willis to call J.C. right now and have both of them meet me halfway to the gate. Hurry."

REN LOADED HIS Winchester and put it in the truck beside him. He called Willis on the truck's CB radio.

"You armed?" he asked the cowboy.

"Yes, and I told J.C. to bring his cannon with him."

Ren chuckled. "It's just a .44 magnum, Willis."

"Looks like a cannon to me. Here he comes."

A big black SUV was barreling down the hill toward them, not sliding in the snow, even though the truck didn't have chains.

"Irritates the hell out of me that he doesn't use chains and never slides off the road," Ren muttered.

"He grew up in the Yukon Territory," Willis told him. "I don't think this much snow even bothers him."

"Who were his parents? Inuit?" he asked, using the appropriate name for Eskimo people.

He chuckled. "His father was Blackfoot. His mother was a little redheaded Irish woman."

"He's not redheaded," Ren remarked.

"Not hardly," was the amused reply.

The SUV pulled up beside them. A tall, lithe man with short, straight black hair approached them. His jacket was pulled back over a huge .44 Magnum, and he carried a small automatic weapon in one big hand.

"What do you think it is?" J. C. Calhoun asked Ren, nodding toward the truck, which was still sitting at the gate, idling.

"I think it's trouble," Ren replied.

"Then let's go start some," J.C. said, and he grinned, showing snow-white teeth.

CHAPTER EIGHT

THE TRUCK DRIVER grinned at them out the window. "Hi," he called in a friendly voice. "Sorry I'm so late, but there was a wreck over on the interstate. We sat for two hours while they cleared it."

"What are you hauling?" Ren asked the man.

The truck driver saw all the guns and whistled. "Hey, I'm not a bandit," he said, tightening his hands on the wheel. "I'm a genuine, run-of-the-mill truck driver making a delivery."

"We didn't order any barrels," Ren told him.

"But, you did. See here. This is the purchase order." He pulled it out of the truck's pocket and handed it across to Ren. "Barrels."

Ren frowned. Then he looked at the purchaser's name. He laughed. "This is Skyhorn Ranch," he told the driver as he handed the paper back.

"Skyhorn?" He frowned and looked around. "That man who gave me directions said to look for a ranch way off the road with a silo sitting far off on one side of the gate and a big tree on the other."

Ren looked around. "Yes, we have those. But so does Nat Beakly. He's ten miles down the road, that way." He pointed east. "His spread is the Circle Bar J."

"Oh, darn." The truck driver sighed. "I'm going to be even later. Well, thanks for the help. Sorry to have bothered you." He noted the guns. "You guys looking to start a war, or expecting an invasion?"

Ren chuckled. "I run purebred Angus bulls here. Some of them are worth millions. We're, shall we say, overly cautious."

"I noticed." The driver nodded toward a prominent camera nearby. "Should I smile?" he asked.

"Only if your face is well-known on the FBI website," Ren said with pursed lips. "We run facial recognition software on everyone who comes near the place."

"Guess it pays to be cautious, huh?" the driver said. His dark eyes darted from one man to the next. "Sorry to get you out of bed."

"We're up all hours," Ren told him. "We have sharpshooters posted around, too." He smiled coolly. "As I said, we're cautious."

"Well, I'll be on my way. Have a good night." The driver waved and backed the truck up to the turnaround. He waved again and tooted his horn as he went down the road.

"Something suspicious about that guy," J.C. said curtly. "He was too curious."

"I noticed." Ren turned. "Check the facial recognition software on this camera and see if anyone turns up."

"You bet," J.C. said.

"Willis, tell the boys to keep their eyes and ears open," Ren added. "If this was a trial run, to see how we responded, there may be another attempt soon. Remember the camera I had checked, between the house and the stable?"

Willis nodded.

"I do, too," J.C. said, looking at him with eyes almost silver, surprising in a face with an olive tan. "Too much to be a coincidence. He might have been on the property earlier and got spooked."

Ren looked at the truck driver in the distance. "I got the feeling that not much would spook that man. Willis, wait half an hour and call Nat Beakly. I'd bet you a full breakfast, including coffee, that the truck never shows up over there."

"I won't take that bet," Willis said, smiling.

"Let's get busy," Ren said.

They turned and went back to their vehicles.

MERRIE HAD COME DOWNSTAIRS to get a glass of milk when Ren walked in, still carrying the Winchester.

"Something's happened! Is he here? Has he found me?" she asked, her young face a study in fear.

He stood the gun up in a corner before he went to her. He took her by the arms and pulled her against him. "It's all right. We've got armed men everywhere. He won't get to you. I promise."

"I'm not a coward, honest I'm not," she said against the soft sheepskin of his jacket. "It's just…I'd rather fight something I can see, you know?"

"I do know." He smoothed his hand over her back, and she stiffened. Odd how the sweater felt, as if it was uneven somehow.

The phone rang. He kept an arm around Meredith as he answered it. "Yes?"

He chuckled as he listened. "Okay, Willis. Thanks. And thank J.C. Guess I'll be buying breakfast for you two in the morning. Sure. Good night."

He hung up. "It was a legitimate mistake. The driver thought we were Nat Beakly's place. He said he'd been held up in traffic, and that much is true. I heard about the wreck on the scanner, had the whole interstate shut down for about two hours."

"Thank goodness," she said heavily.

He tilted her face up and smiled at her. "Go on up to bed."

She made a face. "I want some milk. I'm thirsty."

"I think I might have a milk cow in the pasture off the barn…"

She gave him a droll look.

He just grinned. "If you're going to the kitchen anyhow, how about bringing me a beer on your way back?"

"Sure!"

He went to put the Winchester back in the gun case, which he locked. By that time, she had a cold beer bottle in one hand, unopened.

"Sari says Paul doesn't like anybody opening his beer before they hand it to him. It may be an FBI thing," she added, smiling.

He took the cold beer from her. "Could be. Thanks."

"You're welcome." She hesitated.

"Something else?"

"Why don't you buy cans instead of bottles?"

He leaned down. "Glass bottles eventually disintegrate into the ground. If you drop a can, it's bad for the ecology."

"Simple solution—don't drop one!"

He gave her a sardonic look. "I like the way beer tastes when it comes out of bottles. Cans make it taste tinny."

She grinned. "Can bigot," she accused.

He burst out laughing. "Get some sleep, Cinderella. Tomorrow night, you go to the ball."

"I hope my dress is okay," she said worriedly. "Delsey said it would be appropriate, even though it's, well, unorthodox."

His eyebrows arched. "How unorthodox?" he asked suspiciously.

"It doesn't show anything," she said quickly. "Well, a little of my legs, but nothing else." She flushed.

That flush delighted him. He smiled at her. His black eyes twinkled. "A little of your legs? How scandalous."

She laughed self-consciously. "I guess it would have been, a hundred years ago."

"We'll leave around six tomorrow," he told her. "Delsey won't have to feed us. Which is a good thing. She's sitting with a neighbor who's having surgery tomorrow morning. Delsey's going to spend the night in her room."

"They let you do that?" Merrie exclaimed.

"They do in Catelow," he replied.

"That's such a sweet thing to do."

"The poor woman's scared. She's sixty and she's

never been 'cut on,' as she puts it. Some female problem that requires an operation. She's Delsey's third cousin."

"We don't have any cousins or aunts or uncles," Merrie said sadly. "Sari and I are all that's left of our family."

"Randall and I are pretty much the last of ours. Except for his mother."

"She painted, didn't she?" she asked softly. "It's her studio that you're letting me borrow."

"She painted." He turned away.

"Good night," she said, not pushing her luck with him.

"Sleep well," he said, but he didn't look at her again.

"WHOSE HOUSE IS the party going to be at?" Merrie asked Delsey as the older woman helped pin up her long hair in a style that looked like something out of the forties. It really suited the dress.

"Durward Phelps's place," she replied. "He has mining interests all over, and he owns at least two producing oil wells. He's very rich. But he didn't inherit it. He's like Ren. He worked hard for what he has."

"He must be a nice man."

"He is. But his niece isn't. I hope she isn't going to be there tonight."

"It's that woman, Angie, that Ren was mixed up with, isn't it?"

Delsey nodded as she put a jeweled pin on Merrie's head. "There. Darlin', you could grace the cover of a fashion magazine," she said with genuine praise. "You look lovely."

"You're sure I won't embarrass Ren in this dress?" she asked worriedly.

"I'm positive. Okay, grab your coat. Time to go."

"My knees are shaking, I'm so nervous. I don't know anything about parties or dancing. I've never even been kissed in my whole life!"

Delsey took a breath. "Well, at least you'll know about two of those things when you get home, right?" she teased. "I wish I could be here so you can tell me all about it. I'll be at the hospital with my neighbor. But you can tell me tomorrow, okay?"

"Okay. That's a promise. Thanks so much, for taking me to get the dress, and for helping with the makeup and my hair." She shook her head. "I'm just clueless."

"These things take time. You're going to do fine. But if Angie comes after you, don't you stand there and take it, you hear me?" she added firmly. "Bullies are full of hot air. You fight back and watch how quickly their superior attitude deflates."

Merrie smiled. "I'll remember."

"Go have fun."

As long as she lived, Merrie would never forget the look on Ren's face when he saw her on the staircase.

He'd been looking at something on the screen of his iPhone, but when he heard her coming down the steps, he looked up. His mouth fell open. His eyes absolutely ate her up from head to toe in the elegant red silk dress with its black frog closures and high neckline and side slits.

"I know it's not quite the conventional thing to wear to a party. Even a fancy one," she faltered.

He moved closer. He was striking in a dinner jacket, his hair combed, the faint odor of expensive cologne coming from him, along with the clean smell of soap. He looked devastating.

He lifted his hand and touched her cheek. "You look beautiful, Meredith," he said quietly. "Absolutely beautiful."

She flushed and averted her eyes. "Thanks," she said softly.

He laughed softly. "All right, I'll stop staring. Let's go, honey."

Her heart jumped half a foot at the gentle endearment. He took her hand into his big one and held it tightly as they walked out the front door to where his red Jaguar was parked.

"It's gorgeous!" she enthused.

He smiled as he helped her into the car. "I don't like sports cars as a rule, but this one is exceptional."

He got in behind the wheel, fastened his seat belt, made sure hers was fastened and pushed the button that cranked the car.

"No car key?" she asked, shocked.

"It's a smart key." He pulled the fob out of his pocket and showed it to her. "All electronic. It just has to be somewhere in the car, or in your pocket, to work. There's no real key that goes in the ignition. Put on the brakes, push the start button and go."

"I've never ridden in a Jag," she confessed, fascinated with the wood on the panel and the console. "So many controls! It's like the cockpit of a jet!"

He chuckled. "When we hit the highway, you'll think you're in one."

He pulled up to the gate, used his electronic device to open it, drove the car through and closed the gate behind them. Beside the gate, a camera was at work displaying his image to the computer tech in the bunkhouse.

"Here we go," Ren said, putting the car in gear.

It shot forward on the deserted highway, growling like the jungle beast for which it was named.

"Gosh!" Merrie felt her stomach drop at the speed. "It's fast!"

"Fast, elegant and very safe. Jags are individual. They have quirks. Sometimes they purr, sometimes they roar. Sometimes they just want off the leash." He pushed down on the gas.

"Can we go back for my stomach?" she asked with a grin.

"Leave it there. We'll get it on the way home."

She just laughed.

THE HOUSE WAS ELEGANT for a rural area. It was huge, and it looked as though every light inside had been turned on. There was valet parking at the front door of the brick mansion with its flat facade and high roof.

"All that expense to build it, and no front porch." She sighed. "It's just sad."

"Some people don't like porch swings."

She looked up at him and laughed. "I guess not."

"You do," he teased.

She nodded. "We have a swing and all sorts of furniture that moves. Sari and I could never sit still, so Mandy made sure we had movable things to sit on." She bit her lower lip, staring at the door. "Will there be a lot of people?" she asked worriedly.

He slid his hand into hers and curled it close. "Don't worry about the people," he said softly. "I'll keep you safe."

She tingled all over. Her heart jumped up into her throat at the way he was looking at her. She felt as if she might melt right there at his feet.

He saw that emotion in her. He felt it in himself. He held her hand tighter and led her into the house.

"This is Durward," he said, introducing her to a tall, heavyset man with snow-white curly hair and light blue eyes. "Durward, our houseguest, Meredith Grayling."

"Nice to meet you! Knew some Graylings once. Nice woman. Not impressed with her husband, though. There's Angie! Come here, honey, and say hello to Ren. Be nice," he added in a loud whisper.

The woman was brunette, absolutely gorgeous, with lips so red they seemed stained, and a face that could have graced fashion magazines. Her complexion was flawless, her blue eyes vivid and pretty. The one thing that ruined the picture was the smirk on her face when she came up to Ren, who stiffened visibly.

"Well, hi, Ren," she said in a soft purr. "Found somebody to replace me, huh?" She laughed. "She won't last long. You're no dream lover," she added.

Ren stiffened. His face was like stone.

Merrie curled her fingers closer into his and looked evenly at the other woman. "It's very sad."

"What is?" she asked haughtily.

"That you have so little self-esteem that you have to pull other people down to build yourself up."

Angie sucked in her breath. "I'll have you know that I'm a model! I can have any man I want!"

"Except Ren," Merrie said with a cool smile. She moved closer to him and looked up at him adoringly.

He smiled at her.

Angie turned on her heel and glared at her uncle. "I'm going home! Have Billy drive me to the airport right now!"

"Of course, honey," her uncle, flustered, agreed.

"You little…!" she began, glaring at Merrie.

"Sticks and stones may break my bones, but words will never hurt me," Merrie interrupted, purring in a singsong voice.

Angie made an exasperated sound and stomped out of the room.

Ren put his arm around Merrie and pulled her close.

Durward sighed. "Never could understand her. She's so like her mother. Strange." He glanced at Meredith and smiled. "You handle yourself pretty good."

"Thanks." She moved closer to Ren, who was brimming with pride.

"Go have fun," Durward said. "Don't let my rude niece spoil things for you. There's a live band. Playing music from the forties. You'll fit right in, Miss Grayling. Gorgeous dress."

She laughed. "Thank you."

Durward turned away from them to greet a couple behind Merrie and Ren, and Ren led her into the next room.

"Full of surprises, aren't you?" he teased as he led her onto the dance floor.

"I'm not easily intimidated," she returned. She was nervous. "Ren, I'm not sure about this."

"It's easy. If I can do it, it's easy," he emphasized. He slid his arm around her, cradled her right hand in his and began to move. "Just follow my lead. No, don't look down. Look at me, Meredith."

She lifted her eyes to his and felt swallowed whole. As if the two of them were connected, in some strange way. As if they belonged together. She'd never experienced anything like it in her life.

Ren felt something similar. He'd been apprehensive about coming to the party. He knew if he didn't come, Angie would say he was afraid. No, he was just uncomfortable. They'd been very close, but it had all been an act on her part. He couldn't have known how vindictive she'd be when he had discovered she'd cheated on him and broke up with her. The Facebook fiasco had been very painful. No man liked having a woman ridicule his lovemaking skills. Ren had been embarrassed and angry. But the pretty little rose in his arms had defended him like a lioness. He wasn't used to having a woman protect him. He shouldn't like it so much. But he did.

"That's it," he said at Merrie's ear. "Slow and easy, honey."

It sounded as if he was talking about something

more than just dancing, and Merrie felt an unfamiliar swelling in her body. She tingled all over. Her breath was catching in her throat as he drew her even closer and she felt the press of his muscular body so close to hers.

She'd never been held like this. She'd never known it would feel so... She wasn't sure what she was feeling, but certainly it was arousing. That had to be what the odd swelling was, the frantic beating of her heart, the breathing that sounded like someone was running a race.

She peered up at Ren, only to have her eyes captured yet again, held in an intimacy that she'd never known. It took them a minute to realize that the music had stopped and they were about to be alone on the dance floor.

Ren cleared his throat, took her hand and led her to the buffet table.

"Some food and drink might make this easier," he said in a deep, rough tone.

"Yes," she agreed, still vibrating.

"Want punch?" he asked.

"Please."

He ladled some into a crystal cup and handed it to her. But her hand was trembling. He had to steady it with both his own hands.

"It's all right," he said softly. "There's nothing to be afraid of."

But there was. She looked at him and knew, for the first time, that he was what she'd been waiting for all her life.

She was falling in love.

REN DANCED WITH no one else. It seemed to get easier, the more Merrie did it. She felt more confident as the evening progressed. They moved together as one. The contact was very stimulating, and she couldn't hide the effect it had on her.

She was breathing raggedly as they wound around the dance floor to a slow, lazy rhythm. Ren's hand on her waist moved up a little. She caught it instinctively. The dress was thin and her scars were noticeable, even to touch.

"Sorry," he said gruffly, and moved his hand back down to her waist.

"No, I'm sorry." She bit her lower lip. "There are things you don't know about me," she said miserably.

About her affair with his brother, he was thinking. She didn't like him to touch her in any really intimate way. But she was breathing like a runner. Her heartbeat was almost audible. She was all but trembling in his embrace. Those weren't signs of revulsion.

Almost experimentally, he drew her very close from the hips down. His body had an immediate, almost embarrassing reaction to the closeness, and he felt her stiffen and try to move back.

He lifted his head and looked down at her, but he held her firmly. His eyes were soft with sensual wisdom. "I won't rush you," he promised.

She swallowed. She was very embarrassed. She pushed gently at his chest. "Please?" she asked in a high-pitched, agitated tone. The feel of him like that made her aware of her body in a way she never had been before. She was afraid of how she felt.

He saw her flushed face and took pity on her. He let her put some space between them. She was genuinely unsettled. *What an odd woman*, he thought. Nothing about her added up. Just when he thought he knew her, she threw him a curve.

He gave her a curious appraisal. "I don't know what to make of you, Meredith," he said honestly.

"I'm just an ordinary woman," she said, relieved that he hadn't insisted.

"No. You're definitely not ordinary." He pulled her gently closer and laid his head against hers as they moved to the lazy rhythm. "Not ordinary at all."

She felt her heart trying to jump into her throat. She was so aware of him now, so hungry for something more than his arms around her. But that way lay disaster. She knew what men expected of women. She'd seen risqué movies at home. But she couldn't let Ren see her back. He'd be revolted. She knew what it looked like. She'd seen it in the mirror. No man would want to touch a woman with scars like hers.

So she steeled herself to be less responsive in his arms, to dance without letting him affect her. She was almost successful by the time the party ended and they climbed back into the Jaguar to head home.

SNOW WAS FALLING SOFTLY. It looked as if it might be deep soon. She grimaced. "The poor men," she said absently.

"What do you mean?"

"They'll have to go out before dawn, in all this snow,

to look at the cattle and make sure they have food and water and shelter."

He smiled to himself. He liked it, that she cared about his ranch hands. She cared for him, too, but she was trying to pull away from him. He wondered why.

He parked the car at the front steps of the house and unlocked the door, letting her go in first.

"Feel like a nightcap?" he asked idly.

"A nightcap?"

He turned. She looked up at him with pale gray eyes that held a soft light.

"A nightcap," he repeated, smiling. "Brandy, to be specific. I rarely drink hard liquor." He didn't add that he had, the day he'd pulled off his belt and snapped it, and Meredith had run into the kitchen to hide behind Delsey. He wasn't a cruel man, and he'd never have hit her. But her fear of him still hurt. It hurt badly.

"I've never tasted brandy," she confessed. She sighed. "I've never even had a beer."

"There's a first time for everything," he said, and his deep voice was like velvet.

He went to the liquor cabinet and pulled out two snifters and a square, squat little bottle of amber liquid. He poured just a little into the large rounded glasses and held one out to Meredith.

"You hold the bowl in the palm of your hands. It warms the brandy."

"Oh." She balanced the cold crystal in her hands, which were cold with nervousness. "I guess it's a learning curve," she said mischievously.

"Most of life is," he agreed.

She lifted the glass to her lips slowly and let the liquid touch them. She made a face as she looked up at Ren.

"Give it a chance," he advised with a chuckle.

She forced herself to take a sip. It burned like fire going down. She gasped, almost choking on it.

He couldn't help laughing. "Innocent little lamb," he teased. "I'm leading you astray."

"You really are," she agreed.

"Try it again," he coaxed.

She was reluctant. But she did. This time, the liquid didn't sting as much, and it warmed her whole body as it went down. She smiled. "Okay," she said. "It's not bad."

He lifted his glass to hers and tapped them together. "Cheers."

"Now you sound British," she said with a laugh.

"I served with a couple of SAS boys in Iraq."

"SAS?"

"Special Air Services," he replied. "They're like our Green Berets or Army Rangers. Or the French Foreign Legion. They have a reputation for excellence, and they're famous for the 'Fan Dance,' their rigorous training course."

She smiled at him. "You look hazy," she remarked.

"Is the brandy going to your head, Meredith?" he asked softly.

She put it down. "I'm not sure. I feel *very* relaxed."

He put his own snifter down and moved closer. "Relaxed is good," he whispered, bending his head. "It makes this easier."

His lips brushed over hers, parting them slowly, tracing them in a silence that breathed tension. His hands smoothed up her rib cage, and she caught her breath at the sensations he kindled in her untried body.

She shivered. He liked that response. His lips brushed hers, lightly, again and again, teasing and tempting, while his hands smoothed ever closer to the high, firm rise of her breasts. But he didn't touch them, or even try to. He taunted.

She wanted…more. But she wasn't sure what. Her breath was so ragged that she knew he must hear it, and her legs felt wobbly.

She laughed unsteadily. "I think my legs are going to buckle," she whispered against his mouth.

"That, I can take care of." He bent and lifted her into his arms, carrying her to the big burgundy sofa. He was smiling as his head moved down and she felt the warm, slow press of his mouth against hers.

She closed her eyes as he laid her down and slid alongside her. His chest arched over hers, brushed against her taut breasts while he kissed her with slow, tender intent.

She really should protest what he was doing. One lean hand was teasing just around the edge of her breast. She wanted him to stop. She didn't want him to stop. She wanted him to move his hand over, just a couple of inches, to the taut peak that ached to be touched.

Involuntarily, her body arched toward his searching fingers, and she moaned helplessly.

"Is this what you want?" he whispered.

As he spoke, his hand moved tenderly over her small breast and his fingers found the hard tip and caressed it. She gasped and shivered. She'd never realized that physical sensation could have such an explosive effect on her brain. She stopped thinking altogether.

He felt her resistance lessen, and he laughed softly as he bent to her mouth again. No more pretense, he was thinking. She was his if he wanted her. And he wanted her. Madly.

He moved closer, one long leg moving sensually against hers while he felt for the fastening of her dress at her throat and started to undo it.

He was slow and expert as his fingers moved between the fabric and her skin, brushing, lifting, tempting. By the time he had it unfastened to her waist, she was eager for his hands to go under the fabric, onto the black bra she wore with a half slip under the dress.

"God, you're sexy," he breathed into her mouth as his fingers trespassed under the cup of the bra. "Sexy as hell!"

As he spoke, his hand moved under the fabric, onto the bare skin of her breast. She arched and cried out helplessly with the force of the pleasure.

CHAPTER NINE

MERRIE WAS LOST in Ren. She was so hungry for him that she didn't protest the lean, warm, strong hand smoothing over the bare skin of her breast. When he searched for the front clasp of the bra and unfastened it, she only lay in his arms, waiting, waiting…

He opened the bra and exposed her beautiful, creamy breasts. They were firm and rounded, her nipples dark pink and erect with desire. He traced them gently, then lowered his head.

His teeth grasped one hard nipple. She gasped and pushed at his head and cried out in fear.

He lifted his head. She looked genuinely frightened. It was a good act, he thought. But he humored her. He wanted her, and she was willing. If she wanted to pretend that she was a virgin, maybe it was how she got off with a man.

"It's all right, honey," he whispered. "I won't hurt you. All right?"

She relaxed, nervous but curious and hungry. "All—all right," she managed through her tight throat.

He bent again. This time, his mouth swallowed her up whole and his tongue worked at the nipple, arousing sensations she'd never felt. She grasped his shoulders with both hands, and her nails bit in as he suddenly began to suckle her.

She cried out, moaning as if she were dying, arching up to him, shuddering, crying.

"Don't...stop, oh, please, Ren, don't...stop!" she sobbed.

He had no intention of stopping. His body levered itself over hers and pressed down, letting her feel the hardness of him intimately. His knee moved between her legs as he fed on her breast, almost drunk with her response, with the sweetness of her skin under his lips.

She knew that she should stop him. It was just that it felt so good, so right! The warm brandy had her so relaxed that her mind had gone soft. She was crazy about Ren. And surely it was more than just desire on his part. It had to be. He cared about her, of course he did. It would be all right. She could let him go this far, just this far. It would have killed her to make him stop, when she was so rapt with pleasure that she thought her body might explode.

"Are you on the pill, or do I need to use something?" he asked huskily as his mouth worked its way down her body to her soft belly.

"The pill?" she gasped.

"I don't want to make you pregnant," he said easily.

This wasn't what she'd expected. She forced her body to lie still as she fought to get her dulled brain to work. She pushed at his chest gently. It was bare. When had his shirt come off? She didn't realize her hands were buried in the thick hair that covered the hard muscles.

"Pregnant," she chanted.

He lifted his head and looked at the creamy beauty of her body. "Pregnant." He cocked his head and looked at her with what she dimly recognized as cynicism. "Oh, come on, Meredith, you're Randall's woman. He told me you were. He likes his women hot and experienced. It's all right. He doesn't mind sharing. It wouldn't be the first time," he added with faint sarcasm, and he looked down at her as if she were someone he'd bought for the night.

Merrie suddenly felt cold and sick and ashamed. The physical delight she'd been feeling left as if she'd never felt it. She tugged at her dress and pulled it over her bare breasts. "Please let me up," she said in a tone choked with shame.

"Let you up?" he exclaimed. "For God's sake, you come in here with me, get me hotter than a chili pepper, and now you want to stop?"

She looked at him with sad, dull eyes. "I'm not Randall's woman, Ren," she said miserably. "I'm his friend. Just his friend. I've never…" She swallowed and averted her gaze. "I've never done this with anyone."

"Pull the other one, lady," he said angrily. He got to his feet, raging with unsatisfied desire. "You weren't resisting very much."

She sat up. She felt dirty. She got to her feet and fumbled the frogs on her dress closed, enough to make her decent. She started toward the door.

Ren was furious. He wanted to hit something. "Is it money?" he asked harshly. "You can have anything you want. More dresses like that one, more coats like the ones I paid for."

She winced. He didn't know that she'd paid for them. She might have told him, but she was too sick. The brandy had gone to her head. She loved Ren. She'd thought he cared for her, too. But he thought she was Randall's woman, and that made her fair game for an affair. Angie had also been Randall's woman, she recalled. Ren was used to Randall's women coming on to him, apparently, and he thought Merrie was just another in a long line of brief conquests. He didn't want forever. He just needed a woman for the night. Nothing had ever hurt so much.

"I'm going to bed," she said in a fog of misery.

"You might as well," he said harshly. "I've had too many of Randall's castoffs as it is. You turn my stomach."

She closed her eyes and winced, but she didn't let him see her do it. "I'm sorry," she choked.

"Get out of my sight!"

She didn't realize that it was frustrated desire talking. He hadn't had a woman in months, and his poor, starving body was trying to cope with the loss. He turned away and went toward his study.

Merrie ran upstairs into her room and locked the door. She threw off the red dress and everything under it, threw all of it in the wastebasket. She grabbed some clean clothes and went into the bathroom to shower off the scent of Ren. She knew she'd never be able to face him again, after what had happened.

When she put on clean jeans and a sweatshirt, and

boots, she packed a few things in a backpack. She put on her warmest coat and waited until she heard Ren go past her room to bed.

He stopped at her door, feeling betrayed and angry. But he couldn't get the taste of her out of his mouth. She was like honey. He'd gotten used to having her around. He liked being with her. He loved the person she was. He was sorry that he'd treated her in such a manner. She couldn't help what she was. Maybe she'd loved Randall, and that was why she'd been his woman. He could overlook that. He could overlook anything, if it meant not losing her. He hated hurting her feelings like that. He stood at her door, trying to find the right words to undo the hurt he'd caused. But he couldn't find them. A neat whiskey on top of the brandy had fuddled his brain.

He went down the hall, reluctantly. He could apologize in the morning. Maybe he could smooth things over. She was under enough stress with a killer stalking her. Now she had Ren's unkindness to add to the mix. He was genuinely sorry.

MERRIE HEARD HIS FOOTSTEPS stop at her door. She sat on her bed with her teeth clenched. If he opened the door...but he didn't have a key. She relaxed a little. No, he didn't have a key, and he didn't want her anymore. He'd made that very plain. She wouldn't give out, so he was probably going to tell her to get out. She closed her eyes, hurting, and listened. After a minute, his footsteps continued down the hall and slowly faded. A door closed. Merrie let out the breath she'd been holding.

She brushed away another wave of tears. What had she expected, after all? She knew that he'd been engaged to Angie, who'd been one of Randall's women. Apparently, a lot of Randall's women had stayed here and given their full attention to Ren.

He thought Merrie was like that, too. She'd been out of her mind with delight when he kissed her, held her, touched her. She thought it was love. It was only lust. He wanted her, but only for a night or two. Not forever.

Maybe the sort of love she read about in her romantic novels wasn't even real. Then she thought of Paul and Sari, and realized that it was real for some people. Just not for her. Not with this man. Not ever.

She waited until she was sure Ren wasn't coming back out of his room. She got her small bag, with her credit card and money in it, and opened the door. She'd have to leave everything else; she couldn't carry it. She went downstairs and looked through the phone book for a cab company. There wasn't one in Catelow that ran after dark. So she phoned Billings and had a limo company agree to come and get her. She gave them her credit card number and the address of the ranch, and asked them to please hurry. They said the driver was on the way.

She went out the door, feeling sick. She hadn't left a note, but Ren would know why she'd gone. She was sorry she wouldn't get to tell Delsey goodbye, as well.

Snow was falling harder. She looked around, but there was nobody she could ask for a ride to the main gate, which was at least a fourth of a mile from the highway. Actually, that was the distance from the stables, on another road. The main gate, where the limo would come, looked much farther, and she had to go through two gates to get to it.

Well, they said the longest journey began with a single step, didn't they?

BY THE TIME she got to the first fence, she wished she'd worn gloves and a better hat than her colorful knitted one. Her socks, inside her new ankle-high dress boots, were soaked because the snow came in over them. Her feet felt as frozen as her poor hands.

The gate had a simple latch. She was surprised, because she thought Ren had said that there were alarms that went off when anyone tried to open gates at night. She recalled that he had facial recognition software on hidden cameras that weren't readily seen. Looking around, she wasn't aware of any cameras in the snow-lit darkness. So perhaps they weren't really looking at the gates at this hour of the morning.

She closed the gate back and kept walking. She was shivering from the cold. There was another gate in the distance. Heavens, it was a far walk! In Texas at this time of year, it wouldn't have been a problem. But Wyoming was very different. She wasn't used to the cold and the snow. And it looked as if she wouldn't have the chance to get used to them.

She felt the throwaway phone in her pocket. It was charged, so she could call Paul from the airport and have him bring the Grayling jet up to pick her up. It wasn't involved in the money laundering charges, so, like the racehorses, it still belonged to the family.

She laughed at her own stupidity. She'd been falling in love. But Ren had only seen her as an easy mark, because he thought she was Randall's woman. It was heartbreaking. She'd never felt anything like this before, and she had to feel it for the first time with a jaded man who looked on women as party favors.

She recalled with anguish the tenderness of Ren's lips on her soft mouth, the slow, easy motion of his hands on her body, the patience he took with her. That Angie woman had said he was a terrible lover. Now she knew it wasn't true. Ren was practiced and sophisticated, a master of sensuality. If she'd been the experienced woman he expected her to be, she would probably have had no qualms about sleeping with him. But Merrie was religious. She didn't go with the crowd.

She felt betrayed. She felt cheap and dirty. She wanted her sister and her home. If the killer found her, that would be all right. She couldn't see a future for herself without Ren, and he didn't want her, except one way. It hurt so much that tears rained down her cold cheeks. She brushed them away angrily. He wasn't worth tears.

She kept walking.

REN HAD BEEN sitting under a tree with Meredith in his arms. She was smiling up at him, her eyes full of love. There was an odd ringing in his ears. She looked at him quizzically, and all at once he woke to the sound of the phone ringing.

He picked up the receiver, half-asleep. "What?" he asked.

"Did you know that your houseguest is past the first fence and headed to the main road walking in the snow, without a muffler or even a pair of gloves on?" J.C. asked.

"What?"

He was out of bed in a flash, hunting clothing. "Lock that second gate, and I mean *lock* it," he said shortly. "I'm on my way."

"You bet, boss."

He ran down the stairs, snapping his shirt buttons as he ran. He grabbed a coat and hat and scarf and the key to the Jaguar and darted out the door. The Jaguar was still parked at the steps. He grimaced at the memories it brought back. He jumped into it, cranked it and shot down the driveway.

He keyed the first gate, drove through and closed it, and kept going. He noted that the electronic lock hadn't been put back on. He'd forgotten to do that when they came home, anticipating untold delights with Meredith. It was careless. He caught up to her about a fourth of a mile to the last gate.

She heard the car before she saw it, and she knew who was driving it. She started running, fighting tears.

He caught her easily before she got very far. He picked her up in his arms, ignoring her struggles, and stuffed her into the passenger seat.

"Stay put!" he said icily when she tried to get back out.

Her lower lip trembled. Tears rained down her cheeks. She was too tired to even care, and she felt frozen clean through. She wrapped her arms around her chest and refused to even look at him.

He felt the pain to his toes. He wanted to apologize, but he couldn't find the right words. She looked devastated. That wasn't the way any experienced woman would have behaved. He'd had enough of them to be certain of it. She wouldn't even look at him. She'd left the ranch walking, in a snowstorm. *Pride*, he thought. She was proud. She wouldn't stay where she'd been treated so badly.

"I called a limo service," she said tightly. "The driver will be waiting at the main gate. Please tell him he can charge me for the inconvenience and I'm sorry."

He called up J.C. and relayed the message. He hung up. Soon they were at the front door.

Just as he pulled up, so did Delsey, in a small SUV. She parked next to them and was surprised when they got out, both wearing regular clothes instead of their fancy evening clothes.

"My goodness, what happened?" Delsey asked, shocked to see Merrie crying.

"We had a little blowup," Ren said tautly. "Get her upstairs and into a bath. She's half-frozen."

"I'll do that. Come on, sweetheart, I'll take care of you," Delsey said, putting an arm around her.

Merrie burst into tears, sobbing as she went with the older woman into the house. Ren stood at the doorstep, snow pelting down on him, and he didn't even feel the flakes on his face. It hurt him, to see Merrie like that, and know he was the cause of it.

MERRIE HAD A hot shower, but she put her jeans and sweatshirt back on. Then while she was waiting for Delsey to bring her some hot tea, she took out the throwaway phone and called home.

"Merrie?" Sari asked sleepily. There was a pause. "Baby, it's three o'clock in the morning! What's wrong?"

Merrie tried not to cry. "I had a little...problem here."

"The killer...!"

"No. I had a blowup with Ren," Merrie said, leaving out why. "Can Paul come get me, right now? I'm sorry it's so late, but I can't stay here! I'll ask Delsey to drive me in to the airport in Catelow. It will take a baby jet, I checked." She paused. "I'm so sorry. I know you thought I'd be safer here," she began.

"There's a new problem," Sari said. "I'll let Paul tell you about it when he gets there. It's just as well that you want to come home. We planned to ask you to tomorrow."

"What's happened?" Merrie asked. "You're not in danger, are you?"

"No," Sari said softly. "No, I'm fine. I'm overly protected," she said with a laugh. She paused. Her hand was over the phone and she was talking to Paul. A minute later she came back on. "Paul said he's headed to the airport as soon as he's dressed and gets the pilot out of bed."

"I'm sorry," Merrie began.

"You're my sister. I love you. Shut up."

Merrie laughed. "Okay. Thanks."

"I'll see you soon."

DELSEY BROUGHT IN a cup of steaming-hot tea and put it on the bedside table.

"That will help warm you up. Why don't you have your gown on?" she asked.

"Because I'm going home, Delsey. Sari is sending Paul to get me. He'll be in the airport in about two hours. Can I get someone to drive me over there?"

"Of course you can. Two hours? Commuter planes are pretty slow…"

"We have a Learjet," Merrie said heavily. "It's very fast."

"A Learjet?"

Merrie picked up her tea and sipped it. "Thank you for the tea. I'm going to stay up here until Paul calls. Is that all right?"

Delsey saw more than Merrie realized. She patted the other woman's shoulder. "You know," she said softly, "Ren isn't used to women like you. He's used to who Randall usually brings home. That Angie person was one of Randall's women. Ren thought that since Randall brought you home with him, you were the same sort of person." She grimaced. "I could have told him different, but you just don't bring up subjects like that with him. He's so self-contained." She drew a breath. "He doesn't show what he feels. But he does feel things. He's sensitive."

Merrie sipped tea.

"Well, enough said. You drink your tea. Sure you're okay?"

"Just cold," Merrie said. "I didn't stop to look for gloves or a scarf. I really should have. And my boots are soaked. They were dressy ones. I forgot how deep the snow was." She held up her sneakered feet. "I won't walk far in these, but at least they're dry." She shook her head. "I thought it would be easy to get to the road."

"Nothing easy about Wyoming when the snow starts falling," Delsey replied. "If you need me, you call, okay, dear?"

"Okay."

REN WAS SITTING at the table with a cup of hot coffee that he'd brewed himself. He looked up when Delsey came into the room.

"She's called her sister," Delsey said. "Her brother-in-law is coming to get her. He'll be at the airport soon. I'll drive her there."

Ren felt cold inside. He focused on his coffee. "I see."

"She isn't what you think she is," Delsey blurted out, uncomfortable. "She told me that her father never let her go on dates, not her whole life. She said she'd never even been kissed. She's not one of Randall's women."

Ren paled at the revelation. If it was true, he'd made one hell of a monumental mistake. It was even worse than he thought. He sipped more coffee.

"We'll have someone meet him at the airport and bring him here," he said shortly. "I want to talk to him before she leaves."

PAUL WAS MET at the airport by a man in a truck with the Skyhorn logo on the side, crossed bull horns in a red field.

"I'm Tubbs," the man introduced himself. "The fixed-base operator at the airport here says you're the only customer he's got, so you must be Paul Fiore."

Paul chuckled. "That's me. Okay, let's go."

Tubbs deposited him at the house. Ren let Paul in and shook his hand.

"Merrie says she wants to come home," Paul told the other man. "It's a good thing, too. She's been tracked here. We just found out."

Ren's blood ran cold. "Been tracked here by the killer? How?"

"The charge slip. She used her credit card at a high-end store here. It rang bells with a man we think has been monitoring her for the hit man. He uses all sorts of tech to help him find his targets. He's wily."

"Used her charge card." Ren felt like an idiot. No wonder she hadn't thanked him for her dress and coats. She'd paid for them herself.

He frowned. "She bought some high-ticket stuff recently," Ren told him. "For one thing, an evening gown that was the most expensive thing in the store—and it's a high-end store."

"She hasn't told you anything about herself, has she?" Paul asked.

"Not much, no."

"She's worth two hundred million dollars," Paul said simply, watching the shock run over Ren's face. "Left to her by her mother. She hid money in Swiss banks for both women, so that their father couldn't get his greedy hands on it."

"Two hundred million." Ren couldn't take it in. She was a millionaire many times over. But she didn't act like a woman who owned anything.

"Hey, it's just money," Paul joked. "Could I have a cup of coffee? I worked late on a robbery in San Antonio and I'm about half-dead."

"Sure. What about your pilot?" Ren asked.

"He's got a thermos of coffee and a good book. Hates people. Good pilot." Paul sat down. "How you doing?" he asked Delsey with a big smile. "I'm Paul Fiore."

"Nice to meet you," she said, thinking what a handsome man he was, with that thick, black wavy hair and dark brown eyes.

"Tell me about Merrie," Ren said quietly.

Paul shrugged. "Not much to tell. The old man beat them. Both of them have scars down their backs. He used the belt doubled, with the buckle first."

Ren groaned out loud. No wonder she hadn't wanted his hand on her back at the party. Or earlier, when he'd held her and wondered at the odd pattern on the back of her sweater.

"He was a fanatic. He wanted all the towels to match, to be perfect on the racks. He hit Merrie once for having her bathroom rug off-center. And when she tried to go on a date at sixteen, he had the boy beaten and run out of town. He used the belt on Merrie because she'd dared to let a boy near her."

"What a life she must have had," Ren said heavily.

"No boys, no dates, no parties, nothing except home and television. And church, of course. He did let them

go there. Isabel said that religion was all they had to
hold on to after their mother died. He was a control
freak. And he had a heroin habit to go with a brain lesion. The drugs finally killed him. Well, he had a heart
attack because the drugs had weakened his heart. But
it was drugs, all the same."

"Poor kids."

"They were. The trainer had to keep him away from
the racehorses. He beat one so badly that it had to be
put down. We won the Preakness with Grayling's Pride
this year," he added with a grin. "We're hoping to go
farther with him next year."

"Racehorses?"

Paul nodded. "The Grayling stables are known far
and wide. Their father had his fingers in a lot of pies.
Most of the money he made was illegal, but the girls'
mother left them well fixed. The racehorses were hers.
You know, they'd never had anything fancy in their
lives. They went shopping before Isabel and I married
and bought new clothes. Isabel had been going to work
in a thirty-dollar suit. Before he died, their father refused to let them get even part-time jobs. He died trying to force Isabel to marry a Middle Eastern prince
he'd picked out for her, so that he'd have money for his
defense. Isabel refused to do it. He went after her, but
her bodyguards broke down the door. He died before
they could pull him off. Isabel still blames herself. She
didn't do a thing. He just died."

"I'm sorry," Ren said, his heart bruised and battered
by the things he was hearing. Poor Meredith! And he'd

treated her like an easy conquest. He closed his eyes on a wave of pain that sickened him.

"Could you ask Merrie to come down, please?" Paul spoke to Delsey. He looked at his watch. "I've got to be at work in a few hours. I don't like to cost the government time," he said with a chuckle.

"Your wife must have millions, too," Ren said as Delsey went up the staircase.

He shrugged. "She does. So do I, a really unexpected gift from her father," he lied. Isabel had insisted on sharing her fortune with him, but they'd put it out that her father had left it to Paul in his will, to spare Paul's pride.

"You still work, though."

"Sure," Paul said, chuckling. "I love my job. Isabel loves hers, too. We aren't cut out for cocktail parties and country clubs."

"Neither am I," Ren said. "I like being around the livestock."

"I love horses," Paul confessed. "We don't ride the racehorses, of course, but we have some prize quarter horses that we sell for breeding stock."

"I thought Merrie was just above the poverty line. She doesn't act like a wealthy woman."

"Neither of them do. Isabel said their mother was like that. She wore regular clothing and worked in the garden." His lips compressed. "There's a good chance that their father killed their mother. Isabel wants to do an exhumation and have an autopsy that isn't rigged, like the first one was. Money changed hands and their mother's death went down as accidental."

"Shame."

"It really is. If we do the exhumation, it will just cause the girls more pain, you know? The guy's dead, their mother's dead. Life goes on."

"Or it seems to." Ren looked up as Merrie came down the staircase with her bag, her fanny pack and her big sketchbook.

"Paul!"

She put her things on the sofa and ran into his arms, hugging him. "Thanks so much for coming!"

He patted her on the back. "No problem, kid. If you've got everything, we should go."

"I'm ready."

"I'll drive you over to the airport," Delsey volunteered, seeing Ren's discomfort as he stared with anguish at Merrie.

"Thanks," Merrie said. She hugged Delsey. "Thank you for being so kind to me."

"It was a pleasure. I'll miss you," Delsey said softly.

Merrie laid her head on Delsey's shoulder. "I'll miss you, too."

"Have a safe trip home, honey. Be safe."

"I will. You take care of yourself."

Delsey just smiled.

Merrie turned to Ren with her heart breaking in her chest. Her eyes wouldn't go past his throat. "Thank you for letting me stay here," she said politely. "I can't carry all the canvases with us, but if you wouldn't mind having one of the men pack the stuff up and send it to me, I'll send you an address label. We have a FedEx account."

"All right," he said stiffly.

"I'm ready," she told Paul.

They were at the door, waiting for Delsey to get her coat on. Ren looked at Merrie with regret written all over his face. His eyes were turbulent.

"I didn't know you at all, Meredith," Ren said quietly. "I'm sorry."

An apology was the last thing she'd expected from him. Her face reddened. "Thanks, Ren," was all she could manage. She gave him one last look, winced and went out the door with Paul and Delsey.

Ren stood in the living room, remaining in the same spot for several minutes. All the color, all the life, was suddenly gone from the house. It was empty and gray and lonely.

Until that moment, Ren hadn't realized what he truly felt for Meredith. And now it was going to be too late to mend the heartbreak, to start over. She was going to leave, and her last memory of him would be one of shame and embarrassment.

He groaned out loud as he remembered what he'd done to her, what he'd said to her. He'd made her feel cheap and useless. It wasn't how he felt. Not at all.

He walked back toward her studio and opened the door. There was the portrait she'd done of him. There was the painting of Hurricane. There was a sketchbook nearby with a rough outline of Delsey. There was one of Tubbs as well, and the other men. He was still astonished by the extent of her talent.

He felt at home, here, among her canvases. His mother had loved to draw, although she wasn't the same sort of artist Meredith was. His mother drew flowers. She drew them alone, in pots, on trees, in a garden—always flowers. She drew beautifully. He ground his teeth together. He'd pushed her out of his life over an anguished comment, one that he'd provoked himself with his educated cynicism. He'd hurt her. She'd reacted. It was that simple, but it had colored their lives for years. He didn't forgive people. But he should have forgiven her.

He picked up Meredith's sketchbook and flipped through it. There, on the last page she'd used, was a self-portrait. It was only a sketch, but it touched him. Everything she was, was in that drawing. There was such vulnerability, such compassion, such kindness in those large pale eyes.

"I'm so sorry, honey," he whispered, touching the paper with his fingers. He drew in a long, harsh breath. Without thinking about it, he tore the drawing out of the sketchbook and took it back to his room.

There was a frame shop in town. He'd lost Meredith, perhaps forever. But he'd have the drawing to remind him.

Then he remembered what Paul Fiore had said. Meredith's stalker had been here, and he'd gotten past all the sophisticated equipment Ren had placed around the ranch.

He recalled the truck driver, the one who'd made him suspicious. He thought about Beakly and his financial situation, and he had a brainstorm.

He picked up his cell phone and called J.C.

"Mmm-hmm?" J.C. answered, obviously having gone to bed.

"You can go back to sleep in a minute, J.C. Tomorrow, first thing, I want you to go see Beakly and ask how much the truck driver paid him to say he had a shipment going there."

"What?"

"Just a hunch. It may be nothing."

"Okay. First thing."

"Thanks. Sorry to wake you."

"No problem. It was a pretty lousy dream," J.C. said, and hung up.

Ren turned off his cell phone. He'd get up in the morning, and Meredith wouldn't be at the table for breakfast. She wouldn't be here to ride out with him, to look at the cattle. She wouldn't be sitting in front of the television, knitting.

He closed his eyes on a wave of pain. Of all the mistakes he'd ever made in his life, this was surely the worst. Even worse than Angie and her betrayals.

That brought back memories of how Meredith had defended him from Angie at Durward's party. He wished he could shut his brain off so that he could sleep.

It was almost daylight before he finally went to sleep, and he had barely two hours of it before he was up and moving out with his men. At least being exhausted from lack of sleep helped stop him from brooding about Meredith.

CHAPTER TEN

MERRIE WAS SILENT almost all the way home. She noticed that Paul was very tired, and she coaxed him into closing his eyes, so that she wouldn't have to answer any questions about why she'd called him to come get her.

She'd get enough of the third degree from her sister when she arrived home, she was certain.

The contract killer had found her through her own stupidity. She should never have used her credit card. She recalled Ren's odd looks when she'd mentioned her dress and the coats, and she realized much too late that he still thought she'd used his card for the expensive purchases. Delsey probably hadn't mentioned that Merrie paid for her own things. Of course, Ren didn't know how much she was worth. Maybe if he had, he'd have had reservations about coming on to her so strongly.

She flushed, recalling his hunger for her, his sensual delight in her body. He was experienced, and it showed. She laughed silently. He'd probably had so many women that he couldn't even remember their faces, so she'd had a lucky escape.

Lucky. Sure. That explained why she was still fighting tears when they landed at the airport in Jacobsville.

She wiped them away before Paul could see them and put on a smiling face for him.

The pretense lasted only until she got in the house. Sari was waiting, her arms open. She knew without being told that Merrie wasn't home because of the killer. She'd run from a man she cared about too much.

Mandy was still asleep, Sari told her. "She'll be so happy to have you home. She's missed you so much. We all have. Especially me."

Merrie hugged her. "We've hardly ever been apart. I had fun, learning about ranching. But it's nice to be home again." Tears threatened again.

"Come on upstairs," Sari said. "I'll tuck you in and read you a bedtime story," she teased.

"Thanks," Merrie said sadly. "I could use a little TLC."

"Go to bed, sweetheart," she told Paul with a loving smile. "You can get at least three more hours before you have to wake up for work."

"You're an angel," he mused, smiling. "Thanks."

"Thanks for coming for me, Paul," Merrie said. "I'm sorry I called so late."

"Not a problem, kid," he teased. "I work for the government. I can sleep standing up if I have to."

"He really can," Sari assured Merrie when they were in her room. "I've seen him do it on occasion."

"He's so kind. You're so lucky, Sari," she said. She dropped down onto her bed and let out a sigh. "I wish I was, too."

"Want to talk about it?" Sari asked gently, sitting beside her.

"He thought I was Randall's woman and treated me accordingly," Merrie said stiffly. "When I said no, he thought I was teasing. He was so mad!"

Sari winced and hugged her sister close. "I thought it might be something like that. You should have told him about how we were raised."

"I tried to. I don't think he believed me, even from the first." She drew back, dabbing at her eyes with a tissue from her pocket. "He's not a bad man," she added heavily. "But one of Randall's other women came to stay and seduced him into getting engaged to her. When he found out that she only wanted his money, not him, he broke the engagement. Then she went online and told people he was clumsy in bed."

"That's a rotten way to get even with a man," Sari said quietly. "We've prosecuted cases from people who thought they were harassing someone anonymously and found out differently in court."

"Yes, they never seem to realize that an IP address can be traced," Merrie agreed. She drew in a breath. "Ren asked me to go to a party with him. He knew his ex-fiancée was going to be there." She smiled sadly. "I told her to leave him alone."

"My mild-mannered baby sister actually fought for a man?" Sari teased.

Merrie laughed softly. "Yes, I guess I did. Ren was impressed." The smile faded. "Then we went home." She swallowed. The memories stung. She lowered her eyes. "I thought he cared about me. I didn't realize that a man could be that way with a woman and feel nothing but desire." She looked up with miserable eyes. "I guess I really am stupid."

"I remember how I felt about Paul," Sari replied. "You know how it was for me. He thought I was too young. He wouldn't take me seriously. And he was haunted by a past I didn't even know about. It was a very rocky road to the altar." She grinned. "But look at us now."

Merrie nodded. "You really did have a fairy-tale romance." She grimaced. "Mine is more like a horror story."

"He might improve over time," Sari suggested.

"Not likely. Not where I'm concerned, anyway."

"It's early days yet. Go to sleep. Relax. You're home, now. Nobody is going to hurt you here."

"Are the Avengers still around?"

Sari laughed. "Yes, they are. We've had them putting up more surveillance equipment. And we've got a houseguest."

"We have? Who?"

Sari patted her hand. "All in good time. Get some sleep, honey. We'll talk more in the morning. I have tomorrow off, since I'm doing overtime the day after as a trade-off with one of our other ADAs."

"You're a nice lawyer."

"Aw, shucks," Sari drawled.

Merrie just laughed.

HER DREAMS WERE HAUNTED. She was lying in Ren's arms, drowning in his kisses, when he drew back and threw her aside.

He got up and just walked away, without looking back. She was calling to him, over and over, but he kept walking. She got to her feet and ran. She was wearing a long, expensive, gauzy gown with incredibly high heels. As she ran, she tripped over her long skirts and started falling. She called to Ren to save her, but he was gone. She fell down a hole and turned end over end over end…

She came awake suddenly, her heart shaking her. It was only a dream. But it had felt very real. The falling part, especially. She thought of Ren as he'd been the last time she saw him, drawn and quiet and withdrawn. Paul, she guessed, had told Ren some hard truths about her past. He'd realized then how wrong he'd been about her.

But it was too late to matter anymore. Ren's anger was going to sting for a long time. He might feel guilty that he'd tried to seduce her when he knew how green she was, but that didn't mean he loved her. She remembered the joy she'd felt in his company, the pleasure of just sitting with him and watching the news on TV in the evenings. She'd gotten used to being with him. In the space of a day, her entire life had changed. She knew that she'd never see Ren again, not as long as she lived. Nothing had hurt so much, not even his harsh words.

She wondered if he'd tell Randall why she'd really left. Probably not. He did love his brother. He considered that she was Randall's woman, so he might not want to admit that he'd wanted her. Not that he hadn't had his successes with Randall's other women, as he'd confessed to her.

She went down to breakfast in jeans and a T-shirt, her hair in a ponytail and no makeup on. She didn't care if she looked as bad as she felt.

When she got to the table, she did a double take. There was another man in the room, and it wasn't Paul or the Avengers.

He was broad, with a big nose, high cheekbones and a chiseled mouth. His hair was jet black and wavy, his eyes large and dark. He resembled Paul, but there was a dangerous air about him. Then she remembered. She'd painted him from photographs Paul had given her, as a birthday present he'd commissioned for his cousin Mikey.

"Cousin Mikey," she blurted out, then flushed with embarrassment when his thick eyebrows arched over twinkling dark eyes. "Sorry," she added quickly as she sat down. "I painted you…"

"Ah. The sister-in-law." He grinned. "Yeah. It was a good likeness. The knife on the table beside me was a touch of genius," he added with pursed lips.

"Oh, stop that, she looks like a fire engine already, you dope," Paul said, making a face at him as he joined them.

"Sorry." Mikey chuckled. "Couldn't resist it." He cocked his head and stared at Merrie. "You don't look like I thought you would, baby doll," he added.

"What did you expect?" she asked, curious.

He accepted a cup of black coffee from Paul with thanks before he turned back to Merrie. "A fortune-teller, with a crystal ball. Maybe a kerchief around your head."

Her eyebrows arched.

"I'm a bad man," he mused, and it wasn't an apology or a conceit. "You painted the real me. And you didn't know a thing about me."

"Oh." She managed a shy smile. "I just sort of see inside people. Paul didn't say anything about who you were or what you did. He just handed me the photographs and said you were his cousin, and asked if I could do a painting of you for a present. I said sure."

"Well, it's amazing," he said. "I had it framed and put over the mantel in my living room," he added. "I don't get a lot of visitors, but it's had its share of attention." He laughed out loud.

"What's so funny?" Merrie asked.

"This big mob boss—and I mean, big, he controls half of a state up north—wanted to know who you were so he could ask you to paint him."

Merrie's eyes widened. "What did you tell him?"

"That it was a present, and I didn't know who did it." He became serious as he looked at her with eyes twice as old as he looked. "You don't want to get mixed up with a guy like that, unless it's the end of the world."

"Thanks for protecting me," she said, understanding what he was saying.

He nodded. He stared at his plate and scowled. "Not being rude, but what the hell is this white stuff?" he asked, pointing.

"It's grits," Mandy said as she came back into the room with a wicker bowl of biscuits wrapped in expensive white linen cloth. "Merrie!" she exclaimed. She stopped long enough to hug Merrie. "Oh, it's so good to have you home!" she said, fighting tears.

"I've missed you, too, Mandy," Merrie said, sighing. It was nice to be home, where she really was loved.

"Come on, enough of this." Mandy laughed, fighting tears of joy. "Sit down. I'll get out all the preserves. He—" she indicated Mikey "—will do almost anything for my homemade blueberry preserves."

"Almost anything," Mikey agreed with a grin. "Okay, come on, tell me about grits." He pointed at his plate. "Is it grit, like the stuff you polish stones with?" he asked, poking at the dubious food with his fork.

"It's what you get when you grind up corn," Mandy mused, smiling. "You know about grinding up stuff, don't you, Mikey?" she added, teasing.

He wrinkled his nose. "Hey, I never did that thing they accused me of," he said with faint belligerence. "Putting a guy in a grinder? That's lowbrow."

"Try the grits," Mandy said. "I've put butter in them."

He looked at them dubiously, but he put a forkful into his mouth, chewed and lifted both eyebrows. "Hey. That's not bad. Tastes like polenta."

She laughed. "Told you so."

He shook his head. "Grits. Cowboy hats. Horses and cattle." He made a face at Paul. "What the hell is a good Jersey boy like you doing in a place like this?" he added.

Paul looked at Sari with his heart in his eyes. "Living the American dream."

Sari smiled back at him.

Mikey just shook his head. "Well, you guys can have it. No casinos. No bars to speak of. Not even a decent nightclub. It's the end of the world, that's what it is!"

"We have butterflies and lightning bugs and hay rides and county fairs," Merrie protested. "That's better than nightclubs."

"I'm gonna break out in hives any minute," Mikey promised her, with a belligerent expression.

She just grinned.

Just then, the front door opened and booted feet came marching in.

"Well, we got the new cameras installed, finally," Barton, the broader of the two bodyguards, announced. "Hey, is that grits? You made them just for me, didn't you, you sweetheart!" He caught Mandy by the arm and kissed her cheek.

She blushed. "I did not! I made them for her!" She pointed at Merrie.

"Welcome home, Miss Grayling." Rogers, the taller of the bodyguards, greeted her with a smile.

"Thanks. I hear I had company up in Wyoming," she added. "I did a really dumb thing. I used my credit card at a store."

"Nobody's perfect," Barton assured her as he sat down with his companion.

"Except me," Mikey said, sipping coffee. He glowered at the bodyguards when they looked at him.

"Absolutely perfect," Rogers said abruptly.

"Model of perfection," Barton agreed.

Merrie looked astounded.

"He took down both of them in hand-to-hand combat in less than thirty seconds," Paul said complacently.

Merrie pursed her lips and hid a laugh. "Spec ops, Middle East," Mikey explained with a grin. "I was a bad boy."

"You must be, if you could take them both down," Merrie agreed.

The bodyguards managed to look sheepish and charmed all at once.

Paul chuckled. "They were in the same unit, believe it or not. Afghanistan, and then Iraq."

"Hard times," Mikey said.

"Steel needs tempering, I guess," Paul said.

"I guess," his cousin agreed.

"What sort of cameras?" Paul asked Barton.

"Classified cameras," Barton replied with pursed lips. "Sorry."

"I'm with the FBI, for God's sake," Paul exclaimed.

"We outrank you," Rogers said brightly.

Paul glared at him. "Nobody outranks the FBI. We wrote the book on classified!"

"Oh, yeah?" Mikey said. "Then why don't you know about the flying saucer that crashed in Roswell, New Mexico, and all that technology they found on it? I'll bet they know," he added, nodding toward the bodyguards.

"I know nothing," Barton said blithely.

"I know even less," Rogers seconded.

"They probably even know where the bodies are," Mikey scoffed.

Rogers and Barton exchanged amused looks but remained silent.

"See?" Mikey said, pointing toward them with a fork as he stared at his cousin. "And what do you know?" he added. "How to track down bank robbers!"

"Hey, somebody's got to catch common criminals," Paul shot back. "It's your money we're protecting."

"I don't even have enough money to afford good shoes," Mikey said.

"Oh, my heart bleeds," Paul scoffed. "Sell your Mercedes and buy a pair."

"I like the Mercedes," Mikey said. He looked thoughtful. "I guess I could sell the Rolls. I never drive it anyway. It's too pretentious."

"Too pretentious?" Paul exclaimed.

"Well, it gets you noticed by the cops, anyway," Mikey said. "Really noticed."

"Gee, that could be bad if you're stalking somebody, huh?" Paul chuckled.

"Cut it out," Mikey muttered. "Baby doll over there will think I'm as bad as you tell people I am."

Merrie laughed, because he was pointing at her. "No. You're only as bad as you think you are," she returned. She cocked her head and looked at him warmly. "You're not bad unless people hurt somebody you care about."

A faint dusky color burned along his high cheekbones. "You're sharp."

"Like a tack," she teased.

He smiled. His eyes smiled along with his mouth.

She read so many things in his face. Pain. Terror. Love. Death. Hope. Anguish. Loneliness. "You were very hard to capture in oils," she remarked, thinking out loud.

"Try a net," Paul prodded.

"Stop that," Mikey said. "Or I'll tell them what you did to Grandmama when nobody was looking."

"I was ten!"

"It was still bad," Mikey retorted.

"Not that bad."

"You got such a whipping," Mikey said, smiling as he reminisced. "Poor little Paulie."

"You told."

"I never!" Mikey chuckled. "I just pointed, as you shot that hand up in the air."

"Same difference. I was doing it behind her back!"

"Not after I pointed, you weren't," Mikey replied.

"You bad boys!" Mandy chided.

They grinned at her, looking so much alike that Merrie and Sari exchanged amused glances.

SEVERAL DAYS LATER, Merrie was still brooding about Ren and worried about the killer. Cash Grier had come to the house to talk to Mikey. They went off in a room together. It had seemed ominous, but soon there was muffled laughter coming from the study. They learned later that Cash had been with a spec ops group near where Mikey was stationed during his time in the military. They were exchanging memories, not all of which seemed to be traumatic, judging by the laughter.

But Cash left. Mikey went out. Paul was still at work. Sari had come home for lunch. Merrie was wandering around the house, lost in thought and misery.

The bodyguards were patrolling outside. Mandy was cooking. Merrie was brooding. Sari saw her from the staircase, watching, worrying.

"You've got too much free time on your hands," Sari remarked. "You think too much."

"I can't help it," Merrie retorted. She drew in a long breath and smoothed back her ponytail. "It kind of figures that I'd go overboard for the first man who paid me any real attention, right?" she added. "I was an idiot."

"You didn't know what he thought you were," Sari said. "Randall should have made it clear to him."

"Randall's a sweetheart, but he's flighty," Merrie explained. "He told Ren I was his friend. But we both know how that word gets thrown around these days." She grimaced. "I never thought..." She swallowed. "Well, live and learn. I won't be so gullible next time."

"My poor baby." Sari hugged her. "Why don't you go into town and see Brand Taylor? You spoke about buying him out at the art gallery. This is a good time to sound him about it."

"What a good idea!" she exclaimed.

"You can take the bodyguards with you."

"Oh, for heaven's sake, in Jacobsville? Even a professional hit man would think twice about trying to pop me in the middle of town. If he's even here. I left Wyoming in the middle of the night. He's probably camping outside Ren's ranch, waiting for me to show myself in a window. Paul flew me down here in the private jet, with our own pilot. Even if the killer checked commercial flights, he'd be no smarter, and Delsey drove us to the airport in Catelow. We didn't leave a paper trail. Not even a digital one."

"You could be right. But maybe we should ask the bodyguards first what they think," Sari began.

Merrie kissed her cheek. "It's nice that you worry about me, but now you're going overboard. I'll have the chauffeur bring the limo around. It's got bulletproof glass. And that new driver is an ex-cop, right?"

"Yes, he is. He had references, and we checked them. He's very nice."

"I wouldn't know. You hired him while I was in Wyoming."

"Take my word for it. He's very nice. He also has a concealed-carry permit, and he carries a .45 automatic."

"You're sure he isn't following in Morris's footsteps?" Merrie wondered, alluding to the former chauffeur who was in jail awaiting trial on attempted murder charges for taking two shots at Sari. He'd been one of two killers Timothy Leeds had hired to kill the Grayling sisters, in a failed attempt to torment their father. Leeds had put out the contracts without knowing Grayling was already dead.

"I'm sure. Paul checked him out, too. The driver has relatives in Corpus Christi. They vouched for him. So did the former police chief there, where he worked." Sari smiled. "My, you're developing a suspicious nature. Good for you!"

Merrie laughed. "I guess I am. After what we've

both been through lately, I guess we're all a little twitchy."

"Nice choice of words," her sister replied, tongue in cheek.

"Thanks. I'm also developing a larger and more useful vocabulary." She pursed her lips. "One of Ren's cowboys hit his thumb with a hammer outside the kitchen window and I learned five new words." She grimaced at the memory of Ren.

"You must have enjoyed some part of that visit."

"I enjoyed a lot. There was this poor horse, Hurricane," she added. "One of Ren's men had beaten him very badly. He wouldn't let anyone near him. But Hurricane let me take off the bridle they hadn't been able to remove. He even let me doctor his cuts. Ren was furious, because he'd told me not to go near Hurricane."

"Horses can be very dangerous. You know that."

"I do. But the horse was in terrible pain and scared to death. I think he sensed that we were kindred spirits. Later on, I painted him. And…oh, dear, Willis's wolf!"

"Willis's what? Who's Willis?"

"He's Ren's ranch foreman. He has a pet wolf. It lost a leg to a bear trap, so he rescued it and tamed it. He takes it to schools to teach children about wildlife." She grimaced. "I promised to paint him, but my sketchbook is still at the ranch. I have to send boxes and a label out there. Delsey will package up my stuff and send it on if I ask her to."

"Who's Delsey?"

"She's Ren's housekeeper," Merrie said softly.

"She's so sweet. She was kind to me." She lowered her eyes. "Ren was, too, until…"

Sari hugged her. "Merrie, time heals all wounds, and that's the truth. Listen, it's almost November. Thanksgiving will be here before you know it. We have to order new Christmas ornaments for the tree."

"Ren won't let Delsey put up a Christmas tree, except in her room," Merrie said. "He made me hide my cross under my shirts so it didn't show."

Sari frowned. "Why?"

"His mother celebrates Christmas. He went to one of those liberal colleges up north, and when he went home for the holidays, he made some sarcastic remarks about religion being nothing but superstition and backward people who believe in a higher power. Hurt his mother's feelings. Then she said some things about Ren's father, and he overheard it. He just walked out the door and went to live on the ranch with his father. He pulled the ranch out of bankruptcy and built it into an empire. But he hasn't spoken to his mother since. He holds grudges."

Sari drew in a breath. "That's sad. Sometimes I wish our mother was still alive. She was so kind."

"I think Ren's mother is, too," Merrie said. "He let me use her studio to paint in while I was there. He said she loved to paint flowers."

Sari smiled. "A woman who loves flowers can't be all bad."

"I thought the same thing. I hope he relents someday and talks to her. Delsey said something about his mother having a test and being worried about a biopsy."

She looked at Sari. "Sometimes you think you have all the time in the world to make up, and you don't."

"I know many cases of that. Grudges are sad."

"They are. Ren's so alone," she said softly. "Except for Delsey and Randall he really doesn't have anybody. He's...self-contained. He lives alone, inside himself. He won't let anyone else in. I guess Angie dynamited the last little bit of love he had inside him."

"He might change one day, honey."

"He might not." Merrie was sad. "I thought we were headed toward such a sweet future together. And here I am back home alone." She sighed. "But it could be worse, I guess," she added. "I asked Delsey if she could fix me some grits, and she asked me what a grit was."

Sari laughed. "Paul says they aren't common up north."

"I can't imagine people who don't eat grits," Merrie replied. "It's the seeds of barbaricism!" she said facetiously.

"There's no such word," her sister said.

"Sure there is. I just made it up. It's my word. I own it." She struck a pose. "And don't try to appropriate it, or I'll accuse you of artistic theft."

"Whatever you say. Barbaricism," she scoffed, shaking her head.

"I'm going to take my new word into town and share it with Brand Taylor," Merrie told her. "Come on. I'll be perfectly safe."

Sari gave in with a sigh. "Okay. Maybe you're right."

"I'm always right," Merrie assured her. "I'm an artist. We know stuff!"

"I won't argue with that."

THE CHAUFFEUR WAS kind and polite. Sari had hired him on Paul's recommendation. When the bodyguards weren't around, Mr. Jones was.

He dropped Merrie off at Brand Taylor's gallery in Jacobsville and waited outside in the vehicle for her.

"Miss Grayling," Brand greeted her. He grinned as he shook hands. "I was hoping you might stop by one day. I understand that you might be in the market for an art gallery, and I want to retire to the Bahamas."

"The Bahamas?" she exclaimed, laughing.

"Yes. I'm going to become a professional beach-comber. I may never put on a suit again," he added, indicating the elegant one he was wearing.

"I would love to buy you out, if you're serious," Merrie replied with a smile.

"In that case, shall we discuss options?"

MERRIE WAS ON top of the world when she came out of the art gallery. She and Mr. Taylor had agreed on a price. Of course, an evaluation of his inventory would have to be done, and two Realtors would also chime in on the property itself. Merrie told him she'd match the higher estimate, just to make sure his beachcomb-ing dreams could really come true. He was delighted.

She climbed into the backseat of the limo, her head spinning with dreams and ambitions that she'd never before had a chance to realize. Her father would never have allowed her to buy an art gallery, any more than he'd let her date.

It was going to be a poor substitute for Ren. But she

would have something to keep her busy. Something to help bury her broken heart in.

Maybe eventually she could forget how it felt to lie in Ren's strong arms and feel his mouth devouring hers. He'd been hungry for her, almost starving. It had probably been a long time since he'd been with a woman, she reminded herself. No wonder he'd been starving. It wasn't even personal.

She was so lost in thought that she didn't even realize that Mr. Jones was speaking to her.

"Oh! I'm so sorry! I was lost in dreams of business ownership," she said with a laugh. "What was that, Mr. Jones?"

"I said, where do you want to go now?" he asked with a smile.

"To Barbara's Café," she said. "I'm going to get one of her chocolate cakes to take home for lunch."

"Not a bad idea," he said.

"Absolutely," she agreed.

REN WAS CLIMBING DOWN from the cab of a huge hay feeder, a machine that took the big round bales of hay and churned them up into feed, along with additives, and pushed the feed out into troughs through a long curved tube.

"Hey, boss," J.C. called.

Ren tugged his hat lower and his scarf tighter as he joined the other man. It was even colder than the day before, and snow was still driving down. "What's up?" he asked.

"I went to see Beakly," J.C. replied.

"And?"

"You were right. He was paid two thousand dollars to back up the truck driver's story about a delivery," the other man said curtly.

Ren blew out a breath, idly watching it steam in the vicious cold as it left his warm mouth. "Maybe it's a good thing Meredith went home, after all," he said quietly. It still hurt to recall what he'd done to her. If he thought about it very much, he'd go mad.

"Maybe. I hope they're watching her closely. Contract killers are crafty and meticulous, and they don't usually strike until your guard is down."

"How would you know about that, Calhoun?" Ren mused.

J.C. didn't say a word. He just looked at Ren, his odd silver eyes as cold as the snow around them.

"I'm sure she's well protected," Ren replied. "Her brother-in-law is an FBI agent, and the family is wealthy."

"None of that will matter," J.C. told him. "This man's a chameleon. He popped up out of nowhere, with a disguise that fooled both of us. He came onto the ranch right under our noses and disabled two closed-circuit cameras. Yes, we have it on tape," he added. "We had a hidden camera that he didn't see. It caught a good shot of him, close up."

Ren's cold lips made a thin line. "Print it out. I'm going to fax it to the FBI agent at his office in San Antonio," he said. "It might not do a lot of good. I'm sure they have a pretty accurate description of him by now. But it might help."

"Good idea," J.C. said. "You never know what will break a case wide-open."

CHAPTER ELEVEN

MERRIE LAID HER head back against the seat, smiling at her good fortune. Brand Taylor was quite knowledgeable about art, and he had a reputation for astute appraisal. He'd taught Merrie a thing or two about painting as well, during her infrequent trips to his store to buy her art supplies. He sold them in a separate room of his gallery, Jacobsville being such a small town that he needed the diversity to stay afloat financially.

She hoped he'd agree to stay on long enough to teach her the management end of the business. She knew the art side fairly well. Managing a retail business on a daily basis, however, was another matter. That was going to take some training. She might do well to sign up for a few business courses at the local community college where she'd done her art classes.

But that thought had little appeal. She had no interest in numbers or keeping records. That would turn a new and exciting job into something incredibly boring and tedious.

Alternatively, she might just hire a business manager. Her spirits lifted. Sari had suggested obtaining the services of a good certified public accountant, as well. That wasn't a bad idea. If other people could handle the day-to-day management of the business, Merrie could do what she loved best. She could buy and sell art. And she could paint!

At least worrying about her new business would keep her mind off the one thing it kept gnawing on: Ren. Without him, life lost all color. The thought of never seeing him again made her sick to her stomach. She'd loved him. The way they'd parted was still painful to recall.

When she closed her eyes, she could envision the portrait she'd done of Ren, the one that had captured him so perfectly. He'd been surprised and delighted with the end result. She wondered what he'd do with the canvas now. Probably hide it in a closet, because he wouldn't want to be reminded of her. He wouldn't like remembering how badly he'd treated her, even if he'd only wanted to have sex with her. He was a kind man inside, where he hid that part of himself beneath a gruff exterior.

She knew him down to his bones. He'd been hurt so much that he withdrew from the world, from people. He lived isolated from the world and spent his life taking care of livestock. He loved animals. Animals couldn't hurt you, and his business gave him something to nurture, to protect.

He loved the land as much as he loved cattle. He'd talked to her about his plans for pasture improvement, for experimenting with native grasses and water conservation on his property. He was a good steward of the land. They had a lot in common. Merrie loved gardening and animals, as well. If he hadn't hurt her so badly, she might still be in Wyoming, learning more about him.

But that hadn't been in the cards. He didn't want someone to live with him and love him. He just wanted a woman for the occasional night, when he needed a body. Maybe he'd loved Angie, who'd treated him like dirt. He certainly didn't love Merrie.

She wished she could smother her feelings for him. It would make her life easier. It would take time, she told herself. She couldn't expect a hurt that went so deep to be healed in a matter of days. She just had to get through the worst of the emotional pain, and then she could start to heal.

The limo slowed down. Idly, she glanced out the tinted windows. Mr. Jones was pulling into a parallel parking space near an intersection headed out of Jacobsville. It was at a convenience store, the only spot parallel to the highway, with no other parking spaces around it.

"Mr. Jones, why are we stopping here?" she asked.

He didn't turn his head. "Just need to check the tires, Miss Grayling," he said with a reassuring smile. "It feels like one may be going flat. Only take a sec."

"All right," she said, leaning back against her seat. She hoped he wouldn't take long. She was hungry and eager to go to the café.

She didn't notice that Mr. Jones wasn't bending down to look at a tire. He was speaking on his cell phone and looking out toward the long, straight highway that led to Victoria Road.

He started walking away from the limo. Merrie's

eyes were closed. She didn't see him go. She didn't realize what was happening, even when she felt the impact and glass shattered around her in what seemed like
slow motion. She was being shaken violently. She'd forgotten to put on her seat belt. She was thrown against
the other door from the force of the impact. The last
thing she saw was the formidable grille of what looked
like a huge pickup truck before she fell unconscious.

"WHAT A HELL of a stupid thing I did," Paul groaned
while he and Sari paced the waiting room outside the
surgical suite at the Jacobsville hospital. "What a hell
of a thing! I took a former police chief's word for gos-
pel. I should have checked him out, too!"

"You couldn't have known that he had mob ties,
Paul," Sari said, sliding her arms around him. Her eyes
were red from crying. Merrie was in bad shape. The
impact had bruised her lungs and her stomach. They
were currently repairing her lung and removing her
spleen and appendix, which had been damaged in the
impact. She had badly bruised ribs, and one hip was
traumatized. On top of all that, she'd suffered a mild
concussion. But she was alive. Thank God, she was
alive!

"I should have suspected everybody." Paul hugged
her close. "I'm so sorry!"

She hugged him back. "She'll be all right. Dr. Coltrain is the best surgeon on staff."

"I know. I know, baby."

They sat back down. The waiting was the worst part.
They didn't know what else Coltrain might find when

he went in to repair the other problems. He hadn't said much, but that in itself was a statement to anyone who knew him well. Sari did. He'd been her doctor, and Merrie's, for years.

"Where's Cousin Mikey?" Sari asked.

"Yelling at people," he said simply. "Calling in markers. He's gotten fond of our Merrie."

"He's not such a bad man," Sari said.

"Yes, he is," he said quietly. "But it's good to have a bad man in your corner, sometimes. He's talking to his mob boss buddy. He thinks they might relent if he asks nicely."

"You said that the contract killer would consider it a point of honor to make good on the job he took."

"That's true. But he'll have ties to Jersey," he said. "He may have ties to the big boss. If he does, that man could be induced to put pressure on him to end the contract."

"So there's hope," she said, grasping at straws.

He caught her hand in his and lifted it to his mouth. "There's always hope."

She smiled at him.

He drew in a breath. "Should we call that Wyoming rancher?" he asked. "He was pretty torn up when I told him the truth about Merrie. He had some sort of feelings for her, I know."

"If he wants to know anything about her, he can call and ask," Sari said, still resenting the way he'd treated Merrie.

"I guess so."

Paul went to get coffee for them. Sari rubbed one

eye, and he knew what that meant—a threatening migraine headache. She had them more often when she was stressed. Strong coffee might stave it off until they had a report on the extent of Merrie's injuries.

While he was gone, Sari noticed a tall, well-built man coming toward her in a police chief's uniform. She smiled. Cash Grier was over forty, but he could have passed for thirty. He'd lived a life that many men envied, and he was married to an honest-to-goodness movie star. They had a daughter and a new baby son.

"How is she?" Cash asked, dropping into a chair across from Sari's.

"We don't know. There's a lot of bruising, and she'll lose her spleen and her appendix." She shook her head. "The driver took off. Paul checked him out. He had an ex-police chief lie for him when Paul did a background check."

"Don't feel bad," Cash said. "Anybody can slip up once. We've got a BOLO out for your limo driver," he added coldly. "We'll find him."

"He set her up, didn't he?" Sari asked, still disbelieving what had happened.

"Yes. From the info we've gathered from eyewitnesses, he parked the limo in a spot where it could easily be broadsided by a speeding vehicle, got out, called somebody and walked away just before the impact."

"The other vehicle…?"

"A 1996 Dodge Ram truck, stolen of course. The driver dived out in the nick of time. He conveniently disappeared."

"Of course."

"We're checking area hospitals for a man with a lot of bruises, and possibly broken bones," Cash continued. "Just between us, this guy is too smart to be caught that way."

"That's what we've been told."

"I believe your houseguest knows something about the contract killer," Cash added. "Can I come over and talk to him again?"

Sari managed to smile. "Of course. Come on out to the house anytime you like."

"Thanks. We'll wait until you have some news first, though," he added. He cocked his head. "It's mostly the bruising they'll have to monitor," he told her. "When Tippy was beaten by her stepfather in New York, she was in the hospital for several days. She had bruised lungs. They put her on antibiotics. She did fine. Merrie will, too."

Sari nodded. "Thanks."

"I wanted to...just a sec." His cell phone was vibrating. He stood up, pushed the button and listened, and replied with a grim expression on his face. He put the phone back in its holder. "They just found a body out on the Victoria Road."

"Let me guess. Was he tall and silver-haired and called himself Mr. Jones?" she asked wearily.

He raised both eyebrows. "You're good. Ever thought about getting a job as an assistant district attorney?"

"If I weren't so miserable, I'd laugh," she said with a faint smile. "So I guess there's no way to question him about who hired him."

"Or where his boss went," Cash agreed. "Well, he might have something on him that would give us a clue."

"How was he killed?" she asked.

"Double tap," Cash replied. "Execution-style. First rule of assassination. Kill the assassin."

She just nodded. She drew in a breath. "Oh, I wish time went faster," she moaned.

"When you're my age, you won't be wishing that," he said with twinkling eyes. Paul came down the hall with two cups of coffee. "Hey, chief," he said when he saw Cash. "Want a cup? I can go back."

Cash made a face. "I am a connoisseur of fine coffee. We have a nice little hospital, but that vending machine should be arrested for counterfeiting caffeine products."

Paul smiled. "I want to watch you try to handcuff it."

"It's not as bad as that poor soft drink machine over in Palo Verde that Garon Grier told me about."

Paul lifted both eyebrows.

Cash chuckled. "Happened before he and Grace married. It seems that the machine had a habit of taking money and not giving out soft drinks. So it was accidentally hit with a baseball bat—several times." He held up a hand when Paul started to ask how somebody could accidentally hit a vending machine with a bat. He smiled broadly, then continued. "Garon didn't inquire about the perp, but I'd bet money that he was wearing a uniform at the time."

Paul laughed in spite of himself. "I had a vacuum cleaner once that met with the same sort of accident."

"So did I," Cash replied with a grin. "Kindred spirits."

"I shot mine."

"I stomped mine," Cash said.

"Feeling better, sweetheart?" Paul asked Sari, who was holding the cup of hot coffee against her temple.

"Not a lot, no," she said miserably. "I didn't bring my migraine capsules with me today, either."

"I'll call Mandy and have her send them over with one of the Avengers." Paul stepped away for a moment to place the call.

"I've never had a migraine," Cash said, sobering, "but I know people who do. Tough luck, counselor."

"Story of my life," she replied, wincing. "They get closer together, and worse, when I'm under pressure."

Paul came back. "Mandy's sending them over with Barton," she said.

"Thanks, honey," she said, squeezing the hand he put on her shoulder.

"I'll get back to work," Cash said. "It goes without saying that if Tippy and I can help, we will, even if it's just sitting up with Merrie while she's recovering."

"Thanks," Sari said. "I mean that."

He shrugged. "We have to look out for each other. It's one of the really great things about small towns." He looked at Paul. "You weren't here when I told her," he indicated Sari. "We found Mr. Jones in a ditch near the city limits sign on Victoria Road."

"Dead, right?" Paul asked curtly.

"Very dead. We're backtracking on the truck right

now. It's a rental. The killer left the rental sheet in the glove compartment. Sloppy."

"Maybe he wasn't the contract man."

"You mean, maybe he subcontracted the job?" Cash asked. "Well, it would be a novel approach."

"Tell me about it. I'll do some checking of my own," Paul told him.

"He means, he'll ask Mikey," Sari said with a pale smile.

"Mikey knows stuff."

"Yes, he does," Cash said. "He's got connections, and a mind like a steel trap."

"Cash came out to the house to talk to Mikey," Sari explained to her husband. "Turns out they served overseas near each other, and they have mutual acquaintances," she added.

"We do." Cash chuckled. "Your cousin can tell some stories," he added to Paul. "Amazing, with his history, that he doesn't mind talking to policemen."

"Funny thing, he actually likes cops." Paul chuckled. "He sits in on a regular Friday night poker game back home with a slew of detectives from the precinct near his house."

"I like poker myself," Cash replied.

"Here's a free tip," Paul said. "Don't ever get in a game with Mikey."

"He cheats?"

"He doesn't have to. He's locked out of every damned casino in Vegas, and a couple of big overseas ones, too. I can tell you for a fact that Marcus Carrera meets him at the door if he even walks into the Bow Tie on Paradise Island in the Bahamas."

Cash laughed. "What luck!"

"Yeah. Pity he got barred. But he already had the Rolls by then, anyway. He could buy a small third world country with what he's got in Swiss banks."

A man approaching caught their attention. It was one of the bodyguards, Barton, with a bottle of capsules.

"Mandy said you needed these urgently." He handed the bottle to Sari.

"Thanks," she said with a smile. "It really is a mission of mercy," she told Cash.

"I'll take her word for it, this time," Cash told the newcomer with pursed lips. "I don't trust men who eat sheep's eyes."

Barton rolled his. "Listen, they're an acquired taste which I acquired because it was the only damned thing I could get to eat in the village where I was hiding out."

"Hey, at least he doesn't blow up people with hand grenades," Paul defended him.

"I don't do that anymore," came a deep, amused voice from behind them.

They all turned at once. Dr. Carson Farwalker was standing there in a white lab coat with a stethoscope draped around his neck and a clipboard in his hand.

"Luckily, we're also short on crocodiles in Texas," Cash mused, alluding to an incident in South America when Farwalker and Stanton Rourke had fed a cold-blooded killer to one.

Carson chuckled. "Luckily. Doc Coltrain sent me

out to tell you that Merrie's doing well," he added, the smile fading. "He's putting in the final sutures now. They'll wheel her down to recovery in about ten minutes."

"Oh, thank God," Sari said. Hot, joyful tears ran down her cheeks. "Thank God!"

"Great news," Paul said. "Thanks, Carson."

"They're bringing in your ex-chauffeur," he told his companions. "Dr. Coltrain will perform the autopsy, probably later today. Maybe it will give you some answers."

"Maybe so."

Carson nodded and left them. Cash left a minute later.

Paul pulled Sari into his arms and rocked her. "It's okay, honey," he said softly. "Everything's going to be okay."

"We have to catch the killer," she said at his ear. "We have to. Or next time…"

"Yes. Or next time we might not get lucky. Don't worry. We've got plenty of people hunting him. We'll find him, baby. We will."

LATER THAT AFTERNOON, Merrie opened her eyes in the recovery room and looked up into her sister's face.

"I feel like I fell off a cliff," she said in a weak voice.

Sari squeezed her hand. "I imagine so. You're all right, sweetheart. Dr. Coltrain patched you up. Now all you have to do is heal."

Merrie managed a smile. "So sleepy…"

"You go right back to sleep. One of us will be with

you, all the time," Sari promised. "All the time, Merrie."

Merrie closed her eyes and drifted away.

WHEN SARI WENT back out into the waiting room, Paul had company. A tall, very handsome blond man was sitting with him, sipping coffee and looking morose.

"Hi, Sari," Randall, Ren's brother, said, rising to shake hands. "How is she?"

"Weak, but she'll get better," Sari said wearily. She sat down on the other side of Paul and accepted a cup of black coffee. "This has been a hell of a day."

"Paul filled me in," Randall said. "Why did she leave Skyhorn?" he added.

"She used her credit card in Catelow," Paul said, bypassing the real reason Merrie had begged to come home. "The contract killer traced her to your brother's ranch."

Randall ground his teeth together. "Gosh, I'm sorry. I still think she'd be safer there than here, though. It's so isolated that any movement gets picked up. Although," he added heavily, "Ren's beating himself up over a truck driver who almost managed to get on the property. Paid a neighbor to swear he mixed up the address on a delivery. Ren thinks he was looking for a way in that wouldn't put him under suspicion."

"Merrie's home now," Sari said curtly. "We'll take care of her."

"What's going on?" Randall asked bluntly. "I mean, Ren got drunk. Really drunk. I've never known him to do that, not even when he found out Angie was cheating on him and broke his engagement."

"Got drunk?" Paul asked.

"Stinking drunk, Willis said," Randall agreed. "Couldn't lift his head for a whole day."

Paul had a good idea why the other man's brother had gone off the deep end. He glanced at Sari and realized that she was thinking the same thing.

"I told Ren that Merrie was my girl," Randall said, wincing. "If I gave Ren the wrong impression and caused him to, well, to offend Merrie, I'm very sorry."

"She used her credit card, that's all," Paul said, smoothing it over. "We had to bring her back home after that."

"Yes, but what happened to her today was no accident, was it?" Randall asked worriedly.

"Probably not," Paul said.

Randall shook his head. "I'm just so sorry. I feel like the whole thing's my fault."

"Life happens," Sari said quietly.

"Ren asked me to come by here. I was going to San Antonio to talk to a prospective buyer, anyway. He wanted me to see Merrie and apologize. He didn't say for what."

"He seems to be a few days late," Sari said with cold sarcasm.

"He's not a bad man," Randall defended his older brother. "He's had a hard life and it's made him bitter. But my big brother doesn't go on benders. Your sister means something to him."

Sari softened, just a little. "When she's in a room, I'll tell her," she said quietly.

"Okay. Thanks." He scribbled down a number on a paper from the small notepad in his jacket pocket and handed it to Sari. "That's my cell number. I'm never without my phone. If it isn't asking too much…"

"Yes, I'll keep you in the loop," Sari told him. "And thanks for coming by."

"I'd rather it was under nicer circumstances," he said with genuine feeling. "Merrie's very special. I'm sorry I'm such a rake, you know," he added. "If I wasn't, I might be tempted to try my luck with her. She'll make some man a wonderful wife someday."

"I don't think she's looking along those lines anymore," Sari replied. "She's enthusiastic about buying a local art supply store and gallery here in town."

Randall just nodded. "I see."

"It's a nice little town. Sort of like Catelow," Paul interrupted. "Tell Ren she's going to be okay, will you?"

"I'll tell him. I'll keep you all in my thoughts. And my prayers," he added. He noticed Sari's expression, and he smiled sadly. "I went to college, too, but I wasn't as easily influenced as Ren was. He was fascinated with one of his professors, a female physics teacher who was antireligion. I'm not sure he realized it, but the person more than the subject matter was what influenced him. He had a crush on the professor."

"Merrie and I had little else except religion after Mama died," Sari said with a sad smile. "Your brother may find that his priorities will undergo a radical change one day when he's faced with a loss more personal than a cow or a bull."

"I've been saying that for years. My mother is facing the possibility of cancer treatment. Ren hasn't spoken to her in a long time, but he seems to be softening a little," Randall said. "Whatever his faults, he's still my brother and I love him."

"Merrie and I would have liked a brother," Sari said.

"I'd have liked a sister," Randall replied. "Take care."

Paul shook hands with him and he left.

"You should cut Ren a little slack, honey," Paul said gently. "Men aren't perfect." He pursed his lips. "Well, I am," he amended with twinkling dark eyes. "But you can't hold the rest of the male population up to such exacting high standards, right?"

She laughed and hugged him, laying her cheek against his broad chest with a sigh. "I guess not. If he got that drunk, Merrie must mean something to him," she conceded. "Unless it's just a guilty conscience."

"I never got drunk from just a guilty conscience." He kissed her red hair. "But I did get stinking drunk after I left here that first time, after I'd told your father a whopper of a lie." He held her closer. "I was hurting. I imagine the Wyoming rancher is hurting, too. If he was fighting what he felt, and he assumed Merrie was experienced, he's probably kicking himself for what he did to her."

"If she hadn't come home…!" she began.

He put his finger over her soft mouth to silence her. "Isabel," he said gently, "if she hadn't come home, the killer would have found a way to get on the ranch. Maybe he found a way in that Ren didn't know about, maybe he had a position marked out that gave him access to Merrie's window with a high-powered rifle. This idiot bungled the job. He ran a truck into the limo and didn't kill her. If it was another guy, if the killer is still in Wyoming with his rifle, he might not be aware of the attempt here."

Her eyes widened. "You mean, there might be two killers?" she asked, ice flowing through her veins at just the thought.

"He was watching both places. He might not have known for sure that Merrie had left Skyhorn, but it would be stupid not to watch for her in Jacobsville and Comanche Wells, too."

"What sort of hit man uses a pickup truck as a murder weapon?" she asked.

"Somebody who doesn't know what the hell he's doing, most likely," Paul said. "Mikey picked up a rumor that the contract killer has a distant relative on the wrong side of the law in Houston. That's not too far from here."

Sari wrapped her arms around her chest. "This just keeps getting better and better. Do you think one guard on the door will be enough?" she added. Her face tautened. "And this time, we'd better double-check the background of anybody we get to do security for Merrie."

"I'm two steps ahead of you," he assured her. "I think…"

He broke off as Mikey came down the hall toward

them. He was bareheaded, his thick, wavy black hair glistening, as if he'd been out in the misting rain. He was wearing a suit that probably cost more than one of the two Grayling limousines, a blue pin-striped one with a spotless white shirt and a maroon patterned tie that set off his olive complexion.

As he neared them, they saw a glimmer of amusement in his black eyes that were so much like Paul's.

"Got some good news for a change?" Paul asked as Mikey stopped in front of them.

"Maybe," he said. "How's baby doll?" he asked.

"She came through surgery okay," Sari told him. "She's still in pretty bad shape."

Mikey's face hardened. "The guy who did that won't get far," he told her quietly, glancing around to make sure they weren't overheard. "I called in a marker."

"Hey, now," Paul began.

Mikey held up a hand. "You don't know a damned thing," he told his cousin. "Period."

"I work for the FBI, Mikey," Paul persisted.

"Baby doll in there—" Mikey's head jerked toward the general direction of the recovery room "—is one in a million. And nobody, I mean nobody, hurts her and gets away with it."

"You're a nice man, Cousin Mikey," Sari said softly.

He averted his eyes, looking sheepish. "If I'd met somebody like her years ago, maybe I'd have turned out different."

Paul and Sari exchanged speculative glances.

"Yeah, yeah, years ago, she'd have been in diapers, I know," Mikey muttered. "Just saying. Anyway, the hot rod hitter has a record in Houston for attempted murder. He killed a guy two years ago in what was claimed to be a horrible accident after he ran a truck through his minivan at an intersection."

"Damn!" Paul groaned.

"He got off because the two witnesses suddenly had memory loss and couldn't describe what they saw," Mikey continued. "One of them was driving a brand-new Mercedes shortly thereafter."

"So he walked," Paul muttered.

"He walked."

"I want him alive," he told Mikey firmly. "He might have some idea where the shooter is and what he's planning."

"Not likely." Mikey dropped into a chair next to Paul and leaned forward, his elbows on his knees. "I know the shooter, Paulie," he said softly. "I know how he operates, how he sets up a hit. I've been doing some reconnoitering around your house," he added. "Barton and Rogers went with me. We planted devices in every space he might occupy. He'd have to be a ghost to get through."

"That's at home, Mikey," Paul said heavily. "But Merrie's going to be here for several days. You can't lock down a whole hospital for one patient."

"Think so?" Mikey asked with a grin.

"Okay. What are you up to?" Paul asked, because he knew that grin.

"Oh, I got a few people who are going to be working here temporarily. In fact," he added, nodding toward a man carrying a mop and pail, "there's one of them now."

Paul's eyebrows arched as he noted the way the man was looking around him, as if he were an escaped fugitive.

"Mikey, none of these guys would have their likenesses posted on the FBI website, would they?" Paul asked.

"Well, not in this country, at least," came the amused reply. "Just relax. I'm not even breaking the law. These are honest citizens. The hospital administrator likes them a lot."

"Why does he like them?" Paul asked.

"I just happened to mention how much I support labor unions, and I noticed that this little hospital doesn't seem to have one…"

"God, Mikey!" Paul exclaimed.

"It's all in a good cause," Mikey said. "Keeping baby doll safe. And you know, Paulie, you can get more with a gun and a smile than you can with just a smile." He grinned.

Sari was trying not to laugh and failing miserably.

"See?" Paul said, pointing at Mikey. "That's me, if I'd made different choices in my life."

"He's not so bad," Sari defended Mikey. She smiled at him. "Thanks for everything."

Mikey smiled back.

RANDALL HAD DECIDED that Merrie's accident wasn't the sort of thing he could tell Ren about over the phone, so he detoured through Catelow, Wyoming, on his way to Denver to see another client.

Ren was at the supper table when he arrived. He looked up from the mashed potatoes Delsey was plopping on his plate. They both stared at him.

"You're supposed to be in Denver," Ren commented. His brows drew together. "Has something happened to your...our mother?" he amended.

Randall took a breath. "No. We still haven't heard anything from the biopsy."

Ren relaxed. "Oh. Well, have a seat. Delsey made pot roast and mashed potatoes."

"My favorite." Randall kissed her on the cheek. "You sweetheart!"

"You flatterer." She laughed, moving back into the kitchen to bring coffee.

Randall pulled up a chair and sat down. Ren looked bad. His eyes were bloodshot, and there were purple half-moons under his black eyes.

"You don't look as if you've slept in days," Randall remarked.

"I haven't." He glanced at Randall with faint irritation. "You might have told me that she wasn't one of your lovers."

Randall sighed. "I was trying to protect her," he said quietly. "She's the most innocent human being I ever knew. I was afraid if I didn't say she was my girl, you might...well." He shrugged. "Paul said she went back to Comanche Wells because she used her credit card in Catelow and the killer traced it here."

Ren ate a forkful of roast without tasting it. "He

came to get her. You never said she was an heiress, either. I thought she was poor."

"You should see Graylings. That's where she and Sari and Paul live. The stables are the talk of Texas. They breed racehorses."

"Paul told me." He'd avoided it as long as he could. "Did you see her? Did you tell her what I asked you to?"

"I couldn't talk to her," he replied. It was harder than he'd dreamed it would be.

"Why not?"

Delsey came in with the coffeepot. She set it down. "How's our Merrie?" she asked.

Randall took a deep breath. "They'd just taken her out of surgery when I got there...! Ren!"

Ren had jumped out of his chair and taken him by both shoulders, almost crushing them in his fear. "Surgery? What happened? Is she going to be all right?"

He and Delsey were both hanging on Randall's every word.

"Apparently there were two would-be killers," Randall said, wincing when Ren belatedly loosened his grip. "The one in Texas aimed a pickup truck broadside at the limo that was driven by an accomplice. Paul had checked out the driver, but the source had been paid off."

"Killers? After our Merrie?" Delsey exclaimed, sitting down. This was all news to her, since no one had told her the truth.

"Oh my God," Ren said huskily. "My God!"

"They're looking for him," Randall said. "The driver

was found dead in a ditch just after Merrie was taken to the hospital. They think he may have been paid off. They haven't turned up the driver of the pickup yet."

"My God." Ren's mind was whirling. "What have I done?" he groaned.

Randall didn't know what to say. Apologies seemed useless.

"You'll have to stay here and manage things," Ren said, getting to his feet. "Let Denver slide."

"Where are you going?" Delsey asked.

"To Texas," Ren said, and kept walking.

CHAPTER TWELVE

MERRIE WAS in ICU when Dr. Coltrain went in to check on her. He didn't like her vitals. Her blood pressure was dropping, and she wasn't waking up. He knew that she'd awakened long enough to talk to her sister earlier, but she was backsliding. He didn't know why.

He was really worried. He knew they'd repaired every possible trauma. But even in best-case scenarios, people sometimes died. He didn't want to lose Merrie.

Sari almost went mad when Coltrain came out to talk to them and told her what was happening.

"It's going to be all right," he assured her with more conviction than he felt. "I've had her moved into ICU. We'll keep her there for a day or so."

Sari looked at him with shiny blue eyes, trying to focus on his face. The migraine was better, but she was sick at her stomach.

"I wish you'd go home, honey," Paul said gently, curling her into his broad chest.

"I can't," she sobbed. "You know I can't."

"I'll contact you the minute there's any change," Coltrain said gently.

"Thanks," Paul said.

He turned his attention back to Sari as the doctor strode away.

"You have to have faith," he whispered in her ear. "Don't give up on her now."

Her nails dug into his back. "I'm so scared!"

"Yeah." He held her closer. "Me, too."

As they spoke, a tall man in a shepherd's coat, wearing designer jeans and hand-tooled leather boots, with a Stetson pulled low over his eyes, approached the nurses' desk.

"Meredith Grayling," he said stiffly. "I was told she was a patient here."

Sari looked up with blood in her eye. Before Paul could stop her, she got to her feet and approached the tall man.

"If you're Ren Colter, the door is that way," she said in a scathing tone, pointing toward the exit.

He stared down at her from a drawn, pale face. He winced. "You're Sari, her sister," he said quietly.

She bit her lower lip, then nodded.

Paul came forward and put his arm around her shoulders. He held out a hand to Ren. "She's upset," he said as he shook hands with Ren. "They've taken Merrie to ICU. She's not responding as well as they hoped she would after the surgery."

Ren drew in a ragged breath and averted his eyes. He was dying inside. He'd made so many damned mistakes. He didn't know how he was going to go on if he lost Meredith. It would be his own fault. He'd ruined everything. He'd frightened her, insulted her, sent her running right into the arms of a killer!

"Stop beating yourself up," Paul said. "It won't help. Come and sit down."

"I'll go mad if I have to sit," he bit off.

Sari peered up at him past Paul's broad chest. She saw the anguish in his face, and it softened her. She moved restively. "Randall told you about Merrie."

"Yes." He stared at her. "You don't look a lot alike, but you both have the same eyes. Hers are more gray than blue. Gray, like a fog on the river, early in the morning…" He averted his eyes and tried to swallow the pincushion in his throat. He rammed his hands deep into his pockets. "Have they found the assassin yet?"

"Still looking," Paul said. "We've got people everywhere, including a man who knows the contract killer. We don't think this was his doing. He had no way of knowing that Merrie came home, since we took her in the family jet. We think he's still got your ranch staked out and that he sent a relative to keep watch here. Maybe to take her out if he got the opportunity."

"The relative will wish he'd never been born, I promise you that," Ren said through his teeth.

"Get in line," Sari muttered.

"Ah, ah, ah," Paul cautioned. "I work for the FBI and you're an officer of the court," he told his wife.

"I'll buy you some earplugs," she retorted.

Two men in camouflage came in the door, sidearms holstered, and approached Sari and Paul. But they did a double take when they saw Ren.

Sari gaped as Rogers and Barton came to a stop and saluted the Wyoming rancher.

He chuckled, returning the salute. "What the hell are you two doing here?" he asked them after they'd shaken hands.

"Working for them," Barton said, pointing toward Sari and Paul. "We've been watching the house."

"Never occurred to us that some fool would try to run over a limo with a pickup truck," Rogers added miserably.

"Nobody could have predicted it," Paul told them. "How do you know him?" he asked, jerking a thumb toward Ren.

"He was our company commander in Iraq," Rogers said.

"Best damned commanding officer we ever had," Barton added.

"I wasn't, but thanks," Ren replied. He looked over their shoulders. "Damn!" he said, his lips compressed. "It's old home week."

They all turned as Mikey came walking toward them. He saw Ren and slowed just a little. He grimaced.

"Now, Captain," Mikey began. "It was just a little lumber and a few nails…"

"You walked off with half the lumber in the supply shed to build a canteen at base camp," he said gruffly. "And you installed two women of decidedly odd morals…"

"They were lonely," Mikey protested. "The local cathouse had just closed and they didn't have enough money to make it back to Spain."

"What a bunch of bull," Ren muttered.

Mikey grinned. "You have to admit, sir, that morale went up eighty percent."

"So did STDs," Ren shot back.

"Hey, that's what they have doctors for, right?" Mikey said, his eyes twinkling. He glanced at Sari's red eyes. "What's going on? Something happen to baby doll?" he asked worriedly.

"They took her to ICU," Paul said. "The doctor didn't say much, but she's not responding as well as he wants her to."

"Damn!" Mikey swore.

"They have a first-rate hospital in San Antonio," Ren began.

"We have the best surgeon in two states right here in Comanche Wells," Sari replied. "Dr. Coltrain won't lose her. I know he won't."

Ren nodded. "Okay."

His face was a study in guilt and worry. Mikey frowned. "You know the family?"

"I know Meredith," Ren said heavily. "She was staying with me in Wyoming."

"You're the Wyoming rancher," Mikey said, nodding. "Guess who's camping on your property with an MSR?" he added.

"What's an MSR?" Sari asked.

"Remington Modular Sniper Rifle," Mikey replied. "Accurate up to a thousand yards. Our boy likes it. A lot."

"How did he get onto your property?" Sari asked Ren.

"He does a pretty good impression of a truck driver,"

Ren replied. "He bribed a neighbor to swear he had a delivery there so he had an excuse to pretend he was lost on my land."

"He started out driving semis when he was just out of high school," Mikey said.

"You know him?" Ren asked.

Mikey nodded. "We used to play on the same team. Not anymore," he added coldly. "Nobody hurts baby doll on my watch."

Ren took a deep breath. "When will we know something?" Ren asked.

"When we know something," Paul said philosophically. "We might as well sit down and get comfortable."

"Not us," Barton said. "We turned up something."

"What?" four voices asked at once.

"Well, it's not a lot," Barton replied. "Your police chief had a receipt for the truck rental. He checked it out, and the truck was registered to a man named Ronnie Bates. He lives in Houston."

Paul's eyes narrowed. "Just how did you find that out? Grier doesn't share information when he's working on a case."

"His secretary was filing it," Barton said. "I just happened to peek over her shoulder."

"What were you doing there in the first place?"

Barton cleared his throat.

"Barton?" Paul persisted.

"Okay. I ran a red light. So sue me!" he muttered. "I was paying my ticket when I noticed the receipt. Only one truck rental receipt I know of that anybody would have out in a police station right now. Had to be the guy."

"No wonder Eb Scott likes you," Paul said and chuckled.

Mikey wasn't saying anything. He just listened. But there was an odd smile on his chiseled lips.

Paul stared at him. "Spill it," he said.

"Spill what?" Mikey asked innocently.

"You're smiling. You never smile."

"He was smiling at his disciplinary hearing, too," Ren commented drily. "That was just before a three-star general walked in the door and said that Mikey was pilfering material for the canteen on his orders and who the hell did we think we were? Lucky for him, they let him off with a verbal reprimand."

"Yeah." Mikey sighed, smiling. "The general used to take me to poker games in the back room of the officers' club. He sure liked winning."

Ren just shook his head.

REN HAD A lot of time to think on his way here. He was rethinking a lot of his life, especially the part that pertained to faith. Meredith was a stickler for it. She wore her cross all the time. His brother had faith. His mother...well, she'd never lost hers. Ren had lost his own sense of values in college. Randall had reminded him, gently, that an infatuation with a female physics professor had been instrumental in changing those opinions. When he thought about it, he realized his brother was right.

Faith, they said, worked wonders. He hadn't been in

a chapel in years. But he found the chapel in the small hospital and walked hesitantly into it. He sat down on the back pew and stared at the altar with quiet, troubled eyes. Maybe it wasn't logical. But maybe there was a higher power, a power that concerned itself with humanity and would listen to a plea. He took a deep breath and bowed his head.

Sari, returning from the restroom, happened to look in the chapel and saw the tall Wyoming rancher sitting there, in the back pew. Something knotted up inside her turned loose. If Meredith had that sort of effect on a man, perhaps love could work miracles. She smiled to herself as she continued on down the hall.

AN HOUR LATER, Dr. Coltrain came out into the waiting room. "I don't have anything new to report," he said quietly. "But she's holding her own."

Sari stared at him. "You're still worried," she said, because she'd known him long enough to see through that poker face.

He drew in a long breath. "Blunt force trauma is hard to predict, especially on internal organs. I think she'll be all right. But I can't give you any guarantee."

"I know," Sari said.

"If you want to transfer her over to San Antonio or get a second opinion, I'm game," Coltrain added.

She shook her head. "I think moving her would be a mistake," she said softly. "And she trusts you. So do I."

"Can I see her?" Ren asked quietly.

Coltrain's eyebrows went up, but Sari knew that Merrie had feelings for the tall rancher, even if he'd hurt her. She remembered him in the chapel, with his head bowed. He cared about Merrie, too. Letting him see her might just make the difference. She stood up beside him. "Let him go in," she told the doctor gently. "Please."

Ren looked down at her, surprised. "Thanks," he said roughly.

She just nodded.

Coltrain took him back to the ICU.

"Five minutes," he said quietly. "No more." Then he left them alone.

Ren approached Merrie slowly, then slid his fingers into hers, where they lay so still on the bed. There was a nurse nearby, but she was out of earshot.

She was very pale and her heartbeat seemed faint and threadly when he took her hand in his. Her hand was cold. A chill went through him. He'd been with wounded men in this condition, in combat overseas; men who had these symptoms and hadn't survived. No wonder Dr. Coltrain was worried.

"I'm here, Meredith," Ren said softly, leaning down close to her ear. "Come on, honey. You can beat this. You're tough. I promised to show you branding in the spring on Skyhorn, remember? You have to stick around for that."

She didn't move, but her eyelids flickered, just a bit.

He brushed his cheek against her cold one. "I've got so much to make up to you, Meredith," he whispered deeply. "I don't even know where to start. I'm sorry, for what I did, for what I said. I want a chance to replace those bad memories with better ones. So you have to live. You have to, Meredith." He squeezed her hand. "I'll help you fight. I won't leave you. Not ever again."

He heard her breathing strengthen. He brushed his lips tenderly across hers, feeling the life surge in her, feeling hope reborn.

"I'll be waiting, when you wake up. I'll be right here, honey."

Her eyelids fluttered again. And suddenly, they opened, ever so slowly. She looked at him.

"Meredith," he whispered huskily. His voice broke. He felt the sting of moisture in his eyes as those beautiful, pale blue eyes that seemed almost gray in the light looked back into his black ones. "My own," he whispered, his voice rough with feeling, as he bent once more and touched his mouth against hers. "Come back to me."

She blinked. There was a lot of pain. It was hard to breathe. "Ren?" she asked in a thready voice.

He lifted his head. It was hard to see her, through the hot mist in his eyes. "Yes. I'm here."

"Don't...leave," she managed.

His fingers contracted around hers. "Never!" he breathed. "I'll never go away again!"

She tried to smile, but the anesthetic still had a hold on her. "Okay," she whispered, and her eyes closed again.

Dr. Coltrain walked back into the room.

"She opened her eyes," Ren told the redheaded doctor. "She looked at me and spoke."

Coltrain let out a breath. "Thank God," he whispered.

Ren was conflicted. He looked down at the sleeping woman with turmoil in his heart, in his eyes. "I haven't talked to God in years," he said roughly. "I thought he was a myth." He shook his head. "I've prayed more in the past hour than I have in my whole damned life."

Coltrain put a hand on his shoulder. "There are no atheists in foxholes," he mused. "Or in surgery."

Ren managed a smile. "I want to sit with her."

"She'll be here in ICU overnight, at least. But if she keeps improving, we'll move her out into a regular room tomorrow."

Ren nodded.

"Go tell the others," Dr. Coltrain prodded. "There'll be confetti and noisemakers, but remind them that this is a hospital," he added, chuckling softly.

"Thanks, Doc," Ren said with heartfelt gratitude.

Coltrain smiled at him. "Get out of here. I'm busy."

Ren chuckled. He let go of Meredith's hand. While Coltrain was bending over her with the stethoscope in his ears, Ren went out to tell the others.

"THANK YOU," SARI said to Ren when they'd absorbed the news. She searched his black eyes quietly. "I'm sorry I was so unwelcoming, at first."

"I don't blame you for feeling angry," Ren replied. "I've kicked myself mentally all the way here from Wyoming."

"If she'd stayed, she might be dead now," Sari told him. "Mikey said the man probably had studied every possible site to set up with a sniper rifle on your ranch."

"I wouldn't doubt it, but if he did, he's in for a few

surprises. You remember J. C. Calhoun?" Ren asked Barton.

Barton whistled softly. "Do I remember Calhoun," he agreed. "He works for you?"

"For six years," Ren replied. "We've had a couple of attempts on my purebred bulls. But word gets around. He turned two rustlers over to the sheriff's department, and they were spilling their guts about the operation before they were even questioned." He chuckled.

"Yeah, he has that effect on a lot of people." Barton nodded.

"I don't remember Calhoun," Mikey commented. "I guess he was after my time."

"He came in about the time they transferred you from Afghanistan to Iraq," Ren replied.

"Wasn't a willing transfer," Mikey said. "Even my general couldn't pull enough strings to keep me on the base. I hated Iraq," he added. "They put my squad in charge of ferrying political heavyweights around the city. We didn't lose any politicians, but we lost two of our best guys in an IED attack."

"Nasty business," Ren said. "I was in charge of a sniper unit in Iraq."

"Which is where we met him," Barton said.

"Shots rang out and I called on a live frequency to ask who was the SOB who almost shot my head off when I was headed to base." Ren smiled sheepishly. "Turned out the SOB—" he indicated Barton "—took out a sniper I didn't even see who had me targeted from behind. I apologized profusely."

"You did not," Barton argued.

Ren shrugged. "I said that I might have said a few things I shouldn't," he hedged.

"Coming from him, it's an apology." Mikey chuckled.

Barton grinned. "No argument."

Ren turned back to Sari. "I'm staying with Merrie. I'll sleep standing up against a wall if I have to, but I'm not leaving this hospital."

"Nobody asked you to," Sari replied. She drew in a long breath. "Thanks, Ren. Thanks for coming all this way. And for giving Merrie an incentive to wake up."

"You're welcome," he replied. "I've got a lot of making up to do. I just want enough time to do it."

"That doctor's pretty good," Mikey commented.

"He was good to us when we had to come here for treatment," Sari said with a smile. "Merrie and I were in his office a lot, too."

"Why?" Ren asked, curious.

"Our father could be brutal. We had several incidents while we were both in school," Sari said bitterly.

Ren frowned. "He doesn't sound like much of a father."

"Believe me, he wasn't," Sari replied.

Ren deduced that there was a lot he still didn't know about Meredith. He was just happy that he had a chance to start over with her.

SEVERAL HOURS LATER, they were still in the waiting room. Dr. Coltrain was cautiously optimistic. Sari and Ren had taken turns going in to see her during the very few visiting periods they were allowed while she was still in the intensive care unit.

At midnight, Sari and Paul insisted that Ren come home with them.

"She's going to be all right, but you won't be if you don't get some rest," Paul said firmly. "We'll go back first thing in the morning."

Ren finally gave in. He hadn't slept in days. "They'll call you if something happens with her?" He looked in the direction of the nurses' station.

"Yes, they'll call us," Sari assured him. "They have both our cell phone numbers."

"But it doesn't matter," Paul said with a smile.

"It doesn't?" Ren asked blankly.

Paul nodded toward the door. Mikey walked in with Mandy at his side. She smiled at them and sat down in the waiting room with a big bag of knitting.

"I'll be right here if she needs anything," Mandy said. "Now go home and get some sleep," she added, including all of them in her sweeping gaze. "Nothing will happen to my baby while I'm here."

"Or me," Mikey added, sitting beside her. "Gotta protect the cook, right?" he asked, grinning at Mandy. "Best roast beef I ever ate."

Mandy blushed. "Oh, Mr. Mikey," she protested.

"Best cook in Texas," Paul added, bending to kiss Mandy's cheek. "Thanks, honey."

"I knew you'd never leave if somebody in the family didn't stay here," Mandy said. "Get some sleep. I'll call if there's any change at all. But there won't be.

She's got a reason to live, now," she added, glancing warmly at Ren.

"All right," Sari said. She hugged Mandy. "If you need anything…"

"If she does, I'll go get it for her." Mikey chuckled. "Go home."

They left, still uneasy, but too tired to do much arguing.

REN'S FIRST SIGHT of Graylings took his breath away. "She said she lived on a small ranch," he said as he gaped at the huge mansion, all its lights shining bright and welcoming in the darkness past the white fences and tall mesquite and oak trees.

"It is small, by Texas standards," Sari said with a weary smile. "But we have some of the most famous racehorses in the world. And some great security. FBI approved," she added with a grin at her husband.

"I seem to do better on security than I do on limo drivers," Paul said wryly.

"It was a fluke," Sari said. "He slipped through with some shady support. You couldn't have known."

"Dead right," Barton agreed, sitting in the seat beside Ren, facing Paul and Sari. "Any background check wouldn't have found anything. I'm assuming the contract killer set up the identity check. The guy from Houston sure wasn't smart. What sort of would-be assassin leaves the rental slip for the truck in the glove compartment, for heaven's sake?"

"A clumsy one," Paul said. "And it's going to cost him."

"Count on it," Sari agreed. "When we catch him, Mr. Kemp will turn him any which way but loose."

"He certainly will," Paul said.

ROGERS PULLED THE LIMO up to the front door. They all got out and Paul unlocked the door, swinging it open to polished oak floors with Persian carpets and a crystal chandelier handmade in Italy.

Ren whistled softly. Skyhorn Ranch had comfortable furnishings, but nothing as fancy as this. He noted that two paintings on the wall, which looked like originals, were crooked.

Sari noticed him staring at them. "I did that one," she said, indicating a landscape with a racehorse in the foreground. "Merrie did that one." She indicated a painting of a golden retriever.

"You paint?" Ren asked.

"I move the paintings so that they aren't straight," Sari said, and her face tautened. "Revenge."

"Their father was a perfectionist," Paul explained.

Ren shook his head. "I've got a painting in my office that's looked like that for ages. Putting it straight isn't a priority," he added with a grin.

"Come on up and I'll loan you a pair of pj's," Paul offered. "I don't guess you took time to pack anything."

"Nothing," Ren agreed. "I went straight to the airport the minute Randall told me Meredith was in the hospital."

One glance at his rigid features was enough to make them understand how he'd felt. He still had anguish in his eyes.

"Let's go up," Paul said. "Rogers and Barton will keep watch."

Ren followed the couple up the long winding staircase. "The dog was Meredith's, wasn't it?" Ren asked. "The one in the painting downstairs."

"Yes," Sari said. She paused and turned. "She told you?"

He nodded. "No one has ever hurt an animal on my place. We had a new hire who beat a horse. He could barely get to his truck when I got through with him. I had him arrested and I pressed charges for animal cruelty." He shook his head. "Never understood how anyone could hurt a helpless animal."

Sari just smiled. Apparently her baby sister had picked a winner. Unless it was just guilt that had brought Ren all the way from Wyoming in such a rush that he didn't even stop to pack a suitcase. She admired that haste in him. It proved that whatever he felt for her sister, it was strong.

REN HADN'T EXPECTED to sleep, but he did. The bed they gave him was a king-size one, in a bedroom twice the size of the one he slept in at Skyhorn. He was so tired that he probably wouldn't have minded a twin bed that his feet hung off of. He'd often slept on the ground in Iraq, using a rock for a pillow.

He woke at daylight. He was used to early hours on the ranch. After a quick shower, he phoned Willis to find out what was happening back home.

"Had a little excitement here," Willis said, a whimsical note in his voice.

"What sort?" Ren asked.

"Well, Snowpaw flushed out an intruder."

Ren's heart jumped. "Was he carrying a sniper rifle?"

"Hell! How did you know that, boss?"

"I'm psychic," Ren drawled. "What happened?"

"Snowpaw took off after him, snarling all the way. Even on three legs, he was quicker than the man. He took him down and mauled him a little before he got away. He managed to swipe up the rifle on the way. Jumped a fence flat-footed to escape Snowpaw. The killer was aiming the damned thing at him when I shot at him."

"Did you hit him?" Ren asked.

"No such luck. It was dark and I don't use the rifle that often. But I think I nicked his jacket. It was enough to make him run."

Ren was livid. It was just as Paul had suggested. The hit man had staked out Skyhorn, thinking Meredith was still there. Apparently his cousin in Texas who'd hit the limo Meredith was in hadn't been able to contact him yet. The driver was probably still in hiding, if he wasn't looking for a doctor. Considering the mess the truck was in, the man driving it had at least some injuries.

"When did this happen?" Ren asked.

"Last night, about midnight. We searched this morning and found a couple of places where he'd hunkered down. Near the house, too."

"On the side where Meredith's bedroom was," Ren guessed.

"Maybe you really are psychic," Willis teased.

"Not likely. Get J.C. and a couple of the boys out there and have them stake out every single place a sniper could possibly camp. I doubt he'll be back, but he might be."

"We'll do it. How is Miss Meredith?"

"Not well. But she's still alive, at least, and they think she'll be all right."

"Hell of a thing, somebody hurting that sweet little woman," Willis said. "Snowpaw loved her. He hates women as a rule."

"I noticed. Keep things running smoothly while I'm away. I don't know how long I'll be here. I'm not leaving until Meredith is completely out of danger."

"Will do, boss. Be safe."

"You, too."

REN WENT DOWN to breakfast. He wished he'd brought a change of clothing, but that was no problem. He'd go shopping when he took a lunch break. He had no intention of leaving Jacobsville anytime soon.

Mandy was home, bringing in platters of eggs and bacon and biscuits to the dining room table.

"Meredith's doing well. And Mikey's still there," she told Ren when he joined them. "Sit down and eat before you go back to the hospital."

"Thanks," Ren said, smiling at her.

"I love her, too," Mandy said, amused at his ruddy cheekbones when she said it. She finished putting food on the table.

"Did you sleep?" Paul asked.

"Not much," Ren confessed. "I called Willis at my ranch this morning. They flushed out a man with a sniper rifle, who was camped out near Meredith's room," he added grimly.

"So he doesn't know yet." Paul nodded.

"Apparently not. At least, he didn't know last night."

"Did your men shoot him?" Sari asked.

"Nicked his jacket. But Snowpaw mauled him a bit on the way."

"Snowpaw?" Paul asked.

"Willis's wolf." He smiled sadly. "The first time he saw Meredith, he went straight to her and put his head in her lap, let her pet him." He shook his head. "No other woman on the place could ever get near him."

"That would explain the wolf drawing in her sketch pad that she brought home," Sari mentioned. "The wolf only had three legs."

Ren nodded as he helped himself to eggs and bacon. "Bear trap. We don't use them, but we have a neighbor who does. After Willis went to have a 'talk' with him, he stopped using bear traps." He smiled. "Willis has a temper almost as bad as J. C. Calhoun does."

"Pretty name. The wolf's, I mean," Sari added.

"He's named for a fictional wolf in the online computer game 'World of Warcraft,'" Ren told her. "Willis plays. There's a quest where you have to avenge an orc whose family was killed by ogres. When you complete it, the orc's wolf, Snowpaw, goes home with you to live. It's a sad sort of quest."

"Do you play?" Paul asked.

Ren shook his head. "Don't have time for gaming, or much else. I'm too busy running the ranch."

"I had six calls waiting for me on my iPhone when we got home last night," Paul said, smiling. "All from my colleagues. Even the Special Agent in Charge messaged me. Great group of guys."

Sari agreed. "Family is big with them."

"They've all got kids. Even the SAC." Paul chuckled. He glanced at Sari lovingly. "We're going to try having kids when things settle down around here. Right now, we're focusing on our careers. Sari's an amazing prosecutor."

Ren looked around at the lavish furnishings. He shook his head. "All this, and you both work?"

"You're not starving yourself, I hear," Paul noted, having checked the rancher out much previously. "You work. And at harder stuff than either of us do."

"When I started building up the ranch," he said. "work became everything to me. I only slowed down when I got engaged, about six months ago." His face hardened. "I thought she was crazy about me. Turns out she was only crazy about my money. When I found out, she went on social media to get even." He smiled sadly. "I took Meredith to a party with me, the night you came to get her," he told Paul, and his eyes were dark with regret. "She took my ex-fiancée down in a heartbeat, and never used a single cussword. In fact, she sent her running." His jaw tautened as he recalled what came after. "I was gun-shy," he confessed. "Convinced myself that Meredith was like Angie, because

I thought she was one of Randall's women, too." He shook his head. "Biggest mistake of my life."

"We all make mistakes," Paul said, recalling his own rough road to the altar. He looked at Sari with soft, loving eyes. "Sometimes we get lucky, and we have time enough to correct them."

"That's what I'm hoping for," Ren said. "Second chances."

"She's going to be…" Sari stopped, because her phone was ringing. She answered it. "Hello?"

Her eyes brightened. "Thanks, Mikey. Thanks! Yes, I'll tell Paul." She hung up. "Merrie's still doing okay. And they caught him!"

"They caught who?" Paul asked.

"The guy driving the truck!"

"Where have they got him?" Paul asked. "I want a word with him."

"I want several," Ren seconded, and his expression was ice-cold.

Sari grimaced. "Houston PD got him," she said. "Early this morning. One of Mikey's contacts phoned him. Apparently the would-be hit man felt confident enough to go home. He—" she indicated Paul "—had a BOLO out for him. Houston PD drove right up to his front door and arrested him."

"Great." Paul sighed. "Now we can all argue jurisdiction until one of his buddies comes and bails him out."

"What if he called the killer in Wyoming and told him, before he was arrested?" Sari asked. "What then?"

CHAPTER THIRTEEN

"WE'VE GOT THE best security in Texas on the job," Paul reminded Sari. "Plus we have the Avengers."

Ren laughed softly.

"Well, that's what we call them," Paul said sheepishly. "You know, Barton and Rogers. In the comic books and the movies, Barton was Hawkeye and Rogers was Captain America."

"They're good," Ren had to agree. "Who is this guy Eb Scott, who loaned them to you? Meredith mentioned him to me."

"Eb has a counterterrorism school here in Jacobsville. It's well-known in defense circles. He trains all sorts of people. Even," Sari added with pursed lips, "it's rumored, people from our own government. He has state-of-the-art everything. He's a retired merc. So are most of the people who teach at his school."

"I hadn't heard of it. On the other hand," Ren sighed, "I keep to myself. The ranch is pretty isolated from the real world. We mostly watch movies on DVD or pay-per-view." He hesitated, smiling, his eyes faraway. "I had videos of branding cattle on the ranch. Meredith was watching them while she knitted. Surprised me. She doesn't look like the sort of woman who could bear such things. She's fragile, in a way. But very strong in others."

"She's tough," Sari said. "Daddy would never let us near the bloodstock. We rode rocking horses around the ranch." She laughed at Ren's expression. "Old horses, not purebred ones. He did raise a few quarter horses for sale, but not for long. He fired the only employee we had who knew how to breed them. After that, he went back to Thoroughbreds. Paul and I have revived the quarter horse breeding here, though."

"We keep a lot of saddle horses. It's a big ranch, and we have to have several strings of quarter horses to herd cattle," Ren replied.

"You run Angus, don't you?" Sari asked.

"Purebred Black Angus," he agreed. "Just herd sires and cows and heifers. No beef cattle. I love beef," he added. "But I don't like to raise it." He smiled a little sheepishly. "Hard to eat something you raised from a calf."

Sari smiled at him with real warmth. He smiled back.

Paul checked his watch. "I have to run up to San Antonio, just for a few minutes," he told Sari. "A couple of projects I have to check on. Will you be okay?"

"I'll take care of her," Ren promised him.

Paul relaxed a little. "Okay."

"I'll be fine," Sari assured him. "I have to go by the office on my lunch break and check in with Mr. Kemp." Kemp was the district attorney.

"I'll stay with Meredith," Ren said quietly.

"I'm off to bed," Mandy said wearily as she finished her eggs and bacon and sipped coffee. "I'm sleepy."

"Thanks for sitting up with her, honey," Paul said. "You're the best."

She smiled at them all. "I'll be up in time to cook supper, don't you worry."

JUST AS REN and Paul walked into the hospital, Mikey met them near the front entrance.

"How's it going?" Paul asked.

He grimaced. "Not so good." At Paul's frozen expression, Mikey said, "No, no, not baby doll. It's your guy in Houston, the one with the pickup truck."

"Mikey..." Paul began angrily.

"It wasn't my guy who did it," Mikey interrupted. "Somebody hit the perp in his cell at Houston PD."

"How?" Paul asked.

"They're still debating that. He had asthma real bad. So he drank something that they think was doctored with a substance that he was allergic to. He had a violent reaction to it and they called for a doctor. The guy came in, saw the asthmatic symptoms and gave him a shot of epinephrine."

"That's what they always did for a pal of mine who had asthma," Paul said.

"Yeah, well this guy had an arrhythmia. So the epinephrine sent him into cardiac arrest. They couldn't save him."

"We had a case like that here," Paul said. "Cash Grier's secretary had asthma. She had an attack right in his office, and Carson Farwalker, who was a merc at the time, as well as a former army medic, checked to make sure she had no heart problems before he injected her with it. He said if she'd had a heart rhythm problem, epinephrine would have been fatal."

"Smart man," Ren remarked.

"Very. He actually had his license as a physician, but he didn't tell anyone until after he married Carlie," Paul said, chuckling. "He was a bad man before that."

"You should tell the captain here about the crocodile thing," Mikey told Paul, jerking his thumb toward Ren.

"What crocodile thing?" Ren asked.

"A man named Rourke and Carson fed a man who'd tortured a young woman to a crocodile in Barrera, overseas. Rourke later married the woman. They live here now."

While they were telling him the rest of the story, Sari got up. "I'm going to check with the nurse's desk," she said, smiling as she left them to talk.

"I'm Sari Fiore. Meredith Grayling is my sister," she said to the floor nurse. "Can you tell me how she's doing?"

"She's doing fine, just fine," the nurse replied with a smile. "We've moved her out onto the floor already. She's in room 230. You can go right in."

"Thank you!" Sari said with heartfelt relief. "It's been a very long night," she explained.

The nurse smiled. "I can imagine."

Sari went back to the others. "She's out of ICU and in a room!" she said.

"Which one?" Ren asked immediately.

"Two-thirty. Go ahead," Sari said gently. "It's okay."

He gave her a weary smile. "Thanks."

THEY'D JUST FINISHED bathing Merrie. She was sitting up with a towel over her front, her bare back to the door, when Ren walked in. He stopped dead and turned around.

"Sorry!" he said. "I'll come back later."

He went out the door and Merrie felt tears welling up in her eyes. He'd seen the scars, she knew he had. He wouldn't be back. She was sure of it.

"There, dear, all through," the aide said cheerfully. "Let me help you with the gown. It's nice and clean."

Merrie let herself be placed in the hospital gown, and then she lay back on the bed. She felt dead inside. She'd never wanted Ren to see it!

The aide went out, and Ren came right back in.

Merrie stared at him with shock written all over her pretty face.

"What?" he asked as he stood beside the bed.

"You, well, you saw my back...didn't you?" she asked worriedly, and flushed.

He gave her a sardonic look. "Meredith, I have scars on my own back, and the backs of my legs, from an IED attack when I was in Iraq. Scars aren't important. Being alive, is."

She still stared at him. "Oh," she said in a tiny voice.

He moved to the side of the bed, bent down and brushed his hard mouth gently over her soft one. "Idiot," he whispered, and he smiled.

She was spellbound. She looked up at him with bright, pale blue eyes, full of hope. "You came back."

"Of course I came back," he scoffed. He dropped down into a chair beside her bed. "They found the guy who ran the truck into you."

"Do you have a bat I can borrow? I'd like to speak with him," she said coolly.

"Too late. He's taking up space in the Houston morgue."

"The morgue?"

"He messed up a hit. I expect the man who hired him had him taken care of. Right in his own cell, apparently."

"What about the contract killer? Do they know anything about him?" she asked worriedly.

"He made it on to the ranch last night, apparently before he'd had time to talk to the man he subcontracted for the Jacobsville hit. Snowpaw got him, but he escaped."

"Snowpaw?" She caught her breath. "Is Snowpaw all right? He didn't hurt him?"

"No, he's fine," he assured her, touched by her concern for the animal.

She smiled. "He's so beautiful, and so sweet." Her chest rose and fell. "I hope Snowpaw bit chunks out of him," she muttered. "He won't get back on the ranch, will he?"

"Not anymore. We've got security on our security," he continued. "Nobody's getting past any of us to get to you."

The comment went right over her head. She was

still groggy from the anesthesia and she wasn't quite thinking straight. She studied his lined face. "You look tired."

"You should see everyone else," he replied. "Mandy's gone to sleep. She and Mikey sat up in the waiting room all night while we slept. I was out like a light." He caught her hand and pulled it to his lips. "I didn't want to leave you, but I was dead on my feet."

She studied his hard face with wonder. "You were in ICU," she recalled suddenly. "You were talking to me."

"Yes, I was," he said. His face hardened. "You gave us a scare, honey."

She flushed a little with pleasure. Her pale eyes lit up as they scanned his face.

He smiled. He liked making her blush. "I'm taking you home with me to Wyoming when you get out of here, if I have to fight your whole family to do it."

"Ta-taking me home?" she stammered.

He kissed her soft palm. "We have unfinished business," he said, his voice like deep, soft velvet. The look in his eyes emphasized the words.

"Ren, I don't... I mean, I can't... I..." She ground her teeth together, and her face contorted.

"I know all that," he said easily. "Don't rush your fences. Everything's going to be all right."

"Do you really think so?" she asked worriedly.

"Your brother-in-law is a hell of a lawman," he said. "You've even got the mafia on your side," he added, tongue in cheek. "I like Mikey. He was really worried about you. He said, and I quote, nobody hurts baby doll on his watch."

"Baby doll?"

He chuckled. "That's what he calls you."

"Wow. I wasn't sure he even liked me."

"He likes you." He made a face. "But not too much, or I wouldn't say nice things about him."

She searched Ren's black eyes until the pleasure became too intense. She dropped them to his broad chest.

He squeezed her fingers. "Hey."

She looked up, her cheeks blushing.

"I'm not leaving you," he said deeply. "Not ever, Meredith."

She felt her breath catching in her throat. What his eyes were telling her was almost too wonderful to believe.

"I'm so sorry, honey," he said, a husky note in his deep voice. "So very sorry, for everything."

"You were hurting, and bitter about what happened with Angie," she said. "I understood."

He drew in a breath. "Hurting you did nothing about the bitterness. It made everything worse. When Randall told me you were in the hospital, I headed straight for the airport. What I'm wearing is all I brought with me." He smiled faintly. "So I guess I'm going shopping while you have lunch today."

She smiled gently. It impressed her that he'd dropped everything so quickly to see her. The look on his face was exciting. He wasn't pretending. He really felt something for her.

"Did you stay at Graylings last night?" she asked.

He laughed softly. "Some house," he mused. "Makes Skyhorn look like a shack."

"I love your house," she argued. "It's beautiful inside. It's warm and comfortable, even the furniture just fits. It isn't right to compare houses, anyway. Ours is the way Daddy left it," she added with a cold expression. "Sari and I are going to remodel it as soon as Mr. Leeds's hit man goes away. Which I hope will be very soon."

"I hope so, too, honey. But in the meantime, you have excellent protection."

"You mean our bodyguards."

"Them, too. But it seems that Cousin Mikey has placed a few more, shall we say, unconventional people around here to help out."

"So that's it," she murmured.

"That's what?"

"The nurses said there were some very odd men carrying brooms and mops and pushing trays around the hospital. They weren't sure why they'd been hired, because they didn't actually do anything."

"Oh, they do something. They watch your room."

She grinned. "Mikey's a pirate."

He chuckled. "He's a nice pirate. A good guy to have on your side."

"Yes, he is." She drew in a breath. "They must still be giving me something for pain. I'm so sleepy!"

"Why don't you nap for a bit, and I'll go see what Jacobsville has in the way of men's clothing?" he asked.

"They have boots and jeans and chambray shirts, mostly," she said drowsily.

"I might turn up something a little snazzier than that," he said.

"Not too snazzy, or somebody might mistake you for the hit man."

"I'm too tall," he joked. "It's a known fact that hit men are small and bald."

"Is it, really?" She managed one last smile, then fell asleep.

He got up, dropped a gentle kiss on her forehead and left the room. Right outside it, one man was leaning on a mop, another on a broom. They grinned at him.

He grinned back and kept walking.

HE FOUND AN exclusive men's clothing store, to his surprise, right on the main drag in Jacobsville. He found some pants and shirts and a nice jacket, along with a spiffy new Stetson—the first new one he'd bought in years. He put them in the luxury rental car he'd found on a local lot—it was a surprise to find one in a small town like this—and went into the nearby café for lunch.

He was surprised when people looked up from their meals to stare at him. Feeling self-conscious, he went up to the counter and ordered a burger and fries.

"You're not from around here," a tall, nice-looking middle-aged blonde woman asked, smiling.

"No. I'm from Wyoming," he said as he paid the ticket.

"You're Ren Colter."

His expression was just short of shock. "Well…yes."

"How's Merrie?" a customer behind him asked. "Is she going to be okay?"

"Yes. She's out of ICU now, and doing much better," he said.

A tall man in a business suit, wearing a Stetson about as expensive as Ren's, paused beside him on the way out. "Tell her the Ballengers asked about her, will you?" he asked. "I'm Justin. My brother Calhoun and I own the local feed lot."

Ren grinned and shook hands with him. "You fed out some cattle for me two years ago," he said. "Nice job, too."

Justin chuckled. "Thanks. I'm running most of the business now that my brother won the US Senate race and is now our junior Texas senator in Washington, DC. He's not home a lot."

"If he can find a way to keep government out of our ranches," Ren said, tongue in cheek, "I'll send him a Christmas card every year."

"That's what I told him," Justin agreed with a grin.

"What are you doing loafing around in here?" Cash Grier asked Justin with a mock scowl. "You've got two bull yearlings out on the highway just outside the city limits. Hayes Carson says he's going to cite you for feeding your livestock on county land."

Justin chuckled and shook hands with Cash. "Times are hard and grazing's spotty in the fall," he said. "Come over for supper sometime and bring Tippy and the kids."

"We don't get out much in the evenings," Cash returned. "We sit and watch the baby sleep."

"Been there, done that," Justin said. "All my boys are in college now." He shook his head. "Time flies."

"So true. See you."

"See you." Cash turned to Ren. "You ordered already?"

"Yes."

"Barbara, how about a bowl of chili and black coffee for the overworked and underfunded police department?" he called to her.

"Coming up, Chief." He stuck a five-dollar bill down on the counter and led Ren to a table near the window.

"It's the cops! Hide the automatic weapons!" a cowboy piped up.

"You don't have any automatic weapons, Fowler," Cash shot back.

"How do you know?" Harley Fowler joked. "I might have one in my boot!"

"No self-respecting weapon would stick its muzzle in there," Cash said disdainfully.

"Who's the tall stranger?" Harley persisted. "That Miss Merrie's feller?"

Ren burst out laughing.

"That's him," Cash said, grinning.

"You need a helping hand with that coyote who's stalking her, you just let us know," Harley told him. "We'll put together a posse and go hunting."

"Not in my town, you won't," Cash said easily.

"Not in your town at all, Chief," Harley agreed. "Out in the boondocks!"

Cash waved a hand at him. "Eat your sandwich and go to work, or I'll call Cy Parks and tell him you're ordering up lynch mobs."

"Nope, just coffee and BLTs," Harley said, grinning. "Miss Merrie doing okay, then?"

"She's doing fine, thanks," Ren replied.

"She's a sweet girl," Harley replied. "Drew a picture of my wife. It was so lifelike, I thought it was a photograph."

"She's got a rare talent," Ren agreed.

"Tell her we all asked about her," Harley added.

"Sure thing," Ren replied.

Cash smiled at Barbara as she delivered his chili and coffee and Ren's burger and fries, also with coffee.

"Thanks," Cash said.

"Have to keep the police well fed and happy," Barbara said, "or crime will take a toll on my profits!"

"If you want to keep me happy, go give my speech to the Rotary Club Thursday," Cash said grimly.

"You'll do fine."

"I hate getting up in front of people," Cash replied. "Life was easier ten years ago."

"In a ghillie suit crawling through the jungle? Give me a break!" She laughed, rolling her eyes. "If you need anything else, just call."

"Thanks."

Ren was staring at Cash over the burger. "Ghillie suit?"

"Yes."

Ren bit into his hamburger and washed it down with coffee. "Barton was a sniper in my unit in Iraq. He had a ghillie suit."

"I did it for a living for a long time," Cash replied.

"So did a couple of other local residents, including one of our doctors—Carson Farwalker."

"He was at the hospital."

"Good man," Cash said.

"I had two other men in my unit from here—Cag Hart and Blake Kemp."

"Cag's running the Hart Ranch Properties, head-quartered here in Jacobsville," Cash said. "Blake Kemp is our district attorney for the judicial circuit."

"I heard Meredith's sister mention Kemp. She works for him, doesn't she?"

"Yes. She's just started, but she's good at her job."

"She loves her sister."

Cash nodded. "It was just the two of them against their father." His face tautened as he ate. "Hell of a bad one. I wasn't chief here when the girls were young. If I had been, he'd have been occupying a cell in my jail, and I wouldn't have given a damn how much money he had."

"Meredith told me some of it," Ren said quietly. "She's had a hard life."

"They both have. But with the old man gone, a little sunshine's filtering through. Especially for Sari," he added with a smile. "She and Paul had a hard road to the altar. She wouldn't speak to him when he first came back here. So he picked her up and carried her out to the car and talked to her there."

Ren chuckled. "A determined man."

"One of the best people in law enforcement. His whole family's on the wrong side of the law."

"Mikey."

Cash's eyebrows arched.

Ren shrugged. "I was a company commander in Iraq. Mikey was in my unit. So were Barton and Rogers."

"It's a small world."

"Very." Ren sipped coffee.

"Did you hear that they picked up the truck driver in Houston this morning, and that he's already dead?" Cash asked.

Ren nodded. "Mikey told us."

"Somebody offed him in his own cell," Cash said. "They think he was given something that caused an asthma attack. A doctor hit him with a syringe of epinephrine in his heart."

"He had a rhythm disorder."

"He did," Cash remarked. "My secretary, Carson Farwalker's wife, has asthma. Luckily she doesn't have the rhythm problem. But I did learn what you don't do for asthma if you do have a rhythm disorder."

"So the killer's dead. I don't suppose he knew anything that would help catch the real killer," Ren continued. "We know who he's after. And that he'll probably be on his way back down here pretty soon."

"We have plenty of security," Cash reminded him.

Ren looked him in the eye. "So did JFK."

Cash sighed. "Well, it's unfortunately true that if a man's willing to trade his life for yours, there's no surefire way to stop him."

"What we're hoping is that he doesn't want to trade his life for Meredith's," Ren replied. "If he was suicidal, he'd have died long before now."

"Good point."

Ren finished his burger and fries and his coffee. "I'm going back to the hospital, now that I have at least a change of clothing," he said, laughing softly. "I didn't even stop to pack a bag when I found out about Meredith's accident."

"That will win you points with her people," Cash said with a smile.

"It did. Nice talking with you."

"I'll be over later to see how she's doing."

"I'll tell them."

REN TOOK HIS purchases back to Graylings and changed clothes before he went back into town to see Meredith.

She looked up when he walked into her hospital room, smiling.

"You look different."

"You've never seen me in casual clothes," he replied, indicating his nicely tailored dark blue slacks and black turtleneck sweater under a casual jacket. He had the new creamy Stetson in one big hand.

"You look very nice," she said softly.

He smiled, bending to her soft mouth. He brushed it tenderly with his. "I had a burger and fries and a long talk with the police chief and several strangers."

"You did?" she asked.

He nodded. He tossed the Stetson into an unoccupied chair and sat down beside the bed in another, taking her hand in his. "Many people sent well-wishes. You'll have to ask Grier who they were. I lost count."

She smiled. "I know everybody. Daddy never let us

socialize, but since he died, I've spent a lot of time in town at the café."

"The owner's very nice. She sends her greetings."

"Barbara," she said, nodding. "Her son is a lieutenant in San Antonio PD.

"Did Chief Grier tell you about the driver of the truck?" she asked.

His eyebrows arched. "How do you know about it?"

"Cousin Mikey came in to see me before he left for lunch. He thinks he has an idea, about how to spike the contract killer's guns."

"Does he, now?" Ren asked. "What?"

"He wouldn't say. He says we can talk about it when I get home." She made a face. "I guess that will take a few days, though." She shifted restlessly. "I'm awfully sore."

"Injuries take time to heal," he said softly. "But you'll be better in no time. Meanwhile, you're well protected here, and law enforcement will be on the lookout for any strangers who show up at the hospital."

"How about at home?" she worried.

"Mikey took Rogers and Barton around and showed them where a sniper might set up shop. They've got the whole place covered like tar paper."

She drew a breath and grimaced. "Hurts to breathe a little," she confessed.

"Bruising," he said. "You get that from blunt force trauma."

She studied him, curious.

"You got thrown across the backseat, into the door, by the impact," he explained. "It bruised your internal organs. That's why they have you on antibiotics. They worry about pneumonia."

"Oh. I wondered about that."

He crossed his legs. "You'll mend," he said. He smiled at her. "The worst is behind you, Meredith. It gets better from now on."

"I hope so." She hesitated. "Ren, have you heard anything about your mother?"

He drew in a breath. "No. Randall said they don't have the results from her biopsy yet."

"When they do, will you go, if she asks for you?" she asked.

He looked troubled. He studied her soft hand in his before he spoke. "I've made some bad decisions in my life. You were the worst," he said, his black eyes searching her gray ones. "But my mother was second worst. What she said about me hurt, a lot. But I should have stayed and talked it out. Pride shot me out the door."

"Nobody's perfect."

"Least of all me, honey," he said gently. He smiled at her, aware of the pleasure in her eyes at the endearment. "On the other hand, I was angry enough to found a ranching empire on spite alone. I wanted to make my father successful, show my mother what a big mistake she made in leaving him. I got rich. But money wasn't enough."

"It never is," she replied. "It's nice to have it. But happiness doesn't depend on it."

"I found that out the hard way." He leaned forward. "The worst part of it was leaving my brother behind," he said with a whimsical smile. "I loved Randall from the day he was born. There's nothing I wouldn't do for him."

"He feels the same way about you." She searched his eyes. "He was trying to protect me, telling you what he did, that I was…his." She flushed. "It wasn't true. He was never more than a friend. He never could be."

"I should have known that. All the signs were there." He drew her palm to his mouth. "I was blind."

"You'd been hurt. You thought I was like her."

"Yes, to my cost." He nipped her forefinger with his teeth. "You're nothing like her. She was tinsel. You're pure gold, Meredith."

She flushed. "Thanks."

"I like your sister," he said. "She was ready to do battle with me on your behalf when I walked in. But when she realized what you meant to me, she was less antagonistic."

"What I…meant to you?" she fished.

He drew in a breath. "Listen, I need to tell you…"

She was hanging on every word when the door opened and Sari walked in, oblivious to what she'd interrupted.

"Hi," she said, going straight to the bedside. She smiled at Ren as she bent to kiss her sister's forehead. "How's it going?"

Merrie was still trying to catch her breath, and regretting her sister's bad timing. But she smiled anyway. "I'm better. Just sore."

Sari sighed. "I've been talking to Paul. He says his office tracked the hit man to San Antonio."

Merrie's heart jumped. "Oh, dear."

"Now, don't worry," Sari said firmly, noting Ren's loss of color, as well. "We've got people watching him. Besides that, Mikey's been very busy on your behalf."

"What is he up to?" Merrie wanted to know.

"You'll find out as soon as we get you home," Sari said. "I've made sure that you have plenty of art supplies. Brand Taylor sends his regards and hopes that you'll be well soon."

"I bought him out," Merrie told Ren, then felt guilty at his expression. He looked positively morose. "I'm going to hire a business manager," she blurted out, and he brightened a little.

Then she recalled what Sari had said. "Why do I need lots of art supplies, Sari?" she asked her sister.

"Mikey's on his way in," Sari hedged. "He'll tell you."

Ren gave her a curious glance. She looked guilty.

He exchanged glances with Merrie and turned back to her sister.

CHAPTER FOURTEEN

JUST AS REN was about to speak, the door opened and Mikey walked in. He glanced at all of them, and smiled.

Merrie looked at him with a sheepish grin. "Hi, Cousin Mikey."

"Hey, baby doll," he teased. "You feeling better?"

"Lots, thanks. And thanks for sitting up with Mandy in the waiting room while I was in ICU, so she didn't have to be alone, and everyone else could get some sleep."

"You're welcome."

"If I can ever do anything for you," she began.

He cleared his throat. "Well, actually, about that…"

"What?" she prompted.

He moved closer to the bed, eyeing Ren warily. "Somebody has to have told you that this guy, this cleaner, has a rep in the business for never missing, yeah?"

She grimaced. "Yes."

"And that since he took the money, he feels obliged to do the hit."

"Yes."

"Well, I talked to some people I know, back home."

He hunched his shoulders. "In fact, I talked to the big boss."

Her eyes widened. She and Ren looked at him expectantly.

"The big boss saw the painting you did of me. Remember, I told you how impressed he was with it?"

"I remember," she said.

"The thing is, he really wants a painting done of himself. He says, that if you'll paint him, he'll take care of the cleaner for you."

Meredith's face brightened. "He'll call off the hit?" she asked, excited.

"Something like that, yeah."

"I would love to paint him," she said sincerely.

Ren was less enthusiastic. "Meredith," he cautioned her.

She stopped him midthought. "Ren, we can't watch every door, every window, every street. If he could even get on your ranch, and I know what kind of security you have, he could get anywhere."

"I know that," Ren said heavily.

"It's just a painting." She looked up at Mikey. "He, uh, doesn't have any outstanding warrants in Texas, does he?" Her voice trailed off.

Mikey chuckled. "No. Not in Texas."

"Paul will have a stroke," Ren remarked.

"He won't. Not if it might save your life," Mikey told Meredith. "There's this nice client who wants his portrait painted. He saw your work in a gallery. He thinks you're awesome. He wants you to paint him a picture to go over his mantel. How is that bad?"

"When you put it that way, it isn't," Ren replied.

"See? Nice. Paulie won't mind."

"Dr. Coltrain says I can go home Friday," Merrie began.

"I'll tell him," he replied. "You'll be much better by then. You can sit to paint, right?"

She laughed. She'd probably work from photographs, like she'd done when she painted the picture of Mikey for Paul years ago. "Sure. I'll do it."

"I'll tell him."

"Can he call the guy off before I do the painting?" Merrie wanted to know.

"We'll find out today. I'll be back." He left them, with an enigmatic smile.

SARI WENT TO check in with her office, leaving only two people in the hospital room. "When Paul finds out," Ren said softly, "we're all going to be in the doghouse."

"If he's not wanted in Texas, it's not Paul's problem," Merrie pointed out. "On the other hand, it really is my life. How much trouble can it cause, just one little painting?"

"I hope you're right, honey." He squeezed her hand. "I just want you to live. Whatever it takes. Anything!"

The look in his eyes made her heart jump. She was thinking ahead, not only to a painting that might save her life, but to a new beginning with the only man she'd ever wanted.

"I like Jacobsville," Ren said unexpectedly. He brought Merrie's palm to his lips and kissed it. "It's very much like Catelow. Everybody knows everything."

"Yes." The effect his mouth was having on her pulse was exciting.

He nipped the fleshy part of her thumb with his teeth. "You have a lot of friends here."

"I've lived here...all my life." She sounded as breathless as she felt.

He slid his lips down to her wrist. "I've lived in Catelow most of mine," he said. The taste of her soft skin was making his own heart race. He couldn't remember a woman whose touch gave him so much pleasure.

She was finding it harder and harder to breathe. She looked up into his eyes and felt her heart shoot up into her throat. The look in his eyes was hungry, predatory.

"I've missed you," he whispered. "The whole world went dark when you left Skyhorn."

"I've...missed you, too," she said unsteadily.

He got to his feet and leaned over her, one big hand leaning beside her head on the pillow, his eyes looking directly into hers. "You're not leaving me again," he said under his breath, tempting her mouth with his, lightly brushing her lips in a silence so full of tension that she felt she might explode. "I'll never give you reason to run, Meredith, not ever again."

She couldn't speak. Her whole body felt swollen, heavy. She reached up and touched his hard cheek, fascinated with the look on his face.

"Words can't convey what this can," he breathed, and he bent to her soft mouth.

It was a kiss unlike any he'd ever given her. It was tender, slow, full of respect and caring and wonder. She closed her eyes and her hand slid to the back of his head, to his strong neck, and dug in, holding his face to hers while he explored her soft mouth with his.

She moaned softly, and his mouth became demanding. The door opened suddenly, and they broke apart.

"Time for meds," the nurse said with pursed lips. "Sorry," she added when she noted the flushed looks on their faces.

Ren stood up, reciting multiplication tables in his head, because what he felt was very noticeable.

He cleared his throat. "I'll get coffee and be right back," he told Meredith as he went out the door.

Merrie was still catching her breath. She took the cup that held her pills from the nurse, but her hand was very unsteady.

"He's very good-looking," the nurse teased. "Have you known him long?"

"All my life. Well, not really, but that's how it feels," Merrie corrected with a sheepish smile.

"It was that way with my husband and me," the nurse said. "I knew him when I first saw him. I never understood how." She grinned. "We have three sons. I never knew it was possible to be so happy."

"I'm hoping to discover that for myself," Merrie confessed, and laughed softly.

REN WAS BACK a few minutes later with a cup of black coffee. He dropped into a chair, and grinned. She looked delightfully flustered. Still a little disheveled, too.

"Caught in the act," he mused, laughing at her blush. "We'll be the talk of the hospital. I expect they'll be sending in chaperones soon."

She grinned back. "I don't care."

He laughed. "We'd better keep it low-key until you heal," he mused. His black eyes slid over her body under the sheet. "Things might get too intense for you. Right now, anyway."

"Too intense?" she fished.

"You'll see." He just smiled.

THEY TOOK MERRIE home Friday in the limo. She was still unsteady on her feet, and a little sore, but so much better that she felt like a new person.

When the limo pulled up at the front door of Graylings, Ren got out first, lifted Merrie gingerly in his arms and carried her inside.

"Ren, I'm too heavy. There are stairs…" she began.

He chuckled. "Honey, I heft loads twice your weight every day," he told her, smiling into her face as he walked up the staircase. "You hardly weigh anything. You need to eat more."

"Just what I've been telling her for years, Mr. Ren," Mandy called from the kitchen door. "Welcome home, Miss Merrie!"

"Thanks, Mandy. It's nice to be home!"

"When you're settled, I'll bring up lunch. I made you oyster stew!"

"My favorite!"

"I know," Mandy said, grinning as she went back to work.

"She spoils me," Merrie told Ren. She studied his hard face with loving, soft eyes.

"Looking at me like that will land you in trouble," he murmured.

"Will it, really?" She brushed soft kisses on his hard cheekbone, down to his nose, over to his chin. It was exhilarating to touch him, to kiss him. She clung to his neck. "How much trouble?"

"The kind where I lock the door behind us, and don't come out for a week," he murmured as they reached what she indicated was her room.

He balanced her on one hard thigh while he turned the doorknob and carried her into the room. He closed the door behind them before he carried her to the bed and put her down, gently, on the quilt.

"Home at last," he said huskily.

"Yes." She didn't let go of his neck. He didn't seem to mind. He eased down on the bed beside her and bent to her soft mouth.

She relaxed into the covers, loving the slow, expert way his mouth explored hers. He was tender and hungry. So was she. She sighed under his mouth and tugged at his neck.

"Is this what you want?" he asked softly as he eased down against her, one big hand sliding up her rib cage.

"Oh...yes," she managed in what sounded like an absolute moan of pleasure. She arched up helplessly, wanting something else, something more.

He noted the hard peaks pressing at the front of her shirt and smiled to himself as he started working at buttons.

She wanted what he was doing, but she looked worried.

"Mandy's bringing up lunch soon," he whispered against her mouth as he got the buttons apart and slid his hand inside, slowly, under the frilly little bra she was wearing.

She arched, shivering, as he touched her very gently. Her eyes searched his.

"I'm not playing," he said huskily. "It's no game."

She shivered again.

"You belong to me," he breathed against her mouth as his ground into it. "You're mine, Meredith. My own…!"

She held on for dear life as he took her into realms of pleasure she'd never dreamed of, oblivious to the pain of her injuries, due to the painkillers she was still taking. While she was loving the hunger of his mouth, it shifted abruptly and found its way inside her blouse, under the bra that he'd unclipped while he was kissing her. His lips curved over her bare breast and he suckled her, hard.

She arched and cried out. The pleasure was so sweeping that she shuddered as his mouth fed on the soft flesh with its hard crown. He moved closer, pressing his hips against hers with helpless need, careful even in passion to spare her his weight by resting on his forearms.

She felt the hardness of him with wonder and a little fear. He seemed not quite in control, and she knew she couldn't stop him. She didn't want to stop him. She loved him.

All at once, he moved away from her, his eyes lingering helplessly on the pretty, taut little breast with its rosy hard crown and the faint red marks his mouth had left on her. "Oh, God," he whispered.

He sat up and shivered, groaning with the denied hunger. His body was in torment. He managed to get to his feet and walked over to the window, looking out at the fenced pastures beyond the house. He was trembling with unsatisfied desire.

"I'm sorry," she said, upset by his reaction. She put her bra and blouse back in place. He looked devastated. "I'm so sorry, Ren."

"I'll be all right," he said, his voice calming. "It was my fault. It was too much too soon. You just got out of the hospital." He winced. "Did I hurt you?"

"Oh, no," she said softly, and managed a smile. "I'm still on painkillers," she explained. She could still taste him on her mouth. He was heaven to kiss.

He drew in another deep breath and finally turned back to her. He didn't look angry, she thought, surprised. In fact, he was smiling like a man who'd won the lottery.

"So much for worrying that you'd never forgive me." He grinned.

She didn't understand what he was saying.

"We're volatile together," he said, searching her eyes. "I love it."

She relaxed a little, laughed self-consciously. "So do I."

"When you're back on your feet," he said softly, "we have decisions to make."

She bit her lower lip. "Ren, I'm old-fashioned…"

"Not a problem, sweetheart."

"But…"

The door opened and Mandy walked in with a tray of oyster stew and a cappuccino. "I made your favorite coffee, too," she told Merrie. "Mr. Ren, I've got a nice steak and salad for you and the Avengers downstairs."

He grinned. "Thanks, Mandy."

"You're most welcome. Here you go, sweet girl." She put the tray, with legs, over Merrie's legs, noting without comment her swollen lips and flushed cheeks. "Eat it while it's hot."

"Thank you," she told the housekeeper.

"You're my baby," Mandy said gently. "I have to take care of you."

"I'll go downstairs and eat. Then I'll be back," Ren told Merrie. He smiled possessively.

"Okay," she said, smiling with breathless happiness.

He chuckled as he left the room.

HE WAS BACK after they'd both had lunch. But before he could talk to her, say what he'd planned to say, there was a commotion downstairs.

Ren got up from the side of her bed and opened the door, listening.

"…told you, you can't set up shop like that," Barton was telling someone. "We have security already."

"Well, now you got more," came a deep, gravelly voice. "Where's the kid? And I want to see more of her work. She's good!"

There was an audible sigh. "She's upstairs."

"She do those?" the voice asked. "Nice work!"

Ren imagined they were looking at the two paintings whose frames Meredith and Sari had unstraightened in the hall downstairs.

There were loud footsteps. A couple of minutes later, Mikey came in, followed by a large, imposing man with a scarred face who had a lionish look about him. His face was broad with chiseled lips and wavy dark brown hair threaded with silver. He looked like a wrestler. He was big, threatening. He had black eyes, like Ren.

"You the kid?" he asked Merrie. He smiled, relaxing the hard, threatening look on his face.

"I'm Meredith Grayling," she said.

"Tony. Tony Garza," he introduced himself. "I guess you know him." He jerked a thumb toward Mikey.

She laughed. "He's Cousin Mikey."

The thick eyebrows arched. "He's your cousin?"

"He's Paul's cousin. But he's family," Merrie said softly, and Mikey grinned sheepishly.

"He said you'd do a portrait of me," Garza remarked.

So this was the mob boss? "I thought...well, when I did a portrait of him—" she indicated Mikey "—Paul sent me photographs..."

"Nothing better than the real thing if you're going to do a painting." He sobered. "I'm sorry about what happened to you. Nobody will hurt you ever again. Don't worry about it anymore, okay?"

She flushed. She smiled. "Thanks, Mr. Garza."

"Just Tony," he said easily. "I'm moving in for a few days. Mikey said it was okay. Is it?"

She laughed. "Of course. We have plenty of room."

"They can sleep anywhere." He indicated the two burly men near him.

"We have a bedroom downstairs that's empty and it has twin beds," Merrie told him. "Our bodyguards sleep next door to it."

"Those guys," Tony said, nodding. "I hear they're pretty good."

"They are," Merrie said.

"So are mine. That's Beppo—" he nodded to one "—and that's Big Ben—" he indicated the other.

The men nodded. They didn't smile. There were bulges under their jackets that looked like guns.

"We won't get in the way," Tony added. "There's a good restaurant in town…"

"I don't mind cooking for extra people, if they're here to save my baby," Mandy said from the doorway. "I always make plenty, anyway. I can make homemade lasagna," she added.

"Darling!" Tony Garza said enthusiastically, and bent to kiss her wrinkled cheek.

She flushed like a girl. "Mr. Tony!" she protested.

His eyebrows went up again.

"I'm from Georgia, originally," she tried to explain. "It's how we refer to people…"

"I kind of like it," Tony mused.

She grinned. "Okay!"

"Well, me and the boys will get settled. No rush, about the painting," he added. "Well, maybe a little rush. I hear we've got FBI all over the place already, and the local PD has us under surveillance, not to mention the sheriff's department."

"The FBI is my brother-in-law. He lives here," Merrie explained.

"Oh. Well, he'll be bringing company, I imagine." Tony sighed.

"They won't intrude. I'll make sure of it," Merrie assured him.

He chuckled. "Okay, kid. You're all right," he added with twinkling dark eyes. He motioned to his men and they went out. Mandy followed them with a soft laugh.

"Apparently," Merrie told Ren, "I'm safe now."

"Aiding and abetting," he murmured drily. "If you have to do time, I'll do something to get myself arrested so I can go, too."

"Aw," she said.

He smiled softly. He bent and kissed her lightly. "Matched set," he whispered. "Nobody's breaking us up."

She absolutely beamed.

THAT NIGHT, SHE was worried about being alone. Sari had offered to stay with her, but she assured her sister that she'd be all right. Sari and Paul went to bed, but Merrie lay awake worrying about the hit man. Tony had said she'd be all right, but would she?

The door opened and was left open. Ren came in, wearing burgundy silk pajama bottoms and a loose red robe that matched them. He climbed into bed with her, on top of the covers, and pulled her to him.

"Now go to sleep," he murmured, kissing her forehead. "We both know you won't sleep if you're by yourself."

She caught her breath at his perception. And at his obvious affection. "How did you know?" she wanted to know.

"I'm not sure. Maybe I'm psychic."

"My family…"

"Door's open," he reminded her with a soft chuckle. "It will stay that way."

"Oh. Okay, then."

He rolled over toward her, his face barely visible in the muted light that filtered in from the security lights outside the house.

"You aren't really afraid of me, are you?" he asked under his breath.

"Oh, no," she whispered. "Not at all!"

He smiled as his mouth slowly covered hers, slow and tender. His hand went under the covers, under the soft silk nightgown, onto her warm breast.

She slid her fingers into the thick hair sprinkled over the hard muscles of his chest, loving the way he felt.

He caught his breath.

"Do you…like that?" she asked.

"I like it." His face nuzzled hers as his mouth went to her soft throat and down, over her collarbone, onto the silky skin of her breast. His mouth opened over the hard nipple, and he fed on her hungrily.

She arched, shivering, her breath coming like a runner's.

"Oh, God," he groaned. He stripped away the covers and her gown. His robe slipped to the floor. "Meredith…!"

His mouth was all over her. She writhed on the covers, thanking God she was still on painkillers or she'd be dying of pain. She loved his hunger, holding on as he took her from one peak to another in a veritable fever of need. His mouth slid down her soft belly and pressed, hard, against her soft flesh. He was losing control very quickly. She was so responsive, as hungry as he was. She couldn't stop him. He wasn't sure he could stop himself.

This was wrong. She wasn't completely well. She'd just been in the hospital. Besides that, she'd never live it down, never get over it. She'd blame him. She'd blame herself…

He drew back from her, shivering with denied hunger. "No, honey," he whispered. "Help me."

"What?" she stammered.

He drew her completely against him, trying to ignore the exquisite feel of her bare breasts against his chest, and he hugged her close, rocking her. "Hold on, until it passes," he gritted. "No, baby, don't move… against me like that. It hurts. It really hurts…you understand?"

"Not really," she whispered. But she stopped, just the same, and let him hold her. Eventually, the hunger dissipated.

What seemed a long time later, he moved her nightgown back into place, put her back under the covers, slid into his robe and pulled her close again.

She took a deep breath. She still ached, but not so much. "How did you know…to do that?"

"Back in the dark ages, when I was a teenager, I learned how to dampen down the fires." He chuckled.

"I never liked girls who gave out to any guy who asked. The ones I dated, in those days, were sort of like you."

She didn't like thinking of him with other women. Especially now, when she knew how expert he was at this. He didn't learn what he'd done to her in books. She was jealous.

He brushed her ear with his mouth. "There hasn't been anybody in months. And there will never be anybody else except you. Not as long as I live," he said at her ear.

She caught her breath. What he was saying was profound. "Really?"

"Really."

She smoothed his black hair. "But you stopped…"

His mouth slid against her cheek, down into her throat. "It's a new world, with you. Besides the fact that you're still recovering from an attempted hit, I don't have anything to use, and I don't want you to look back with regret on our first time. When we make a baby, it should be after we're married. Don't you think?"

"Married!"

He lifted his head and gave her a sardonic look. "You're a virgin. And your family is all over the place. Can you imagine what your sister would do if I seduced you?"

There was a sound outside the room. "Well, I imagine she'd have you taken out to sea and tossed overboard with an anchor tied to one leg," came Sari's amused voice from the doorway.

"Damn," Ren sighed. "Caught in the act!"

Sari burst out laughing. She came into the room

in her nightgown and robe and turned on the bedside light. She gave them a smile.

"Well, no need to ask if you were planning to do the honorable thing. You both have clothes on and the door's wide-open. I gather Merrie couldn't sleep?"

"No, I couldn't," Merrie said with a faint laugh.

"I was just telling her a bedtime story," Ren prevaricated.

"That might be true, except for the way you both look," Sari mused.

"You might try not to look so self-righteous," Merrie shot back with a grin. "Or don't you remember what you did to Paul in the Bahamas the night you were rescued? And you didn't leave the door open!"

Sari blushed. "Mandy talks too much," she said.

"So it's the pot calling the kettle black," Merrie added, laughing.

"I guess so. Well, if you're okay, I'll just go back to bed," Sari said, her blue eyes twinkling.

"It really is okay," Merrie assured her. She looked at Ren with her heart in her eyes. "He wants to marry me."

"He does?" Sari asked, surprised.

"He does," Ren replied, looking at Merrie. "More than he wants to go on breathing."

"Well!" Sari exclaimed. "So I guess you'll be living in Wyoming."

"There's Skype," Merrie replied, beaming. "And we'll come and visit. You can come out to Wyoming."

"There's Skype," Sari agreed. She smiled and nodded. "I want you to be happy, sweetheart. Even if it's in Wyoming."

"Thanks, Sari," Merrie said softly.

Sari sighed. "Back to bed. Apparently you're going to be working tomorrow."

"Apparently so," Merrie said. She wiggled her eyebrows. "Isn't it exciting? We have the Godfather right in our own house!"

"Make sure you do the best painting you've ever done in your life," Sari teased.

"You bet I will." She drew in a breath. "It's such a relief, you know. God bless Mikey for setting it up."

"I'll agree with that," Sari said. "Good night."

They echoed her good-night. She left the door open on her way out.

Ren tugged Merrie closer to him. "Go to sleep," he said softly. "When you finish the painting, we'll decide on wedding dates and places and rings and things."

"Okay." She snuggled closer. "I've never been so happy in my life."

"Neither have I, honey," he whispered, wrapping her up against him. "Neither have I."

THE NEXT MORNING, Merrie set to work in her studio. Tony Garza was a fascinating subject to draw. His face was like a stone carving, all chiseled features. He looked like a statue that Michelangelo might have sculpted.

She mentioned it to Tony and he chuckled.

"What's so funny?" she asked, adding a line to the sketch she was making as a preliminary to the painting.

"Michelangelo was one of my ancestors, so the story goes," he told her.

"Wow!" She laughed. "I'm impressed."

He glanced at her without moving his head. "That painting you did of Mikey. Did your brother-in-law tell you what Mikey did for a living?"

"No. He just gave me the photos and asked me to do a painting. I added the details myself."

"How did you know? I mean, the knife on the table, the red curtain, the darkness behind him...really profound."

She smiled sheepishly. "I don't know. I just...sort of see inside people, to what they really are. Mikey was hard, because I don't usually work from photos."

Tony cocked his head. "How are you going to paint me?" he asked. "What sort of background?"

"I don't know yet," she told him honestly. "I start working, and it just...comes out on the canvas."

"Well," he replied with a faint smile, "I guess we'll both learn something when the time comes."

She smiled. She was wondering about the result herself.

SUPPER WAS RIOTOUS. The Avengers, Paul, Mikey, Tony Garza, his two bodyguards and a tall, good-looking man who came home with Paul but wasn't introduced all sat down at the table. Mandy was laughing to herself as she laid the table with edible goodies. The star dish was, of course, lasagna.

"This is just like my mother used to make," Tony

exclaimed when he tasted it. "Woman, you should open a restaurant!"

"Can't." Mandy sighed. "The girls would starve. Besides, Barbara, who owns Barbara's Café in town, makes it even better."

"It's delicious, Mandy," Merrie said.

The others agreed with Merrie and Tony.

Paul looked around him and shook his head. "My God, aren't we a crazy group? It's like an episode of *Law and Order*," he mused.

"I got a cousin who guest-starred in an episode," Tony volunteered. "He played a cop." He made a face at Paul. "We disowned him."

Paul chuckled. "I know how that goes," he murmured.

"Yeah, you turncoat," Tony joked.

"I'm not so bad," Paul defended himself. "I attract beautiful women." He leaned over to kiss his wife.

"No, honey," Sari protested, "I attract gorgeous men. I mean," she added, "just look around this room!"

All the men chuckled. Even the mystery man who'd come in with Paul.

"Are we allowed to ask whose side he's on?" Merrie piped up, indicating the tall, handsome man sitting next to Paul at the table.

Everybody looked at him. Tony Garza pursed his lips. "Well, he ain't FBI, I can tell you that," Tony said and went back to his lasagna.

"How do you know?" Paul asked, surprised.

"Because I've been investigated by most of them

over the past twenty years." Tony chuckled. "I never forget a face."

"Is he right?" Merrie asked the stranger.

The man, who was tall, with dark, thick black hair and dark eyes, grinned at them. "I'm not FBI," the man said in an amused voice, almost as deep as Tony's. "But I do wear a white hat."

Ren just laughed. "I could tell you who he is, but I won't."

"How would you know?" the unidentified man asked.

"Your cousin is a friend of mine. He's the sheriff up in Catelow." He chuckled. "His last name is Banks. His cousin who lives in San Antonio is named Colter."

"Busted." Banks laughed out loud.

"Yeah, he's from the misfit agency."

"I'm a Texas Ranger," Banks replied. "But I'm off duty. And I'm here because I wanted to meet your houseguest."

Now they were all staring at Banks. Even Tony Garza.

CHAPTER FIFTEEN

"You wanted to meet me?" Tony asked Banks, because the man was staring at him. "Why?"

"You saved the life of a friend of mine, a couple of years back," Banks replied. "He was in on a bust in Jersey, a big one, involving organized crime. One of the perps had him dead to rights, on the floor with a .45 aimed right between his eyes. You stopped the man from shooting."

Tony frowned. Then he nodded. "Yeah, I remember. The guy with the .45 was one of mine." He smiled sheepishly. "I know what happens when you pop a cap on a Fed," he added. "Not good for business."

"Whatever the motive, my friend appreciated it. I just wanted to tell you. He can't. He's still undercover. Not," he added wryly, "in Jersey."

Tony chuckled. "Well, he's welcome. But I didn't have noble motives or anything. It was just good business."

"They say you paint," Banks said to Merrie.

She smiled at him. "It's just a hobby, but I love it."

"I'd love to see some of your work," Banks added.

Ren slid his hand over hers at the table. "*We'd* love

to show it to you," he said, making sure Banks knew he was with Merrie.

Banks got the idea at once and grinned. "Sure, I'd love that," he replied.

Ren went with Merrie, who was still weak, to see the studio where she worked, on the back of the house. Her canvases lined the walls.

Banks whistled. "This isn't a hobby," he argued. "It's a full-fledged career. I've never seen anything like it."

"Thanks," Merrie said softly.

He shook his head. "You see right into people, don't you?" he asked absently. He was looking at a painting she'd done long ago of Mandy.

She smiled. "It's a blessing and a curse."

"More blessing than curse," Banks replied. He glanced from her to Ren and grinned. "The good ones always get snapped up right away," he added.

Merrie flushed. Ren pulled her close and kissed her hair. "Yes," he said warmly. "They always do."

She worked on Tony's portrait for the next few days. It was slow going, because she had to take frequent breaks. But it was going well. Tomorrow she'd add the details she'd decided on, and let Tony see it for the first time.

She and Ren were still sharing a bed at night, with the door wide-open, to the amusement of the rest of the household.

Late one night, he recited a poem to her, his deep

voice thrilling in the soft darkness, lit only by a night-light.

"*...and still the darkness ebbs about your bed. Quiet, and strange, and loving—kind, you sleep. And holy joy about the earth is shed. And holiness upon the deep.*" Ren finished the poem.

"Oh, that's lovely," Sari said from the door.

"It's Rupert Brooke," Ren called, laughing. "You recited one of his poems to me back home," he reminded Merrie. "He was one of my favorite poets in college. He was killed in World War I. This is from a poem called 'The Charm' that he wrote."

"I wish my husband would read poetry to me, but I don't think he even knows a poem," Sari teased.

"I do so know a poem!" Paul protested, joining her. Both were in pajamas. Paul grinned down at her. "Ready? Here goes. 'There once was a man from Nantucket...!'"

"You peasant!" Sari exclaimed, and hit him. He took off running, laughing, and she took off after him, laughing, too.

Merrie laughed into Ren's throat, clinging to him. "They're so happy together," she murmured sleepily. "It's good to see them that way. It was a hard few years, for both of them."

He drew her gently closer. "You and I will give them a run for their money," he whispered at her ear. "You color my world, Meredith. I'd do anything for you."

"Anything?" she teased.

"Absolutely."

"Then recite another poem," she said softly.

He laughed, then kissed her, tenderly. "Okay. Here goes." And he found another poem in his memory.

TONY GARZA JUST STARED at the portrait at first, both big hands in his pockets, his head cocked to one side, his dark eyes narrowed and quiet on the painting.

Merrie had captured him perfectly in oils. The background was surprising. There was a window behind him, where a garden could just be seen, part of which was covered with trailing vines on delicate stakes. On one of the vines were ripe red tomatoes, so lifelike that the viewer could almost taste them. Tony was perching on a desk. His big hands were beside him, on the edges of the oak desk. His fingernails were immaculate. There was a ruby ring on his little finger. There was a faint scar on the back of one hand, a carved symbol that Merrie hadn't understood, but she painted it there anyway. There was a chain, like that of a watch fob, at his waist. It was gold. On the end of it she'd painted a Celtic cross—an odd thing she hadn't understood, either, because she couldn't picture Tony being religious. On the wall behind Tony's head was a small black silhouette of a woman's head in a framed painting. The background of the entire painting was a rich, lush burgundy, with folds like velvet along both sides.

Tony let out a long, long breath. He shook his head. Merrie just watched him. She knew he loved it.

He turned and looked at her with affectionate dark eyes. "You really do see deep, honey," he said softly.

"Can you tell me what those things mean?" she asked. "If it isn't prying too much, I mean."

His thick eyebrows went up. "You painted it and you don't know what they mean?"

She shook her head, her eyes as innocent as a child's. "I just sort of paint what comes to me."

He laughed softly. "A true gift." He turned back to the painting. "I love to cook. I can make lasagna, too, although mine isn't as good as Mandy's. I grow my own tomatoes and herbs. I like to garden." He hesitated. "The scar on the back of my hand was put there by a rival gang member when I was about fourteen. He meant to kill me, but a friend of mine stopped him just in time. The symbol is his gang's sign."

"You never had it erased," she commented.

"It reminds me that, no matter how sure we seem to be, life is full of unexpected things. It also reminds me not to get too cocky about my own abilities." He paused. He dug his fingers deep into his pockets and made fists there. "The cross on the watch fob is my mother's. She was Catholic, deeply religious. I don't wear the watch very much. Just for special occasions. But I leave the cross on its chain, to honor her. She prayed for me every day of her life. She always hoped I'd turn into somebody…better…than I was." He shrugged. "People are what they are. You can change stuff on the surface. Inside, not so much." He turned to her. "It's a masterpiece. I want to pay you for it."

She smiled and shook her head. "I don't ever charge for my work," she said.

"I know you live in a nice house, but your dad lost everything to the Feds because of what he was doing," he began.

She laughed softly. "My mother had all the money. She left Sari and me millions in her will. So, I really don't need the money. But if you want to do something with what you'd have paid me for the portrait, suppose you donate it to your mother's church?"

He smiled with genuine affection. "I really like you," he said softly. "If I'd had a daughter, I'd have liked her to turn out just the way you are."

"That's the nicest thing anybody's said to me in a long time," she said softly.

He just grinned.

"YOU'RE SURE THE hit man won't come along after you're gone and pop her when nobody's expecting it?" Paul asked Tony worriedly.

"Not a chance," came the reply. "That's all handled. You see the portrait she painted of me?" he asked.

Paul nodded. "Best work she's ever done, and that's saying something."

He cocked his head. "You won't get in any trouble for letting me stay here?"

"Nah," Paul drawled. "I just told people that you were wandering the streets looking for handouts and Merrie let you stay until she could find you a proper home." His eyes were twinkling.

Tony hit his shoulder with a big fist. "Watch your back."

Paul chuckled. "You going to stay for the wedding?" he added. "Ren's marrying Merrie in three days. They went to get a marriage license this morning, and to buy rings."

"Three days? Why not," Tony said. "I got no place special to be for a while."

"Then you're invited. And Merrie has something she wants to ask you."

"Does she? What?"

"She'll tell you tonight."

WHEN MERRIE ASKED HIM, Tony had to avert his eyes so that nobody noticed their sudden brightness. Merrie asked him to walk her down the aisle.

"It's okay, if you'd rather not…" she began, afraid she'd insulted him somehow.

"I'd be honored," he managed in a rough tone. He swiped at his eyes with the back of one big hand before he turned back to her. "I mean that."

She beamed. "Okay, then. Thanks!"

He drew in a breath. "You're welcome. I'll have to rustle up a proper suit. Hey, Big Ben," he called to one of his men.

"Sir!" the man replied.

"Drive up to San Antonio and find me a tux with all the works. Don't forget cuff links."

"Yes, sir!"

"You know the size." He pulled out a gold card and tossed it to the man. "Call me if you have any problems."

"Sure thing, boss!"

"A tux?" Barton asked, having come in at the end of the conversation. "You getting married, Mr. Garza?"

"Nope. I seem to be the father of the bride," Tony replied with twinkling eyes.

"Really?"

"Really," Merrie assured him. "Never mind that I'm blonde and he's not," she added facetiously.

Tony laughed uproariously.

"What is it?" Merrie asked.

"Oh, God." He could barely stop laughing. "Listen, when you two have kids, guess what that will make me?" He waited a beat. "The Godfather!"

"I wouldn't touch that line with a pole," Barton said, tongue in cheek, and he kept walking.

THE PERFECT WEDDING GOWN for Merrie was found in Marcella's boutique in town. It was acres of white lace over white satin, with a long train and a fingertip veil topped by a tiara. It had long sleeves and a rounded neckline. It made Merrie look like a fairy princess, Sari said as she helped her try it on.

"I still can't believe it," Merrie said. "I mean, I ran away from Wyoming because I thought he hated me."

"Obviously, that wasn't the case. Plus he's marrying you in a church," she added.

"That was the biggest surprise of all."

"It wouldn't be, if you'd seen him sitting in the chapel at the hospital," Sari replied somberly. "From what you'd told me about him, it was an indication of how deeply he felt about you."

Merrie nodded. "He's changed. It's a very good change," she said softly. "But he still hasn't really said what he feels."

"Paul didn't, either, but I knew," Sari replied. "It was in the way he looked at me. It's the same way

Ren looks at you, sweetheart," she added. "You're his whole world."

"He's mine, too."

"That was nice of you, to ask Mr. Garza to give you away at the wedding. He isn't what he seems, is he?"

"Not at all. I hoped you wouldn't mind," she said. "I wouldn't have wanted Daddy to give me away. But I really couldn't ask anyone else locally, for fear of hurting someone's feelings. So Mr. Garza seemed the perfect choice. I'm still surprised that it touched him that deeply."

"Mikey says he was married years ago and his wife died young. He wanted kids really badly but they never had any."

"Maybe that's why."

Sari smiled. "Maybe so. Now we have to go shopping for casual clothes."

"Nothing risqué," Merrie said. "We're going to Tangier for our honeymoon. I don't want to make people uncomfortable. Attitudes are very different over there."

"As if you ever wore anything reckless in your life!" Sari chided. "You'll fit right in in Morocco."

"It's such an exotic place for a honeymoon," Merrie sighed. "I'm shell-shocked. Two months ago I was so miserable. I'd never even been on a date!"

"How times change." Sari laughed.

"You think it will be okay, traveling so far away?" Merrie worried. "Tony says I'm safe, but I'm still worried."

"If Tony says you're safe, then you're safe," Sari

replied. "Believe me, if he called off the contract, it's called off. Nobody sane would refuse him."

"Okay, then." She laughed. "Oh, I'm so happy!"

Sari hugged her. "I'm so happy for you!" She hesitated. "Ren had a call from Randall today, didn't he?"

"Yes. His mother's biopsy was positive," she replied. "I'm going to make sure we go and see her before we leave for Morocco. Since we're going in our own jet, and the hotel reservations were made, at least we don't have to worry about getting seats on some overcrowded plane."

"Does he want to go and see his mother?" Sari asked.

"Actually, I think he does. Randall said he'd been mellowing toward her for some time now." She smiled at Sari. "Families should stick together, when they can."

"They should." Sari smiled back.

THE WEDDING WAS a big event. The small Methodist church in Jacobsville, where Sari and Merrie had attended for years, was packed to capacity. Reverend Jake Blair, the pastor, smiled at the odd assemblage occupying the bride's side of the church. There were some equally odd people on the groom's. Some were still wearing combat gear, having only had time enough to swing by for the wedding on the way to active duty.

Merrie was so happy that she was almost floating when Sari put the finishing touches on the pins holding up her long blond hair.

"There," Sari said. "You're perfect!"

Merrie stood up. "I'm so scared," she blurted out,

and then flushed, because she wanted to marry Ren more than she wanted anything in the world.

"It will be all right," Sari assured her. "Everybody's scared, darling. Everybody. It's a big step. Just take a deep breath, and relax."

Merrie took a deep breath. She wished it had relaxed her.

She went out to find Tony Garza, handsome in the latest wedding finery, waiting for her. She went up to him, smiling, and took his arm.

He shook his head. "You're the most beautiful bride I've ever seen, next to my own late wife. You look gorgeous."

"Thanks," she said with a shy smile.

"Now, you hold me up and make sure I don't fall, because I'm real nervous," he whispered at her ear.

She laughed helplessly. The wedding march started and all eyes turned to the back of the church. Merrie let Tony lead her to the altar, where a nattily dressed Ren was waiting for her.

THE SERVICE SEEMED to be over in no time. After they said their "I dos," Ren kissed her with breathless tenderness. Merrie looked up at him with her heart in her eyes. He brushed away her tears and kissed her again. They ran down the aisle to cheers.

The fellowship hall was as full as the church had been. Barbara's Café had catered the event. Ren fed Merrie cake while the photographer they'd hired took candid shots for their wedding album.

"Nice turnout," Cash Grier said with a grin, his

beautiful redheaded wife, Tippy, on his arm. "I think I see a few familiar faces from the FBI's Most Wanted list," he added in a low tone.

"That's no way to talk about my adopted father," Merrie teased.

Cash sighed. "We all have our crosses to bear. See the tall, dignified gentleman standing with Hayes Carson and his wife, Minette?"

Merrie and Ren glanced at the sheriff and his wife.

"He's known far and wide as El Jefe," Cash whispered. "He runs the biggest drug cartel in the Northern Hemisphere."

"What?" Ren exclaimed on a laugh. "And you haven't arrested him?"

"He hasn't broken the law in Jacobs County," Cash assured him. "He has a brand-new granddaughter. He's not risking that for business. Not on this side of the border, at least," he added, tongue in cheek.

"You never know about people," Tippy commented. "You look beautiful, Merrie," she added. "Congratulations. I hope you'll be as happy as we are."

"Thanks," Merrie said softly.

Ren agreed, squeezing Merrie's hand. "I hope we have fifty years," he told Merrie. "Maybe more, if we're lucky."

She sighed and looked up at him with pure adoration, just as the photographer snapped a photo. It would go into the wedding album as her favorite of them all.

REN AND MERRIE stopped by his mother's house on the way to New York, where they'd catch the plane to Belgium. From there, they'd fly to Casablanca, and then on to Tangier. It would be a long trip, but Merrie and Ren had wanted someplace exotic and memorable. North Africa seemed to be it, for both of them.

Ren's mother, Retha, was small and delicate, with blond hair and brown eyes. She was so overcome with emotion to find Ren standing in her living room that she almost passed out. Tears formed in her eyes as she approached him.

"It will be all right," Ren said haltingly, going to take her cold hands in his. "I've been doing some research. If it's confined to that one area," he said delicately, "it's almost one hundred percent certain that you'll recover."

"Oh, I hope so," Retha said huskily. She studied his hard, lean face. "You look...different, Ren. It's been so long."

"Too long," Ren replied quietly. "I should have stayed, that Christmas. I did the wrong thing by taking off."

She managed a smile. "Sometimes God tests us. Everything happens for a reason. I'm just very happy that you came to see me."

He drew in a long breath. "So am I."

Retha's eyes went past him to the pretty blonde woman on her sofa. "And who's this?" she asked.

"Meredith Grayling Colter. My wife," he added gently. "We were married this morning in Jacobsville, Texas. That's where she's from. She's an artist."

"Like me," Retha said, beaming. She went over to

Meredith and hugged her. "I wish you joy and happiness with my son."

"Thank you," Merrie said softly. "I'll take good care of him."

Retha's eyes brightened a little too much. She forced a smile. "I'll hold you to that."

Merrie pulled her close and hugged her, rocked her while Retha cried. "There, there," she said softly. "Everything will be all right. I'm so looking forward to having a mother again. I lost mine when I was a child. And you paint, too! I've been using your studio at Ren's ranch."

Retha pulled back, wiping away tears as she laughed. "Randall told me you have genius in your fingers. He said you paint people as they really are."

"I guess I do. I love my work."

Retha touched her soft blond hair. "After raising two boys, I'll love having a daughter," she said gently.

Merrie grinned at her.

"When are they doing the surgery?" Ren asked.

Retha winced. "In two weeks. I'm a nervous wreck already. They'll be doing reconstructive surgery at the same time. I'll take a long time to recuperate."

"We'll be here for the surgery," he said, glancing at Merrie, who nodded. "You can stay with us at Skyhorn, if you like," Ren said a little stiffly. "We'll take care of you."

Retha was conspicuously surprised. "You...would let me come there?"

"You're my mother. Of course you can come there. It's your home, too."

"It was, once. I've made a hash of my life," Retha said quietly. "I did things the wrong way. But if you can forgive me for hurting you…"

"It's my place to ask forgiveness," Ren interrupted. "I hurt you more."

Retha stared up at his face. "It's time we both left the past behind us. We have a much happier future to look forward to."

He smiled gently. "Yes, we do." He drew her against him and rocked her, quietly, while she wept.

It was a long and tiring trip to Tangier. They arrived in the wee hours of the morning. It seemed to take forever to get through passport control and customs. It had been fortunate that Merrie had applied for, and been given, a passport before her father died. Her father had arranged it, because he'd planned to marry her to a cousin of the Middle Eastern prince he'd picked out for Sari.

"We'll have to walk to Tangier from here," Merrie said wearily. "There won't be a cab in sight at this hour of the morning."

"Yes, there will," Ren assured her. "Don't worry."

Sure enough, when they got outside the airport, there were cabs waiting out front. The driver put their bags in the trunk, invited them into his cab and sped toward the city.

Merrie, who'd never been overseas in her life, had found every single part of the excursion exciting. She was drooping a little now, but she sat up to look at the beautiful lights that trailed the highway all the way into town. There were people on the streets, some in long robes, some in European dress, all moving along lazily and stopping to talk to people they knew.

The cab pulled up at a hotel with no indication that it was a five-star hotel, which was what Ren had assured her it was.

But when they got inside, the luxury was unmistakable. Merrie was fascinated by her surroundings, so much so that she barely noticed Ren signing them in. A bellhop came forward to escort them up to their room.

The room had shutters that opened onto the courtyard below, where sculptured gardens and a swimming pool were visible in the security lights. The air smelled of unfamiliar spices and sea air. Meredith drew in a long breath before she closed the window again.

"It's so beautiful here," she told Ren sleepily. "I can't wait to go exploring."

"Neither can I," Ren said, tongue in cheek. "But I'd rather wait until you're awake, for the sort of exploration I have in mind," he teased. "You're dead on your feet, honey."

"I guess I am. I'm sorry." She sighed, leaning against him. "I didn't get much sleep last night from being nervous about the ceremony. I was so afraid I'd slip on the hem of my wedding gown and fall into the pews."

"But you didn't." He laughed.

She yawned. "I'm so sorry!" she groaned. "I wanted to be awake...!"

He pulled her close and kissed her softly. "We have the rest of our lives. Tonight, you rest. Okay?"

She smiled against his broad chest. "Okay, Ren."

SHE AWOKE TO the smell of fresh, hot coffee. She followed the scent up with her eyes still closed, aware of a deep chuckle...

"It's good," he told her as he handed her the cup and steadied it in her hands. "I just had mine. If you'll get dressed, we'll go down to breakfast. I understand that it's something of a special buffet that they put out for visitors."

"I'm starved!" She laughed.

"Me, too. So hurry. I'll wait for you outside."

She looked after him worriedly. He'd gone out, wearing slacks and a green casual knit shirt, without a backward look. She was eager for him, although there was still a little niggle of fear in the back of her mind.

He'd gone without having a woman for months, and he wanted her badly. Didn't that mean he was likely to lose control and hurt her? She'd heard horror stories from other girls when she was in high school, about how their dreams of love had been turned to ash in a bed with an inconsiderate lover.

Not that Ren would be inconsiderate. She flushed with pleasure, remembering their first encounter on the night of the party. She tried not to remember the way it had ended. Ren had been furious.

But that same man had come to the hospital, had sat with her, encouraged her, never left her for a minute, even when she went home. He'd been with her every night, to make sure she felt safe and protected.

Could he have wanted to marry her just from a guilty conscience, about the way he'd treated her? She didn't think so. He might feel bad, might apologize, might even come to the hospital to see how she was.

But the confirmed unbeliever who'd gone into a chapel in the hospital when she was in critical condition wasn't a man who felt nothing more than guilt. It was a life-changing event for him. It had changed him.

It had changed her, too, seeing the happiness he felt just being with her. He didn't like other men near her. He was possessive. She smiled to herself. She wasn't going to admit it, of course, but she loved the fact that he was possessive of her. She felt the same way.

She got up and put on a yellow patterned sundress. It fell to her ankles in soft folds, and the bodice was held in place by spaghetti straps. The back was high, covering the scars she carried from her father's brutality.

It had surprised and delighted her that Ren didn't mind the scars. That was another indication of how he really felt about her.

She picked up her small purse and went out the door after Ren.

CHAPTER SIXTEEN

THE BUFFET WAS EXTRAORDINARY. They found every breakfast choice known to man, including several kinds of fresh bread, fruit and, most surprising, bacon and ham. Since Tangier was largely Muslim, it was unusual to find pork on the menu. The server, wearing a red fez, laughed and explained that they made the concession for foreigners, who were allowed pork in their diets.

They ate on the hotel patio, a delightful place with delicate chairs at round tables, set with linen and fine china and utensils. There were flowers on every table, and a fountain that resembled an American birdbath in a recessed floor nearby. Merrie, who'd never traveled abroad, found her surroundings fascinating.

She pumped their waiter for information. He told them about nearby tourist attractions.

"We also have a driver and a Mercedes, which will be placed at your service while you are here," he said, smiling. "Just tell him where you want to go. You must see the *souk*, in the old part of the city. It is unique. You can sample mint tea and buy handmade rugs and carpets."

"I can't wait!" Merrie enthused.

As they listened, loudspeakers began the call to

prayer. It echoed through the city, a sweet and beautiful song.

"That's so beautiful," Merrie told the waiter.

He smiled. "We belong to different religions, but we are alike, I think, in some ways," he added, noting the cross she was wearing. "We have beliefs that we cherish, in a world that wants to do away with religion."

"I do not plan to give up mine," she said with a pert smile.

"Nor I, mine," he replied. "So we have this in common, no?" And he grinned.

"EVERYBODY HERE SPEAKS so many different languages," Merrie exclaimed as they toured the caves where the Barbary pirates stashed their loot centuries before. They were Berbers, as most of the population of Tangier was. "I feel absolutely ignorant. Did you notice that our driver was fluent in French and Spanish and even Japanese. Not to mention that he speaks perfect English!"

"Europe and Africa have more nationalities than America does. Europe has so many countries in close proximity, and many of them holiday here. The people who work in tourism have to speak a lot of other languages."

Her hand curled closer into his as they walked. "I should learn Spanish, at least," she mused.

"It would come in handy." He looked down at her. "Will you be satisfied, living in Wyoming?"

She looked up at him with her heart in her eyes. "I'll

be satisfied wherever I am, as long as I'm with you," she said softly.

His breath caught at the look on her face. He moved just a step closer. Her lips parted helplessly. He looked down at her bodice and saw two hard little points. His body began to throb.

Merrie's breasts felt tight. The fabric was cloying. She wanted to feel the soft breeze on her body, without clothing. She wanted to lie in Ren's arms in the daylight and experience him in every way.

He turned to their driver and forced a smile, saying that they had an appointment and needed to go back to the hotel. They could come back here and explore more another day.

The driver smiled and drove them back to the hotel.

Ren didn't speak. His throat was too tight. He held Merrie's soft hand in his, curling his fingers sensually into hers, his breath unsteady as the big car ate up the miles. He was on fire. He'd never wanted anything as much as he wanted his wife. His body was in agony.

Merrie felt the tension in him. She was just as hungry as he was. The time it took to get to the hotel, through the lobby, back to their room, was an anguish of anticipation.

He closed the door behind them and locked it. His face was like stone.

Merrie loved the way he was looking at her. She reached up and untied the strings that held her bodice up. She let it fall, drowning in Ren's wide, shocked eyes.

"Meredith," he choked. He went to her, lifted her

in his arms. His mouth slid over the hard nipple, teasing it with his tongue, as he swallowed it up and began to suckle her.

"Oh...Ren," she choked, clinging to him.

He pulled the covers off the bed, tossed her into the middle of it and went down with her.

She arched under the hungry insistence of his mouth as he explored her in a silence that vibrated with tension. She felt his mouth on her flat stomach, her hips, down her long legs. He smoothed it over the inside of her thighs, loving the helpless arching of her body, the moans that were music in his ears.

He undressed her between soft kisses, gentling her, arousing her so that she wasn't afraid. She was so hungry for him that she couldn't be nervous. It surprised her, that she was so passionate. She hadn't realized how she might be with a man she loved.

His mouth came down on hers, insistent and sweet. She felt him touching her where no man ever had, and she gasped.

"I know," he whispered against her mouth. "It's embarrassing. But it's necessary. And it's going to be sweeter than you know. Sweeter than honey, my darling," he breathed as he began a rhythm that had her crying out, surprised at the sudden pleasure he kindled.

"My...gosh!" she managed.

"And it's only the beginning," he whispered as he worked his magic on her untried body.

He watched her the whole time, wild to have her, but determined to make sure that she was ready for him. He nibbled at her lower lip as he quickened the rhythm and watched her cry out, shuddering at her climax, the first of her entire life.

"Ren!" she sobbed as the pleasure ebbed away.

"I won't stop," he whispered. "Just a minute."

She watched him undress, so enthralled that it wasn't shocking. She wanted all of him. Her hips undulated involuntarily as he turned to her, magnificently aroused.

He moved onto the bed beside her. His mouth found hers, as his fingers probed her in a soft, delicate place. She shivered a little, but she opened her legs for him.

His hand moved again, bringing the pleasure back. But it was elusive this time. She arched up, her body demanding in its awakened state, her eyes half-closed, displaying the hunger she felt for more of him.

"Yes," he said under his breath. His mouth found hers as he probed again. This time, the path was easy. His tongue went slowly into her mouth, in the most intimate kiss he'd ever shared with her. As it played with her own, his hips moved between her long legs and she felt him in a way she never had before, with nothing except skin between them.

"Slow and easy," he whispered into her mouth as he began to possess her. "Relax, sweetheart," he said huskily. "Try to relax."

"I'm…trying," she said unsteadily. She was looking straight into his eyes as he entered her. "Oh, Ren, it's so…"

"Intimate," he finished for her. "Yes. It's…intimate." His teeth ground together. He had to slow down. It was her first time. He didn't dare rush it, although he was wild to have her. He felt her body accept him, felt the warmth of her as he went deeper, deeper, deeper…

"Ren!" She arched up toward him, the quick, hard rhythm of his hips creating a tension in her that was frightening. She clung to him, begged him not to stop, pleaded with him to end it, end it, end it… And then she arched and begged him to never end it.

He drove into her, holding nothing back. He was as helpless as she was, anguish arching him down into her as he sought an end to the tension that was breaking his body in two. He almost had it, almost, almost, almost! He ground his hips down into hers, arched his back and cried out, sobbing as fulfillment burst inside him, inside her, and he convulsed over and over again in a maelstrom of pleasure unlike anything he'd experienced in his life.

She felt him at the moment he found pleasure. She found her own, almost at the same instant. She cried out with the shock of it. There were no words that could describe the throbbing, almost painful pleasure that racked her body. She was dying in the heat of it. She shuddered and shuddered, her body echoing the satisfaction it was giving him. She'd been afraid that it would hurt. She couldn't feel pain. The pleasure was so high, so stabbing, so complete that she existed for a few endless seconds as only a part of Ren. Then, so quickly, the pleasure left. She shivered, moved frantically, trying to get it back.

"Shh," he whispered. His hips moved gently against hers. The tiny movement fulfilled her all over again. He watched it happen, smiled with delight as her face contorted, as she sobbed, arching up to him, shuddering each time the climax came back.

But soon, he stilled and forced her to also.

"You'll get sore," he whispered tenderly, smiling. His mouth smoothed all over her face, drawing the tears into it, soothing her with his hands as they slid under her, against the scars on her back that didn't seem to bother him at all.

"I never thought," she began. "I never dreamed…" She shivered. "It was like dying, the pleasure was so strong."

"Yes." He kissed her eyelids.

She opened her eyes and searched his lean face above her. "I was afraid, at first."

"So was I, honey."

"You were?" she replied, surprised.

"You were a virgin," he replied softly. "I was afraid that I might hurt you. It's been so long for me, I was afraid I'd lose control and scare you."

She reached up, tracing his face with her fingertips. "I didn't think it would be so…" She managed a smile. "I can't find the words."

"Poets have been trying for generations," he mused. "Nobody can find the words." He brushed his mouth over hers. "Lie still. If we overdid it, this may be uncomfortable."

He began to lift away from her. She winced. He winced, too, but he rolled over onto his back with a long sigh. "Sorry," he said.

"It's okay. I couldn't stop."

He turned his head and watched her, watching him. "Am I shocking?"

"Well, yes. Sort of," she said. "We study anatomy, in order to paint lifelike portraits. So I know basic stuff, like where the muscles attach and where other…places are." Her eyes found him. She sighed. "But you don't look like any of those pictures," she added shyly. "You look like some of the Greek statues they have in museums. Only better."

He chuckled. "Don't do that. I'll have ego issues."

"I don't mind." She moved close to him, glorying in the feel of skin on skin. She snuggled close. "Now I'm sleepy again."

"Me, too. We'll sleep for a while, then we'll go exploring some more."

"I want to explore you some more," she murmured. "But I'm…"

"Sore," he finished for her. He chuckled. "It's okay. I can live on today for a long time."

"So can I." She hesitated. "Ren? Are you sore, too?"

He laughed. "A little." He turned his head and looked down at her. "I enjoyed getting that way, Meredith," he said when she looked guilty. "And we have all our lives to make up for lost time."

She smiled tenderly. "Okay."

He drew her close, pillowing her head on his shoulder. "I forgot to ask if you wanted me to use something."

"Use something?"

"Birth control," he said drowsily. "So that I didn't make you pregnant."

She drew in a long, delighted breath. "My goodness!"

He lifted his head to look into her eyes. She was beaming. Radiant. He chuckled softly. "Okay. I guess you're old enough."

"I'm definitely old enough," she said pertly. "Besides, if we have enough kids, the family ranch won't go on the market the minute we die."

He burst out laughing. "No. I guess that's a valid reason to have kids."

"Of course it is."

"You haven't really lived, sweetheart," he said after a minute. "You've been a virtual prisoner at Graylings. Don't you want to see some of the world before you're tied down with kids?"

"I am seeing the world," she returned. "We're in a very foreign country, and we'll see several more on the way home." She sat up, proud in her nudity, loving the way his hands explored her. "I'm a homebody," she added gently. "I have no great desire to travel or found a business empire or even become a famous artist. I just want to live on the ranch with you and make a home for you. A real home," she added quietly.

He ground his teeth together, trying not to show what he was feeling. He'd been an outsider most of his life. He loved Randall, but they'd never truly been a family, not with Ren ignoring their mother all of these years. Meredith had changed all that, brightened the dark corners of his life, made him happy. He couldn't remember ever being really happy before, not even when he thought he loved Angie.

"I'm sorry, I guess I'm being pushy..." Her voice trailed off, her confidence waning when he didn't answer her.

He drew her back down into his arms and turned, so that he was propped over her. "I've never had a real home," he said huskily. "Delsey tried to make one for me at Skyhorn, but it was a shaky one, at best." He smoothed back her disheveled blond hair. "I love the way you look right now," he whispered huskily. "Disheveled and disturbed, because of me."

She smiled up at him, tracing his stubborn chin. "You disheveled me," she said.

"Emphatically," he mused. He traced her swollen breasts, lingering on the taut little mauve peaks. "You're the most beautiful woman I've ever known. Inside and out."

"That's nice flattery," she teased.

"It's not." He bent to kiss her breasts. "I want to make a home with you. I want babies. I just want to be sure that you won't regret not having some freedom, too."

"Freedom is just a word." She sighed. "People who are truly free don't want roots or commitment." She smiled. "I want a real life, one with roots and stability and babies. That's freedom to me."

His fingers tangled in her long hair. "I can be difficult."

"So can I," she returned. She linked her arms around his neck. Her expression became serious. "I love you so much, Ren," she whispered, surprised at the emotion she saw in his eyes as she spoke. "More than anything in the world."

Ruddy color stained his high cheekbones. His jaw tensed as he looked at her, sketched her with his eyes, delighting in her beauty, in the tenderness she radiated. He leaned his forehead against hers. "I'm not sure I've ever said the words to anyone," he whispered huskily. "But I…feel them, when I look at you, when I hold you." He drew her against him, enfolding her so close that she could feel every inch of him against her. "Is that enough for you?"

She felt the joy rise up in her like a fountain overflowing. She laughed softly and clung to him, tears rolling down her cheeks. "Oh, Ren! Yes, it's enough. It's more than enough!"

He felt the moisture and lifted his head. "Why are you crying?"

"I was afraid you only wanted to sleep with me," she blurted out.

He gave her a sardonic look. "No man is crazy enough to marry a woman just for one night in her bed," he mused. "Especially not a virgin."

She stared at him. "Oh."

"You don't know beans about men. I love it." He grinned. He bent and kissed her hungrily. "Why do you think I was so out of bounds with you the night of the party?" he asked. "I knew that I'd die for you. I was fighting what I felt, because I was afraid. After that business with Angie, I got gun-shy. You seemed too good to be true."

"Did I?" she asked, breathless.

"Then Randall kept telling me that you were his woman." He grimaced. "I thought he meant you really were his, in every way. I was mad as hell. I felt trapped. I never meant to hurt you so badly," he added, regret in his tone, in his black eyes. "I felt like kicking myself when they told me you were trying to walk in the snow to the front gate, to get away from me. That was when I really knew what I felt. And it was too late."

"I thought you hated me," she confessed.

"I hated myself. You were in danger already, and I let you put yourself in harm's way. The killer had access to my land, and I didn't know it. He could have shot you where you stood," he added huskily. "I thought about that, after you left." His eyes closed. "I would have died with you, Meredith. Because nothing I have in the world would ever make up for your loss."

"Oh, Ren!" She curled against him, her arms tight around his neck. "That's exactly how I feel!"

He hugged her close. "Paul came to get you. He told me the truth, about what you went through at home. I got so drunk after you left," he said, sighing. "I never hated myself so much."

"I tried to hate you, too. But I never could. I went home in so much pain!"

"You'll never know how I felt when Randall came by to tell me you'd been hospitalized. I went crazy. I flew straight to Jacobsville." He made a face. "I thought Sari was going to have me on toast. She was furious. But when she saw how torn up I was, she backed down a little. She loves you very much."

"We're sisters," Merrie said gently. "All we had was

each other, in that torment of a life. I love her just as much."

He wrapped her up against him. "We had a rocky start," he said. "But things are going to be better now. For both of us."

She drew in a drowsy breath, so happy that she could have died of it. "I just hope that Tony Garza was right, about the killer. I don't want to die and leave you. Not now, when we've just really found each other."

His arms tightened. "He promised. I don't know him, but Mikey does. He said that Tony has more power than we realize, and that if he makes a promise, he keeps it."

"I feel a little better," she said. "It's scary, knowing somebody wants you dead. They said that Leeds man who hired him is having a hard time in jail. He's not all there, and he loved his mother so much. Our father killed her. It's a mess."

"Things will work out the way they're meant to, in spite of us," he said with a smile in his voice. "I'm happy not to have to be worried about losing you every minute of the day."

"Me, too." She sighed. "I'm sleepy."

"We'll drowse for a bit. Comfy?"

"So comfy!" she enthused.

He chuckled and kissed her soft hair.

THEY WERE LIKE children together, on fire with love of life and each other. Ren took her into the shower with him and bathed her, then coaxed her to do the same to him. They held hands on the way downstairs, in the

car, while they were being tourists walking around the
most exciting city in Africa.

Every day, Merrie fell more in love with her husband. He lost his constant worried look and began to
relax. They shopped and strolled and rode camels and
went to the bazaar and spent the rest of the day looking at expensive rugs, although he made her rest often.
She was still weak and sore from her recent trouble.
They chose carpets that they both liked and had them
shipped back to Wyoming. Along with the rugs, Merrie found beautiful embroidered caftans for herself
and Sari and Delsey and Mandy, and even Ren's little
mother, and had them sent home, as well.

"It's been the most exciting, wonderful trip I ever
took," Merrie told Ren as they were on the way to the
airport.

He squeezed her hand. "Yes, it has for me, too." He
smiled at her. "We'll come back again."

"I'd love that," she said, and meant it.

THEY WENT TO Texas first, to see how things were going
at Graylings.

Cousin Mikey was sitting in the dining room with
Paul and Sari and Mandy when they walked in.

"What, no Avengers?" Merrie teased as she hugged
her sister and Paul.

"No need," Mikey said, chuckling. "You're in the
clear, baby doll," he told Merrie with a gentle smile.
"Tony sent word back from Jersey that the situation
was taken care of."

"I'm so glad." Merrie sighed. "It was nice of the killer to agree to give up the contract."

"Sure it was." Mikey didn't meet her eyes. He glanced at his watch. "I'll miss my flight!"

"You can fly home in the family jet," Paul said. "You're family, right?"

Mikey chuckled. "I guess I am." He pursed his lips as he looked at the newlyweds. "No need to ask if you two had fun."

"Morocco was extraordinary!" Merrie said. "I'm going to paint it!"

Ren pulled her close. "We'll order more paints and canvases," he assured her.

"Don't be a stranger," Paul told Mikey.

He shrugged. "I might visit occasionally," he mused. He looked at Merrie and grinned. "I hear Tony's telling people he's got an adopted daughter who paints like one of his famous ancestors."

She grinned. "That's sweet of him."

Mikey tapped her nose. "Just don't forget that people are what they are, kid," he replied. "Don't expect Tony to sing in the church choir and help little old ladies across streets."

"He may be a bad man, but there's some good in everyone," she reminded him.

"More good in some people than in others," he added with a sly look at Paul, who returned the look.

"Come tell us all about the trip!" Sari enthused.

"I'll say goodbye, for now." Mikey kissed Merrie's cheek, and Sari's, and shook hands with the men. "I'll head for the airport."

"The limo will take you," Paul said.

"Thanks again," Merrie said.

Mikey smiled. "You're a nice kid," he replied. "Don't let life disillusion you too much."

"I'll try," she promised. "You try not to be so gloomy."

He shrugged. "Leopards don't change their spots. See you."

"What did he mean, about leopards?" Merrie asked when they were drinking coffee and eating Mandy's sour cream pound cake.

Paul sighed. "There's been a development. Sort of."

Merrie's eyebrows arched.

One side of Paul's chiseled mouth pulled down. "They found the contract killer."

"They did?" Merrie exclaimed. "Are they going to prosecute him? Will I have to testify?"

"He won't be arrested," Paul said. "See, they found him, but he's in an oil drum in a river in Jersey."

Merrie's mouth fell open. Ren winced.

"Nobody knows who did it," Paul assured her. "We can speculate, but we'll never really know."

"Tony?" Merrie asked slowly.

Paul shrugged. "Anybody's guess. If I were guessing, however, I'd wonder if the contract man decided his reputation was more important than Tony's orders. You don't say no to Tony."

Merrie felt faint. "You mean, the man was going to kill me anyway, to fulfill his contract, so that his reputation would remain intact?"

"That's what Mikey thinks," Paul replied. "He doesn't know," he was quick to add. "It's an educated guess."

Merrie touched her own throat. "I felt so safe…"

"You were always safe," Paul said. He looked at his watch. "That reminds me. Since I sent Mikey in the limo, I'll have to drive over to the airport in San Antonio. The plane should be landing soon."

"Plane? What plane?" Merrie asked.

"The Avengers are due back from Morocco. Well," he added when he saw Merrie and Ren's expressions, "we didn't dare take a chance without knowing for sure where the hit man was, right? So Rogers and Barton went on your honeymoon with you. They were very discreet," he added with a grin. "They stayed in the same hotel, but they were wearing robes and sporting fake beards. Since they both speak Berber, they blended right in!"

"Good grief." Merrie burst out laughing.

Ren grinned. "I never spotted them. Good camouflage."

"They kept their distance. But if anyone had threatened you, they'd have found him. Even in Morocco."

Merrie leaned against Ren's shoulder and smiled. "They, and my adopted dad, have taken good care of me." She was grateful, although she spared a single regret for the contract killer who was dead. On the other hand, if he was still alive, there would have been other assignments, other poor victims. In the end, she felt, it was God's will. However he'd died.

"Taking care of you will be my job from now on," Ren said softly.

"So it will," she teased.

REN'S MOTHER HAD her surgery. The surgeon told Randall and Ren that he'd removed every trace of cancer. A few weeks of radiation and chemo, and she'd be good as new.

Ren and Merrie stayed with her in Chicago while Randall took care of Skyhorn business and visited when he could.

"You're turning into a fine rancher," Ren teased, hugging his brother while they waited for their mother to come out to the waiting room, after undergoing her last treatments. "I'm proud of you."

Randall flushed. "High praise, coming from you. Thanks."

"It's your ranch, too," Ren said, smiling.

"Well, I'm more of the junior partner. But I think I'm getting good at marketing."

"Best ever," his brother replied.

"Production sale in three months, you know," Randall reminded him. "We'll have to put on a fine spread for all those hungry ranchers we're persuading to buy our bloodstock."

"We'll manage. Right now, I'm looking forward to the holidays," Ren said, surprising everyone. "We'll put up a tree and have turkey and dressing. The works."

"Do you feel all right, Ren?" his brother asked.

"I've never felt better." He looked down at Merrie with love beaming from his black eyes. "It's going to be the best Christmas we ever celebrated. Mom's coming with us, too."

"So many changes, in such a short time," Randall said. "My head's spinning."

"So's mine." Ren chuckled, smiling at his wife. "But not from the changes."

Merrie pressed close to him. "It really is going to be the best Christmas ever," she said softly. She sighed. "What a nice, big, sturdy present I got, early," she added. She looked up at Ren with sparkling eyes.

Ren chuckled. While Randall went to help their mother out to the car, Ren turned to his wife. "You can unwrap him whenever you like, too," he whispered outrageously.

"Ooooooh," she murmured. "I like unwrapping him!"

"He likes it, too," he whispered. "He also bought you an early present."

"He did? What is it?"

"A radio. A loud radio."

She frowned. "What?"

He gave her a sardonic look. "Delsey happened to mention that we need to speak to Willis about his wolf making those loud moaning sounds."

She flushed red.

"Your husband enjoys that moaning very much," he teased. "So he bought you a loud radio to drown them out. From everybody except me," he whispered huskily. "So tonight, we'll unwrap each other and see how hot things can get."

"Burning hot," she teased.

"Blazing hot," he agreed with a grin.

HOURS LATER, REN'S MOTHER settled in her room, Delsey looking after her, and Randall out with the livestock.

Ren pulled Merrie into his room and locked the door behind him.

"Santa won't mind if we unwrap our presents early, will he?" she gasped as Ren tossed her onto the bed and kissed her between the removal of outer layers of clothing.

"He won't mind at all. Trust me. We're friends. I asked him already. Do you like that?"

She arched up, gasping. "Better turn that radio on," she said.

He turned it to a country station and raised the volume. "High enough?" he mused as he found bare flesh and invaded it with his warm mouth.

"Maybe. Do that again."

"This?"

"Definitely...this!"

He rolled onto her when their clothes were tossed haphazardly all over the floor, his body as hungry for her as it had been the first time, in Morocco. He aroused her quickly, urgently, and went into her so hard that she cried out with sweet anguish as the pleasure bit into her.

"It just gets...better," he ground out, driving into her hungrily.

"And...better," she managed.

He carried her up to heights they'd never achieved, sweating and gasping as she responded wildly to his passion. When the culmination came, she almost blacked out, it was so profound. He arched down into her hard, with a furious rhythm. She met it with equal desperation, drowning in the fever they kindled, an-

guished pleasure arching her in a posture so strained
that she thought she might break into a thousand pieces.
And past that was a new and higher satisfaction that
they'd never achieved before. She sobbed all the way
through it, pleading with him not to stop, as she cli-
maxed over and over and over again.

Finally, the tension snapped, and they lay together,
kissing softly, caressing each other, in an aftermath
that vibrated with exhausted delight.

"Never like that," he whispered unsteadily. "Never
in my whole life."

"Definitely never in mine," she whispered back.

He drew in a steadying breath and rolled over onto
his side, taking her with him. The music, forgotten,
droned on. He reached up and turned the volume down.

"I like the radio," she remarked. "We should listen
to it more often."

He chuckled. "Yes, we should."

She smoothed her fingers over his hard mouth. "I
love you."

"I love you back."

She drew in a long, satisfied breath. After a short
silence, she said, "I love having your mother here."

"So do I. We're putting up the tree tomorrow."

"Do you have decorations?"

"Sure. A lariat here, a spur or two there, some bri-
dles and bits..."

She hit him. "We have to have decorations."

"I'll sacrifice Willis. He can go and buy you some
pretty things to put on it. And a tree, while he's about it."

"No."

"No?"

"Picking the tree is the most fun of all. You and I have to do that."

"We do?" He smiled against her mouth. "Okay. But you'll owe me."

"Mmm." She sighed. "What will I owe you?"

"At least one very loud radio song."

She burst out laughing. "You can have two."

He pulled her close and turned out the light. She was still smiling, there in the darkness, close to the tall gentleman she loved.

* * * * *